Betrayal

Tim Tigner

Copyright © 2013 Tim Tigner

ISBN: 0615926118
ISBN-13: 978-0615926117

For more information on this novel or Tim Tigner's other thrillers, please visit timtigner.com

This novel is dedicated to a man who never betrayed anyone, my father, my teacher, my friend, Professor Steven S. Tigner.

Chapter 1

FBI Counterterrorism Response Team Headquarters,

Quantico, VA

SPECIAL AGENT ODYSSEUS CARR looked up at the graying tiles of his boss's ceiling and began counting to ten. He almost made it to three. "What do you mean, I can't brief my men? They're putting their lives at risk, commander. Big risk. These aren't stone-throwers you're asking us to kill. These are the guys who took out the World Trade Center."

Commander Potchak stood. He was a head shorter than Odi but built like a fireplug, and every bit as tough. "What's your point?"

Odi leaned forward and rested predatory palms on the edge of Potchak's metal desk. "My point, sir, is that we're giving up a crucial advantage if we don't rehearse. I want to give my men every available advantage. They deserve no less."

Potchak did not twitch or blink. He just stared back cold and hard for a couple seconds and then said, "If you're not up to it, Agent Carr, I'll give Echo Team to Waslager. He's been itching to go international. You can sit this one out—in isolation of course."

Odi wanted to leap over the desk, grab his boss by the ears and put a knee through his smug face, but he knew that would not help his team. Instead he bit back his frustration and tried to suck it up like a good soldier. "That won't be necessary, sir."

Potchak turned and spat a thick river of tobacco juice into his trashcan, making Odi forget his own frustration for a moment to pity Jose the janitor. "Good," Potchak said. "Now, if you'll take your head just a little bit farther out of your ass and break this task down, you'll see that I'm not ordering you to give anything up. The physics of the assault are the same whether it's Hogan's Alley or I-fucking-ran. A building is a building. A grenade is a grenade. Considering that you used to be the Bureau's top Explosive-Ordnance-Disposal pro, you should know that. All you need to rehearse effectively are models of the buildings and the lie of the land. Both are at your disposal, so I don't want to hear any more whining."

Odi felt his stomach quiver with a pluck of doubt. He moderated his tone and reminded himself that Potchak was usually a reasonable man. "May I ask why, sir? Why the unusual level of secrecy? Surely you don't think anyone on my team has links to al-Qaeda?"

"Oh Jesus, Carr. I'd have thought you'd understand that by now. Have you learned nothing about the way things really work these past two years? Counterterrorism is not a military matter; it's politics. By limiting foreknowledge to the mission leader and myself, some politician feels that he's protecting either his source or his ass. Probably both. I don't know who the source is, or even the politician for that matter, but I'm damn sure that whoever reconned that complex risked his ass to do it. So I'm not without sympathy."

Fighting back the urge to tell his boss what he thought of that, Odi picked up the satellite map to busy his hands. The complex in question consisted of three old cinderblock buildings in Nowheresville, Iran. It would take each of his two-man teams less than two minutes to run their building's perimeter, firing modified M441 high-explosive Rocket Propelled Grenades. In the dead of night, it probably would not matter that the complex was in Iran. The commander was right about that. But Potchak was making a big mistake. A bureaucrat's mistake. The instant things deviated from plan—and things always deviated from plan— being in Iran would make all the difference. As a hardened field operative, Potchak knew that. This discrepancy bothered Odi, but he was not going to risk losing his team-leader slot over it. "What did this secret source say about sentries?"

Potchak spat again and then sat down, signaling a truce.

Odi followed suit.

"There are usually just two men armed with AKs. One guards the entrance to the central building; the other walks a perimeter patrol. You'll have no problem taking them out with synchronized sniper shots. Use those shots as a starting gun, as your team's cue to begin the assault runs."

Odi nodded. "An eight-man team might make more sense than the standard seven. If you'll loan me Johnson, he and I could do that synchronized sniping from polar perimeter positions and then provide cover while the teams make their assault runs."

Potchak cracked a wry smile that warned Odi he would not like what came next. "You've got the right strategy, but the wrong man. You're getting Waslager. He'll be your second sniper … and your second in command."

Odi felt resentment run down his spine like boiling oil, but he could not stand up and get in his boss's face again. He had already played that card. He bit his tongue while taking a moment to analyze the situation. The core problem was that nobody on his team liked

Waslager, or worse yet, trusted him. He was a self-serving loner and a politician. Odi knew that was exactly why the brass did like him. The question he should be asking, Odi realized, was: Why did they like Waslager on this mission?

He set that thought aside for later and latched onto a negotiation tactic. Since aggression was out, he would try to back-peddle. "On the other hand, if I wait to shoot until the path of the second guard passes the first, I could take them both out—probably with a single shot if I use high-velocity rounds. Then we would only need—"

"Forget it, Carr," Potchak interrupted. "You're getting Waslager."

Chapter 2

Asgard Island, Chesapeake Bay

FBI DIRECTOR WILEY PROFFITT set his wineglass down a little too quickly. A drop of blood red wine sloshed out onto the virgin white tablecloth, spreading with ominous portent. He was more nervous than he realized. He picked the glass back up and took another sip before locking his lover's gaze. "How would you like to be First Lady?"

"Of the United States?"

"Um hum." He grinned, feeling better already and enjoying the confused look that danced across Cassi Carr's amber eyes.

She instantly picked up on his mirth and mirrored it. "Does the Director of the FBI know something about Anna Beth Carver that the rest of us mortals have yet to learn?"

"Actually, it's Aaron Dish," he said deadpan.

She leaned toward him conspiratorially. "The First Lady is having an affair with the Vice President?"

Wiley shook his head. For six months he had kept his earthshaking secret, neither hinting at the future that awaited them nor alluding to his secret pact. It felt great to share the big news with Cassi at last. He decided to start with the background, give her excitement time to build. "Dish has a health condition. He won't be joining Carver on the reelection ticket."

"I see," Cassi said, clearly not believing him but apparently willing to play along. Her eyes twinkled. "So how does that make me First

Lady?"

"It doesn't," he said, shaking his head as she feigned disappointment. "You're going to have to wait five years for that. In the meantime, it makes you Second Lady—come a year from January anyway."

Wiley saw a flash of confusion cross Cassi's brow. She appeared unsure if he was being goofy or serious. "Dish really is sick? Carver really asked you to join him on the ticket?"

"Yes and no," Wiley said. "Yes, Dish really is sick. And no, President Carver has not asked me to be his running mate—not yet. But he will."

"Oh, and why is that?" She asked.

Wiley leaned forward so that his lips were an inch from Cassi's ear. He paused there to inhale her sweet perfume before whispering the prophecy. She was wearing a new scent. "Because terrorism is going to top the American agenda."

She pulled back, sobered by his words. Her parents, after all, had died on 9/11. "You really are expecting an attack?"

"I am. You know all those homeland-defense speeches I've been giving of late …?"

She nodded.

"They weren't just typical keep-'em-scared politics."

Cassi took a moment to chew on that one. He watched the gears spinning frantically behind her worried brow. "Maybe at one level they weren't" she finally said, thinking out loud. "But nonetheless, it is because of those speeches that you think Carver will put you on the ticket. They were what earned you the Antiterrorist Czar epithet."

Wiley raised his wine glass in a toast. "To your deductive powers."

Cassi returned the gesture, but he could see that her mind was still focused on working through the implications of his revelation. When she looked up at him wide-eyed, he knew that the other shoe had dropped.

"I'll be Second Lady?" She asked, her voice a choked whisper.

Wiley tried to smile but his lips would not move. He tried to nod but couldn't. Panic gripped him like a cold iron glove. He could not move his head.

As he struggled, Cassi continued, blissfully unaware. "Are you asking me to marry you?"

Wiley realized that a cold hand was clamped over his mouth. He endured a second of complete disorientation and then he understood. His conversation with Cassi had been a dream. The intruder in their bed, and the icy palm clamped over his mouth, were real.

Wiley's eyes bulged in horror as the dark shadow over him shifted in silence. A prickly lump filled his throat as a muscled arm drew back. Fully awake now, Wiley strained to pierce the darkness, searching for the glint of the knife that would complete the picture and end his life. All he saw were fuzzy shadows. Part of his mind latched onto the fact that Cassi was sleeping beside him. The need to warn and protect her surged within his chest, but the heavy quilt, the vise across his face, and the fear in his heart pinned him like Christ to the cross.

As he prepared to buck and lunge, the bedside lamp clicked on and Wiley recognized the intruder's face. His tension drained. He should have guessed.

Wiley looked over at Cassi the instant the palm backed off of his mouth. She was sound asleep. At least she appeared to be ...

"Halothane," his visitor supplied, reading Wiley's thoughts. "Like chloroform only safer."

"And more aromatic," Wiley mumbled to himself, recalling the perfume in his dream. Slowly, he returned his gaze to the midnight caller and voiced the obvious question with his eyes.

Stuart's answer was matter-of-fact. "We need to talk."

Stuart Slider was the invisible man. Compact, sinewy, and average of face. Every time they met he struck Wiley as unexpectedly small. He also enjoyed the annoying ability to appear and disappear at will. Or so it often seemed. Wiley was beginning to detest that trait.

"What the devil are you doing here in the middle of the night?" Wiley asked. "Do you need another hole in your head?"

Wiley had been secretly working with Stuart for six months now, but this was the first time that Stuart had set foot on his Chesapeake island home. Or, Wiley reflected, at least it was the first time that he knew about.

"We need to talk," Stuart repeated. "Unseen, uninterrupted, and alone." He stood, canted his head toward the door, and said "Let's go to your study. No sense giving Sleeping Beauty here bad dreams." Without waiting for a reply, Stuart reached out and extinguished the bedside lamp.

Wiley followed obediently, more out of curiosity than any feeling of subservience. They walked down the plushly carpeted hall to the room at the end. The massive oak door to his soundproofed study was ajar. An eerie glow leaked out into the hall from the three-hundred-gallon aquarium within. The ghoulish atmosphere seemed to suit a halothane-assisted secret midnight rendezvous, so Wiley did not turn on the lights when they entered.

Sleepless fish cast darting shadows about the room as pale moonlight trickled in from the east. Wiley sought his favorite armchair, a black-leather recliner. As he sat he discovered a steaming Starbucks cup waiting on the end table beside his right arm. Unbelievable, he thought. Stuart had never been to his island home before, and yet there the cup was—a low-fat latte no doubt—just what he wanted, right where he wanted it.

Setting the creepiness factor aside, the latte was both a thoughtful and insightful gesture. Yet its primary effect was to fan Wiley's flame. The invisible, unflappable Stuart Slider did not drink coffee or tea or cola. He did not smoke. He did not drink. Wiley was not entirely certain that he even slept. Yet he was always awake, alert, and controlled. What a bastard.

Wiley picked up the familiar cup, more irritated at himself for being weak than pleased to have his fix. It was still hot despite the trip from the mainland. Stuart must have planned even that detail in advance and packed a thermos. Meticulous and a bastard. Wiley took a sip, nodded a perfunctory thanks, and gave his guest a get-on-with-it look.

"Is it true what I've heard about this room?" Stuart asked.

Despite the latte, Wiley wanted to go back to bed. He wanted Stuart to get to the point and then get out. But he knew from experience that playing along would get him there faster than resisting. "What have you heard?"

"I heard that the Secret Service turned your study into a fortress because you refused to have the Proffitt family's ancestral estate updated with the technology and security advances of the past hundred years."

Wiley rolled his eyes. "For an organization whose purpose is to protect national icons, the Secret Service has surprisingly little respect for history or tradition. I'm glad that I only had to deal with them that one time. They call it a panic room. It was a compromise." He reached out and picked up a large universal remote control off the coffee table. "Allow me to demonstrate. First I'll type in the code to let the system know that this is not an emergency, and then ..." He held the square red button down with his thumb. After three seconds of constant pressure the door to the study swung shut. Hidden bolts scraped into place as titanium louvers began to lower over the bulletproof windows with a motorized hum. "Now we're safe from everything up to and including shoulder fired missiles."

Stuart looked about the room. "You've even got a bar and a bathroom in your bunker. Not bad. What's through that door?" He pointed to the corner.

"It's just a closet."

"What about the cavalry?"

"If I had not told the system that this was a test, then the Hostage

Rescue Team would automatically be summoned from Quantico by a beacon hidden in the roof." Wiley pressed and held the red square again. The lockdown procedure reversed.

Stuart nodded in appreciation and then assumed a contemplative expression.

In that dim light, with his black-clad form framed against the black-leather couch, he appeared as little more than an intense set of eyes. The sight made Wiley think of an alligator in a tar pit. An alligator in a tar pit, he repeated to himself. Now there was the very definition of a Beltway lobbyist.

"I've come with news," Stuart said.

Wiley raised his eyebrows.

"I've resigned my job as executive director of the AADC to work full-time on your campaign. We decided that the time had come, now that things are under way."

Wiley did not want to talk about the American Association of Defense Contractors or the things that were now under way. In fact he had specifically asked The Three Marks to keep him out of that loop. Thus far his only tactical contribution to things had been supplying them with a list of useful names. He hoped to keep it that way. Still, Wiley did not fail to notice that Stuart's "we" did not include him. "That's awfully generous of you. Did we agree to give you your old job back after the campaign?"

Wiley saw genuine emotion flash across Stuart's face in response to his words. That was a first. Despite playing poker for decades to hone exactly that expertise, however, Wiley could not tell which emotion Stuart had shown. Was it disappointment ... or anger?

"I won't need my old job back after the campaign," Stuart replied.

"Oh? And why is that?"

"Because, after the campaign you are going to be Vice President—and I am going to be your Chief of Staff."

Stuart's statement hit Wiley mid-sip and he choked, coughing and spraying latte over the front of his scarlet pajamas. Stuart did not bat an eye at his discomposure, and Wiley figured that the bastard probably had his timing planned. "Is that what you came here to tell me?" Wiley asked, mopping his chin with his sleeve. "Is that why you broke into my home in the middle of the night, drugged my girlfriend and dragged me out of bed—to talk about your career?"

"No."

"No?"

Stuart shook his head.

Wiley felt his stomach drop.

Chapter 3

Tafriz, Iran

AS THE WOMAN carried her daughter out, Dr. Ayden Archer wiped the sweat from his brow with a soiled rag. He still had a few clean ones left from last night's wash, but he wanted to save those for the kids. He ventured a peek into the alley before the door swung shut. The line stretched to the far end and disappeared around the corner. He knew it was time to make the mark.

"Please come in," he said in Farsi, holding open the door. The next woman in line bowed slightly, her baby cradled tight. Though she would not meet his gaze, Ayden knew that there was joy in her eyes.

"I'll be right back," he said, grabbing a bottle of iodine and stepping outside. He hated this next part of the daily ritual, but years of experience had taught him that it was the only way.

He walked east down the dusty alley, counting children as he went, offering silent smiles. It always amazed him how orderly they waited. He had not posted rules, yet the configuration never changed. Six days a week the sick children rested side-by-side along the northern wall in the thin ribbon of shade while the mothers stood across from them, baking beneath their chadors in the merciless Iranian sun. If only the women were allowed to rule the country, he mused.

When his count reached thirty children he stopped. Five more hours at six children per hour would take him to eight o'clock. He crouched down before a two-year-old girl. Lily was her name if he remembered correctly. He said, "Hello Beautiful," and stroked her hot cheek with the back of his hand. He took the cap off the iodine and wet the tip of his index finger. He drew a semicircle on her forehead and added two dots. To him it was a smiley face, but if asked he would say it was a moon and two stars. Turning to the mother he said, "Your daughter will be the last patient of the day."

He proceeded to mark the remaining foreheads, also with a smiley face but this time adding a third star for a nose. When he first began the practice he had numbered them, but he changed to the friendlier system when he found that no one tried to cheat. Mutual suffering bred solidarity when testosterone was not involved. As he drew he explained to the remaining mothers, "I will not be able to see your children today, but they will be first in line tomorrow. With these marks you need not come early, so let your children rest. I will see the first at eight o'clock." Ayden knew that this was like the seatbelt announcement on airplanes —everybody present already knew the rules—but he repeated it anyway. By his reckoning, little ceremonies kept you sane.

As he walked back toward the entrance to his one-room one-man free clinic, Ayden felt a chill despite the heat. The day was soon approaching when he would not draw smiley faces with noses. His funds were dwindling. After five wonderful, horrible years, his clinic would have to close.

He felt tears begin to well.

Hope had knocked on his apartment door a few months ago. He had looked through the peephole to see an exceptionally charismatic face beaming from a bush of long tousled hair and punctuated with whirlpool eyes. "Word of your good works has spread far, my friend," the man who introduced himself as Arvin had confided. "If you had the resources, the backing shall we say, would you be willing to do more?"

Looking at the stoic figures now standing patiently in the sun with sick children clinging to their legs, Ayden knew that he would do anything to keep his clinic afloat. Anything. At this point Arvin's generous offer appeared to be his best and only chance, but he had not encountered the opportunity to earn that support. Not yet. Stepping back into his clinic, he prayed that someday soon he would ...

Chapter 4

Airborne over the Turkish-Iranian Border

"WE'RE THIRTY MINUTES FROM TARGET," the pilot's voice blared over Odi's headset as the C-141 began banking north. "Potchak has just confirmed that the mission is a go."

Odi looked around. Only Waslager had heard the announcement. As deputy team leader, he was the only other team member tuned in to both the group and command frequencies. Waslager, deputy team leader, that really fried his bacon. Odi had to struggle not to show his anger to his team. They were tighter than sardines and packed just right, but Potchak had stuffed one more fish into the can. A bad one. Something was rotten in Denmark.

Odi slid his headset switch to enable the whole team to hear his voice and pushed Waslager from his mind. "Listen up. Final reminders for anyone whose thoughts are still stuck on last night's girl. That turn you just felt was our little birdie rounding the southern tip of the Turkish-Iranian border. We're flying north along that border now.

"We hit the wind in approximately twenty-eight minutes. Your chutes are set to deploy automatically at fifteen thousand, but keep your eyes on your altimeter; those puppies have been known to malfunction. You got that O'Brian? Don't go spacing out on me."

"Aye, aye, sir. While we're on the subject, could you remind me: do I pull the black tab or the silver one?"

"Just don't pull the little fleshy one and you'll be fine.

"Anyhow, gentlemen, once you've checked your canopy, begin steering west. I'll be the first out the door and will be wearing my infrared flasher. Line up on me. Remember, the longer we ride the wind, the shorter we have to hump. And don't forget to drop your pack when you hit a hundred feet. If we've navigated right, the terrain will be bald as Mitch's head, so we won't need to worry about getting hung up in trees. If you do forget, your fifth point of contact will be a dozen grenades. Take my word for it gentlemen, that would be enough to ruin anybody's day.

"Once you're safely on the ground, confirm with your codename designator and 'OK.' No real names. No chatter. We'll regroup on my position. Understood?"

"Understood," came six voices. Waslager just nodded.

"Good. Stick to the plan, and we'll be back in Incirlik for breakfast. Any questions, now's the time."

"What's the target?" Flint asked, mindlessly shaving the hair on his forearm with the oiled blade of his Ka-Bar knife.

Odi smiled, pleased to be able to share this information with his team at last. "In a move reflective of their devious, scum-sucking nature, our buddies in al-Qaeda have disguised a training camp as a hospital." The men all jeered—except Waslager. What was it about that guy? Odi wondered. He wished Cassi were there. His twin sister would have Waslager's number in no time. She could always read people—at least when it wasn't personal, he thought with a shrug. When it was personal, Cassi was blind as Oedipus.

"Camp al-Qaeda is located on the outskirts of what was a mining town back when there was copper in them thar hills. Now Tafriz is little more than a farming village, although it's still got more infrastructure than anyplace else around."

"How similar is the camp to the complex we've been training with?" O'Brian interrupted to ask.

"It's virtually identical. Everything will be just as we practiced. The size and layout are like our mock-ups. Their construction is cinderblock instead of wood, but that's inconsequential to your grenades.

"You'll each fire ten modified M441 grenades at ten second intervals, spacing them at ten meters each. I know you guys could pull this off in half that time, but we've slowed it down to allow cooler heads to deal with the shit that tends to happen. So remember not to rush. You hear that Derek. No rushing. I would hate to ruin a flawless mission with a casualty from friendly fire.

"Waslager will take out the roving sentry on the western apex of his route. That will be the starting gun, at which point I'll drop the sentry on the central door and you'll all commence your runs.

"Each team will use its first salvo to take out their building's main entrance and the floor directly above. That will seal the building up and minimize any chance for Omar to escape—not that those unlucky few who do wake up are going to have time for more than a rushed Allahu Akbar, but we absolutely cannot have any witnesses, so we're not taking any chances."

"Waslager and I will provide covering fire as you move in case anyone shows his toweled head, although I seriously doubt that there will be any need.

"If nobody screws the pooch we should be reassembled at the fallback position just three minutes after go. Once everyone is there, I'll signal for pickup. Then we've got a two-click sprint to the other side of a nearby hill, during which a Blackhawk will skim in from the Turkish border for rapid extraction."

As Odi finished, Adam pointed over his shoulder to the jump-door lights. Odi looked up to see that the pilot had changed the indicator from red to yellow. He felt the belly-fish begin to thrash. "Everyone on your feet."

Chapter 5

Asgard Island, Chesapeake Bay

"YOU'RE NOT HERE to talk about your career?" Wiley asked again, trying to maintain a neutral voice.

"No."

"Then why the devil are you here, Stuart?"

"As I said, we need to talk—unseen, uninterrupted, and alone. There's something I need to know. Something we need to discuss."

"Out with it then," Wiley commanded. He had had enough.

Stuart nodded once. "Very well. Are you in love with Cassi?"

"Pardon me?"

"Are you ... in love ... with Cassi?"

"I am."

Stuart gave another single solemn nod. "You started seeing Cassi six months ago, shortly after we ... began our collaboration. I didn't say anything at the time. Perhaps that was a mistake. Frankly, based on her history, and yours, I didn't think it would last."

Stuart's matter-of-fact monotone bothered Wiley, but he kept his mouth shut. The sooner his campaign manager cum chief of staff got to the point, the sooner Wiley could go back to bed.

"I have to admit that this is the first move you've made that I simply do not understand." Stuart paused. He appeared to be weighing how to clarify his statement but then shook his head in surrender. "We are just twelve months out from the election now. Carver's team finalized the running-mate short-list today. It's down to three names." Stuart held up his fist, palm toward Wiley. "Jefferson Wallace." He raised one finger. "Arthur Hayes." He raised a second. "And you." He gave Wiley a gun-barrel point instead of raising the third finger. Then he opened his hand for a shake. "Congratulations, Director Proffitt. You are officially in play."

Wiley smiled despite himself. He shifted his grip on the latte and took the Washington insider's cool hand, amazed that Stuart had acquired such a secret. A short list like that would only be known to the President and his top two or three advisors.

After they shook, Stuart continued. "Meanwhile, it's no secret that

Mills will top the other ticket. And I'm ninety-five percent sure that he will select either Anders or Metcalf to run as his VP." Stuart gave an open-palmed shrug and settled back in his seat, implying with tone and demeanor that Wiley could easily fill-in the rest.

Wiley drew a blank, but he was not about to let the smug SOB get one up on him. Not here. Not in his own house. He took a long sip of latte, inhaling deeply to maximize the punch of the nutty brew. He tried to think. Anders was the two-term Governor of Georgia and Metcalf was a four-term Florida Senator. Both had solid backgrounds, but neither eclipsed his two terms in Congress, four years in the Virginia governor's mansion, and current service as Director of the FBI. Both Anders and Metcalf were married ... Was that it? Wiley wondered. Did Stuart want him engaged? No problem. Why had he gone through all the drama to ask? Stuart was hardly the sentimental type, but then everyone has his quirks. Apparently marriage was the one thing besides power that was sacred to the man. Wiley found that nice to know, and tucked it away for future reference.

Having discovered his reptilian campaign manager's soft underbelly, Wiley changed his tactics. He wanted the satisfaction of hearing Stuart vocalize his feelings. "Go on, Mister Slider."

Stuart gave him a direct, icy stare. "Anders is six-foot-four, Metcalf six-five ... and Cassi is six-one. You however are a relatively puny five-ten-and-a-half—in heels. You cannot run on a power platform while appearing substantially shorter than everyone else in the game. Try it and you will become a caricature, a political Chihuahua, a late-night joke."

Hearing those words, Wiley felt as though he had been sucker punched.

Stuart did not give him time to breathe. "I can deal with Anders and Metcalf. You won't ever have to stand right next to either of them, although I'm sure their campaign managers will try shamelessly. But Cassi ... there's no way to avoid that money shot. The comparative picture of you will have longer legs than hers. 'Which Proffitt wears the pants?' 'Who's really on top?' 'Wittle Wiley Wannabe.' The tabloid headlines will be your deathblows.

"It all comes down to this, Director. Either you forget about Cassi Carr, or you forget about the Oval Office. Those are the only two options." Stuart folded his hands across his chest.

But there weren't two options. They both knew that.

Wiley closed his eyes. He would have to leave Cassi.

Stuart said, "I'll give you until Monday to do it."

When Wiley finally opened his eyes he found that Stuart had vanished. For once he appreciated the man's magical talent.

Checking over his shoulder more than once, Wiley walked over to the wall safe, spun through the combination, and withdrew a small box. It was robin's-egg blue and approximately two inches cubed. He untied the white silk ribbon, tilted back the lid and stared. It was beautiful, he thought, as unique and flawless as the woman for whom it was intended.

Wiley had found the perfect engagement ring a month ago. For weeks he had enjoyed the anticipation of a spontaneous proposal. Holding that joyous secret in the palm of his hand made him feel like a Christmas-morning kid. In fact, he had cradled it hopefully in his pocket on six separate occasions, ready to take a knee. But the moment had never been just right. His latest plan was to propose at dinner tomorrow night. He had picked the perfect restaurant and even dropped a few hints. Tomorrow was now out of the question, of course. As was the next five years ...

For a fleeting second, Wiley wondered what Stuart would have done if he had already proposed. Then he remembered that Stuart had violated Cassi that very night. He had drugged her in her sleep just so that he could deliver his news with panache. Wiley decided not to pursue that line of thought any further.

He closed the Tiffany lid. It gave a final, fatal clap. He re-tied the white bow and secured the box in the safe. Turning his back on one future in favor of another, he staggered across the study to the adjacent bath ... and threw up.

Chapter 6

Downtown Alexandria, Virginia

"WHAT DO WE HAVE?" Cassi asked, trying to focus on the job at hand while still reeling from a shock of her own.

Officer Foster looked down at his notebook and smiled, "We got us some fans of The King." He cleared his throat. "Elvis Aaron Adams got laid-off from the canning plant today. Came home to find his wife —Priscilla, I kid you not—in bed with another man. Now Elvis is threatening to kill them both with his shotgun. For about ten minutes he was screaming his head off and throwing things, during which the widow who lives next door called us. Then things went silent."

"Have any shots been fired?" Cassi asked, remembering that this was the second time she had negotiated with a man named Elvis and wondering if that could be pure coincidence.

"Not a one."

She nodded a couple of times as she processed the situation and then said, "Tell me about Elvis." On any other day, she would have enjoyed the humor inherent in that sentence. Today she was not feeling the least bit whimsical. Officer Foster seemed to sense her mood.

"He's Caucasian, forty-three years old. Five foot six. Two years ago when his driver's license was issued he weighed one-forty-five."

"Does he have a record?"

"Not even a parking ticket."

"Do they have children?"

"The neighbor says no. She says it's just the two of them living there."

"How long ago did he return home?"

"About forty minutes."

Cassi nodded as her processor kicked into overdrive. Forty minutes was a lot of cooling off time. It was also plenty of time to get worked up into a murderous frenzy or plunged down into a suicidal slump. Neither option looked good for Priscilla or her paramour. She decided to see how astute Foster was.

"Is Elvis a drinker?"

"The widow said yes, but when I pressed her on what that meant she admitted that it's just a few beers on a Friday night."

Cassi said, "Nice work," and pulled out her cell phone. "What's his number?"

"They don't have a land line and both their cell phones are switched off."

She cringed. That was bad news. "Thank you Foster. I've got it from here."

Per regulations, Cassi knew that she should remain out of shotgun range. That would mean negotiating through a bullhorn. Whereas some of her colleagues preferred the authority of that technique, she used it only as a last resort or if drugs were involved. Her preference was always to try to connect with the perpetrator on a personal level. Without a phone, that meant she had to get close, close enough to Elvis for each of them to read the inflections in the other's speaking voice.

She had a decision to make. If her analysis was correct, Elvis was highly unlikely to shoot first and ask questions later. Yesterday that would have been good enough for Cassi. Today she was not sure. She had awakened at Wiley's feeling funny. Then she had watched with teary eyes as a white urine strip grew a blue stripe. If she risked her life today, she would be risking two.

A silenced scream emanating from the house made up her mind. She would ignore the regulation. Cassi ran to the front door and stood shielded by the frame. "Good afternoon, Elvis," she said in a loud but friendly tone. "My name's Cassandra Carr, Cassi for short. I'm here to help you. Would you please step toward the door so we can talk?" Pretty please with sugar on top.

Elvis did not offer an immediate reply. That was to be expected. He needed a minute to make up his mind. Cassi tried to focus on something else to keep from getting nervous while she waited, like whistling her way through a graveyard. It was not difficult. Her personal life had the sad, magnetic draw of the best soap operas. The irony of the latest development leapt to mind. During a recent interview on *PoliTalk*, Wiley had used the fallibility of condoms to make allegorical reference to homeland defenses—Was ninety-nine-percent efficacy good enough?—unaware that one of his own little soldiers had recently crossed enemy lines. If this were not so serious she would find it funny.

How would he react? She wondered. Would he be thrilled or horrified? Angry or overjoyed? Would he spurn her or propose? Surely he would propose now, Cassi figured. That was what she wanted, more than anything. But did she want it this way? The answer came immediately, soft but solid like an elephant appearing beneath a magician's wand. No. No, she did not want to get Wiley this way.

The opening of a window on the second floor shook her back to the present. She stepped back for a better view and simultaneously plotted her course of retreat. She would beat feet at the first sign of a shotgun barrel. Unfortunately, she realized with a sinking heart, there was no suitable shelter anywhere close—just a thin lamp pole and a couple of scraggly bushes. The corner of the house was her only safe bet, and that was twenty feet away. The prudent thing for her to do would be to run there immediately.

Elvis preempted her bolt. "You can help by leaving, all of you."

Cassi paused. It was a good sign that Elvis did not open with a threat. To her that indicated that violence was not the first thing on his mind. Furthermore, his request showed that he was anxious to escape. She replied, "I'd be happy to leave. So would all my friends."

Elvis did not react immediately. He was waiting for her conditions. Cassi wanted him to accept the fact that there would be conditions, so she waited for him to ask. As she stood there on the concrete stoop beside the small dilapidated house, the focus of twenty sets of battle-ready eyes and one hostage taker, Cassi's thoughts again drifted to her own condition.

She could not tell Wiley about the baby. Not now. Not until he proposed. And that meant that she could not tell her employer either. They were one and the same. Standing there in the shadow of a crime she wanted to feel good about her decision. She wanted to rest easy knowing that she had made it for the right reasons. But she did not. She felt guilty. She felt guilty because deep inside she was glad for the excuse.

Cassi was a leading contender to replace Jack Higgins at the end of the year when he retired as head of the FBI negotiations unit. Ever since he had announced his intentions she had tried not to court disappointment by thinking about it too much, but that was impossible. Running the negotiations unit was her dream job. And regardless of the psychological defenses she was trying to construct, she knew that she would be crushed if she did not get it.

Cassi did a quick tally of the math. She would be in her fourth month when Higgins' successor was announced. Since this was her first child, she could probably keep her condition hidden until then if she dressed loosely enough. She was not completely comfortable with the ethics of springing the news the same month she got the promotion, but then there was no chance that they would give her the promotion if they knew she was pregnant, and that was not fair either. Was it?

"Okay. Then go on. Leave."

Cassi snapped back into the negotiation at the sound of Elvis's strained voice. "It's not quite that simple, Elvis. First I need you to throw me your gun."

"Don't treat me like a fool."

"I don't think you're a fool, Elvis. I think you're a good man in a bad situation. You've been betrayed. I know you're a decent guy. I know you don't have a record. I just want to keep you from acting foolishly in a moment of anger. I don't want you to do anything that would ruin the rest of your life. Let's face it. If she betrayed you, she's not worth it."

"Will you let me go?"

"I will."

"I can just get in my car and drive away and you won't try to stop me?"

"Not if you didn't hurt anybody. Not if you leave the gun behind. You didn't hurt anyone, did you Elvis?"

"Nothing but a couple of slaps."

"Slaps they deserved."

"Damn right."

"Then you're a free man. Go ahead. Leave the unworthy bitch. Start a new life. A better life. Or wait for her to come crawling back once she realizes what she's lost. Your choice."

Again there was silence. Cassi was worried by the lack of sound coming from the house. Normally the two hostages would be making some noise, trying to connect with the police lest they be forgotten once the bullets started to fly. She hoped that they were just scared into silence.

What would she do if Wiley did not propose soon? Cassi wondered. With the baby growing inside her, she could not wait too long. He would resent the position she had put him in even more if he found himself inextricably trapped. She knew from her counseling days that such a situation could open an emotional rift between them that would drain the intimacy from the rest of their lives.

"I'm coming out," Elvis said, his voice just behind the door.

"Smart move, Elvis. Smart move. Just do me a favor. As you walk to your car, keep your hands in plain sight."

Chapter 7

Tafriz, Iran

"THIS IS RABBIT ONE with an emergency transmission for Brer Bear," Odi said, focusing on keeping his voice down. He knew that sound would carry dangerously well through the inky Iranian night.

"Roger, Rabbit One. Patching you through to Brer Bear."

Odi hated working through the secure satellite switchboard. It cost too much precious time. He tapped a nervous foot and looked over at Adam. His best friend added to the tension by pointing to the luminous dial of his commando watch.

Odi nodded and mouthed, "I know."

Potchak has stressed that he would measure the success of their mission as much by their ability to extricate undetected as by their tactical success. He had drummed deniability into Odi's head. "Deniability tops your scorecard. Deniability is what counts. Deniability, deniability, deniability."

Odi got the message. He had to make the demolition of the buildings look like an accident, like the tragic explosion of the unstable ordnance secreted within. As mission commander, he knew that the composition of their rocket propelled grenades had been modified with that conclusion in mind. Their equipment, their uniforms, everything was either an Asian knockoff or Soviet surplus. All of it was readily available throughout the Middle East. Including his bloody phone.

"Brer Bear here, Rabbit One. Go ahead."

Odi flashed a thumbs-up to Adam and the other six members of the assault team as they sat on their packs spitting chew and trying to look more bored than scared.

"We have a situation. The Briar Patch appears legit. Repeat, the Briar Patch appears legit. There are no sentries present, and we just observed an ambulance." His teammates all rolled their eyes at Odi's grandiose description of the donkey cart. He just shrugged his shoulders sheepishly and looked away. "It brought in a farm boy who had just lost a foot. Looked like he had stepped on a mine. He was met by medics and rushed inside. I recommend that we abort pending further intel."

"Negative on the abort, Rabbit One. You are to proceed as planned. Intel is confirmed. Don't fall for the window dressing. Skullduggery like that is what has kept this training camp operational for years."

Odi knew that Potchak was a hard ass, but he had not expected pushback. Command usually favored live input from the field over anonymous intel reports. "Sir, I'm prepared to do the recon myself, right now, alone." As he spoke, Adam snapped his fingers to get Odi's attention and then met his eye with an are-you-crazy stare. Odi turned his back. "Won't take me more than ten—."

"Negative, Rabbit One," Potchak broke in. "For one, you don't have ten minutes to throw away. You need to make it to the extraction site before first light. Secondly, I refuse to give those bastards a hostage. I'm not going to watch them cut off your head on the evening news while I try to explain that you had a hunch that the thick and exhaustive report compiled by the Middle-East desk was one-hundred-eighty degrees off the mark."

"It won't come to that, sir. I'll order my team to proceed as planned with or without me at," Odi looked at his watch, "oh-three-hundred. Just give me those ten minutes."

"You sound dead set on checking this out, Rabbit One."

"Time doesn't wash off innocent blood, sir."

Odi waited impatiently through a pregnant pause.

"Pass the phone to Rabbit Two."

Odi smiled and handed Waslager the phone as he remembered the Chinese proverb to beware of what you wish for.

As Waslager listened to the commander, Odi's team drew around, their habitually stoic faces contorted with concerned looks. "What are you planning to do?" O'Brien asked.

Odi had been in and out of the shit with these guys more times than any of them could count. With Waslager otherwise occupied, there was no need for Odi to dilute his words. "Before we propel ninety-six grenades though those cinder walls, I want to be damn sure that they're landing on terrorist wannabes, rather than sick children's heads."

The six nodded once in unison as Odi continued. "I think this is one of those situations where intelligence reported what it was asked to report, kind of like Iraqi WMD. The source of the intel was probably some Iranian kid who would make up anything for a Benjamin. And knowing how things have been going down at recruiting, that report was probably analyzed by some Pentagon conscript with three weeks on the job." Odi decided not to mention Potchak's lack of surprise at his mention of the hospital's operational status.

He removed his BDU top and untucked his tee shirt as he spoke, altering his silhouette so that it would not appear like a soldier's. He laid aside his Chinese M4 and slipped his Beretta into the small of his back. "Hopefully I'm wrong. But taking out a hospital is not something I care to live with for the rest of my life."

Odi finished the simple transformation by untucking his pant legs from his boots. Then he removed two flashbang grenades from his pack and slid them into the pockets of his pants. "If you hear one of these, that means I'm in the shit. You are not to wait for me, and you are certainly not to come in after me. You are to move ahead immediately with the original plan." Odi met each man's eye and waited for a confirming nod.

"I don't mean to sound too dramatic. All I am going to do is take a casual perimeter walk around the two flanking buildings. I'll look for telltales of a terrorist training camp, anything military, from boot marks to bullet casings to concealed cameras or guards. Without the two sentries to worry about, Waslager can cover me through his sniper scope instead. That way we'll be right back on plan if I am challenged."

"With the exception of you hauling ass in the opposite direction, I hope," Flint added.

"Nothing I like better," Odi replied, flashing a brilliant smile. "If I don't see anything incongruent with a hospital, I'll pop my head through the central building's main door and—"

Waslager cut Odi off by clearing his gravelly throat. "Listen up," he said, in a voice that was dangerously loud. "Commander Potchak has just relieved Agent Carr. I am now Rabbit One. So get off your asses and lock and load. We're hot in sixty seconds."

Everyone turned to look at Odi.

Chapter 8

The Horus Club, Washington, D.C.

THE DEAF WAITER raised an eyebrow as Wiley polished off his Scotch.

Wiley nodded and another drink was on the way. When Stuart arrived, it would appear to be his first.

Wiley had come to their rendezvous early. He needed to decompress. Although his heart and mind were working full time on his campaign, he was still the Director of the FBI. He had another full plate.

To manage the juggling act, Wiley had hinted to his deputy director that he was not planning to stay in office very long. When the time came, he would be happy to reward Carl's diligence and loyalty by recommending his indispensable right-hand-man as his clear and obvious successor. Given Wiley's close relationship with the immensely re-electable President, Carl was tripping all over himself to pick up Wiley's slack. Actually, Wiley knew that Carl slyly farmed-out most of the additional load. That was not difficult. The FBI had five major departments plus a dozen or so adjunct offices and committees, each headed by a savvy bureaucrat eager to rise still higher.

The scheme was working, but Wiley still lived beneath an enormous load of stress. Stuart contributed to it. Although Stuart technically worked for Wiley, it usually felt to Wiley like it was the other way around. His campaign manager always seemed to be the one holding trump. Plus Stuart radiated an intellectual superiority that made him awkward to command. Wiley could make requests of Stuart, but he had never managed to dictate.

Still, tonight he would try again. He had chosen the ultra-exclusive Horus Club so that he would enjoy the home-court advantage. In his heart he knew that tactical advantages would gain him nothing, but it was his habit to try. The analyst in him knew that whatever tack he chose, whatever methodology he employed, all Stuart had to do to get his was way was to pull out a recording.

He might do exactly that, Wiley thought. Like a communist dictator parading his armaments for all to see. But probably not. There was no point in reminding a person of something he could never forget, and Stuart did nothing without a point.

Wiley recalled the scene as it had played out six months earlier. The AADC's lavish yacht. The three billionaire CEOs. The suspense. The arrogance. The grace. No, he would never forget their first meeting …

~ ~ ~

"It must have hurt," the fat Texan scoffed, "losing your reelection bid."

Wiley kept his eyes steady, his face void of emotion. "I landed on my feet."

"Indeed you did. Director of the FBI—that's not a bad consolation prize. Still, handing the keys to the Governor's mansion over to that snot-nosed tree-hugger had to hurt."

"What's your point, Mark?"

"Relax," Mark Abrams said, his jowls bouncing grotesquely as he patted Wiley on the shoulder. "We're on your side. In fact, we invited you here to make you an offer."

Rather than ask, Wiley wedged his cigar in his mouth and raised his chin. He did not like being led down the primrose path, toyed with, or manipulated—even by billionaires. Let them get on with it.

Abrams looked him dead in the eye and locked his gaze. Without looking away he said, "How would you like to be President?"

"Of the United States?" Wiley blurted back, sending his Cohiba to the teak decking.

Mark Abrams, the head of Armed Services Industrial Supply and arguably the most powerful of the three CEO's present, flashed him a tight-lipped smile but did not say a word.

Wiley cringed inside, berating himself for his sophomoric slip even as he struggled to regain his composure. He shifted his gaze to Mark Rollins. Then to Mark Drake. And finally back to Mark Abrams. "What do I have to do?" He asked.

"Commit." Abrams replied without pause.

Wiley knew that he had asked the right question. Abrams' tone was stern but he was secretly pleased. Wiley could tell. He sensed the relief of a man who had just drawn to an inside strait.

"Irrevocably," Rollins added. "You need to commit irrevocably—both upfront and blind—that you will see the campaign through to the end."

In silence, Wiley studied Rollins, CEO of the gigantic defense conglomerate that bore his name. Rollins was the tallest of his three hosts, and like Drake was thinner than Abrams by half. None of them were puppy dogs, but Wiley sensed a genuine cruel streak in Rollins. His pampered features were pleasant enough, but the man had evil in his eyes.

Mark Drake jumped into the conversational void. "The problem is this, Mister Director. Even with all the technological advances coming from companies like ours, there is still only one means available for untelling something." He lowered his voice. "A most-primitive means."

"So before you reveal your plans, I have to sign a blank check," Wiley summarized.

"Precisely." The three Marks spoke as one.

Their proposition was clearly take-it-or-leave-it but Wiley was not sure he wanted to know what either taking it or leaving it would mean. He shifted positions surreptitiously to scan the floor behind the bar for a bucket of wet concrete. Drake and his fellow defense contractors clearly were not referring to money when they spoke of a check. Wiley wished they were.

"That check has just three words on it," Abrams added, picking up on Wiley's thoughts. "And we need to hear you say them, aloud and with conviction, before we proceed."

Wiley raised his eyebrows in query.

The Three Marks—Abrams, Drake, and Rollins—clarified slowly and in unison while Stuart looked on in satisfied silence. "Whatever … it … takes."

Wiley took a deep breath. He thought of the White House—east and west wings—and of traveling on Air Force One. He pictured the red carpets, the gala dinners, and the saluting Marines. He thought of the power. He thought about what it would be like to literally be able to summon anybody in the world to spend the weekend with him at Camp David. The offer The Three Marks made might come with a price, but Wiley doubted that there was a man alive who could resist signing that check.

As he repeated the three fateful words, never in a million years would he have guessed that the first victim of that pledge would be Cassi …

~ ~ ~

"You're looking pale," Stuart said, jerking Wiley back from memory lane. The man had slid into the armchair across from him without

Wiley's notice.

Wiley turned his eyes to meet his campaign manager's, but did not comment.

"What could be so urgent," Stuart continued, "that it could not wait until tomorrow and yet was not important enough for you to think of when we met this morning?"

Wiley hardly considered Stuart's midnight invasion of his home a meeting, but he needed a congenial atmosphere, so he let that discrepancy pass. He leaned back and tented his fingers contemplatively before he spoke hoping to get Stuart to do the same. "I want you to reconsider your position on Cassi."

Stuart did mirror his posture, leaning further back into the burgundy leather to digest the request, but he made no verbal comment.

"I'll grant you that her height is a problem," Wiley continued, "but I think it's less of a liability than going into this race single would be. I don't have to tell you that the public wants a family man in the Oval Office."

Stuart seemed to ponder the words for a moment, and then he leaned back into the conversation. "Historically, you're right. But times are changing. More and more voters are single. The divorce rate has topped fifty percent. The average American voter is personally aware of the tradeoff between work and family. Most female executives have had to sacrifice family for their careers. With the pump thus primed, it's easy to argue that twenty-first century America needs the undivided attention of its President. Your bachelor status could actually be an advantage. There's certainly plenty of room for spin."

As Stuart snatched his best arrow from the air and snapped it over his knee, Wiley felt despair creeping back into the crevices of his soul where seconds before he had nurtured hope. But he was not ready to fold, not yet. "You might be right, but you might be wrong. Surely you will agree that it would be better if we didn't have to take the chance?"

Stuart nodded once, but remained silent. He wanted more.

"I want you to meet Cassi. Get a feel for her. I think she could add a lot to the campaign. She is a psychologist and a negotiator. She is bright as the sun and she glows under pressure. Women will admire her. Men will respect her. Even kids will like her. She's gutsy—practically a hero. Talk about potential for spin ..."

Stuart shook his head. "Her image isn't nearly as important as what she does to your image. You're the one who needs the votes, not her. She diminishes you when you need to appear larger than life."

"And I'm saying that, despite the height, I look better next to her. See for yourself. Join us for brunch tomorrow."

Rather than dismissing the suggestion outright as Wiley had feared, Stuart stared at him for a minute in silence. Wiley could practically see the wheels spinning behind those dark eyes. He felt a surge of hope. Time passed. The fireplace crackled and a log fell. Finally Stuart spoke up.

"All right. I'll take a look. I'll meet you for brunch with an open mind. But if I say no after seeing the two of you together, she's gone. No rebuttal. No tears. Agreed?"

Wiley sensed that this tenuous capitulation was the best deal he would get. He feared that it would not be enough. Once again he was facing a point of no return. He gave a parting glance to the life he used to know and then he said it. "Agreed."

Chapter 9

Alexandria, Virginia

CASSI CONTINUED CHANNELING her frustration into sit-ups even though she was well past a hundred. At least trimmer abs would help to camouflage her condition, she thought, grasping for consolation. It looked like she was going to need it. She paused to wipe the sweat from her brow and ended up shaking her head in frustration. Despite her instincts all signaling to the contrary, Wiley had let her down again.

She had been positive that last night was finally going to be the night. Absolutely certain. The timing would have been poetic—coming the very day she learned that she was pregnant. Her intuition wasn't just the wishful thinking of a desperate woman's romantic mind, she told herself. All the signs had been there. He had reserved a prime table at La Chancery, an elegant, intimate restaurant with exquisite French cuisine. He had confirmed her availability not once but three times. And he had shown interest in what she was planning to wear. Those were objective indicators, right? Plus she had seen him fumbling in his left pants pocket a dozen times of late, as though fondling a little treasure. A ring perhaps? God, she hated to catch herself reading into everything like a pathetic schoolgirl. She wiped more sweat from her brow. She had already been in her gown when he called to cancel. "I'm sorry Hon," was all he had said for an apology. "It's urgent business."

He had not even congratulated her on her successful negotiation with Elvis.

Gripping the receiver with flustered fingers, she had wanted to scream, to yell, "You promised!" But instead she gracefully offered to cook him a gourmet brunch in the morning. By her reckoning, he had paused a second too long before accepting. But he had said yes. Thus far she had taken everything Wiley had told her at face value. If he had said no, she admitted to herself with not a little shame, she would have spent the night searching for the other woman.

Although their discussion was twelve hours ago, her resentment still burned. She knew that it was the job and not Wiley that was to blame. She understood fully well that resentment was a negative, destructive emotion. But she could not help it. She was a six-foot-one, north-of-thirty woman with a PhD and a badge. Single men who could cope with and complement that combination were rare as honest politicians.

Cassi looked at her watch and berated herself. As a result of her neurosis, he was just fifteen minutes away and she was all worked up and sweaty. Jumping to her feet she caught sight of her panting form in the mirror. It struck her that a good brunch could be even more intimate than a candle-lit dinner—given the right music, a cozy atmosphere, and the proper state of undress.

She ran through the shower and then applied a dusting of makeup and a dab of perfume before slipping back into the cream silk pajamas she had been wearing an hour earlier. The lingerie was not particularly revealing in the classic sense, but it hugged her in all the right places. She had found that there was something about the way flesh bounced under silk that attracted men's eyes like a fishing lure. Twirling before the mirror she decided to go for broke and leave all but one of the buttons undone. She might as well show off her flat stomach while she could. As an afterthought she grabbed the bottoms from a pair of pajamas that Wiley had left in her closet but never worn. Then she ran to the kitchen. She would suggest that he change.

To her own astonishment, Cassi had the candles burning and Norah Jones singing before the doorbell rang. It was amazing what you could accomplish given the proper motivation. She tossed her hair to give it extra body, checked the lie of her top, and opened the door with a sultry "Good morning."

Wiley was not alone.

"Good morning yourself," Wiley said, kissing her cheek. "Cassi, allow me to introduce Stuart."

The third wheel held out his hand. "Stuart Slider."

Stuart struck Cassi as either a European gymnast or a wrestler, but given that he was with Wiley, she knew that he was neither. He wore black Bally loafers, black jeans, and a black sweater that hugged his compact but muscular frame like the label on a bottle of Guinness. She recognized his casual appearance as being anything but. That man had given serious thought to his wardrobe, carefully crafting his image.

She disliked him at first sight.

Cassi shielded herself with the door as they entered so that she could discreetly button her top. When she turned back around after locking the door, Stuart held out a magnum bottle of Veuve Clicquot Yellow Label with a manicured hand while giving her a look that made her think that he could see through silk.

"Why thank you," she said. "How considerate."

"Stuart is an old friend passing through town," Wiley said. "He called last night, but as you know, I was too busy to catch up. So I took the liberty of inviting him along this morning. I hope you don't mind?" As he finished he apparently noted her pajamas for the first time and added. "I suppose I should have called."

"No problem," she said. "We're casual here. As you can see, I'm running a bit behind. If you'll grab some champagne flutes from the cupboard and set one more place, I'll run to the bedroom to change."

~ ~ ~

Wiley and Stuart did most of the talking during brunch. Cassi had the oddest feeling throughout that they were putting on a show, although for the life of her she could not fathom why. Adding to the strange atmosphere, she could not escape the feeling that Stuart was studying her—not as a sex object, but more as a rival. She never caught him in the act, and when he addressed her their conversation was pleasant enough, but for some reason she still felt the urge to smack those rimless silver spectacles off his taught face. That was not fair of her, she knew. It was Wiley who had done the inviting, so if she was going to be mad at anyone it should be him. But even for a psychologist, logic was not always emotion's master. She wondered if the emotional rollercoaster she had been riding these past twelve hours was the pregnancy hormones kicking in. If so, she was looking at eight long months.

The other odd thing about Stuart was that he kept taking pictures of her with Wiley. He explained it away as his hobby, his passion really was how he put it. But Cassi was not convinced. Stuart did not strike her as a passionate man.

Cassi made an effort to take her mind off analysis and back to the conversation at hand, but it was hopeless. The topics they selected were at once too deep for Sunday brunch and yet too shallow for her mood. What did she think about foreign troop deployment? Was she a defender of the second amendment? When they shifted to a woman's right to choose she would have choked on the champagne had she not been just pretending to sip. Rather than answer she excused herself to urgent business in the kitchen.

Since she could not suddenly begin refusing alcohol without provoking the obvious question, Cassi had decided to fake it. At the table she raised the glass to her lips without actually drinking. Then she would surreptitiously soak up half her flute with her napkin and exchange the napkin for a fresh one each time she went to the kitchen. She was pleased with herself for devising such a clever ruse.

As she returned to the table with warm cinnamon rolls, Stuart turned to watch her approach and said, "I've heard of lofts, of course, but I've never actually been in one before. How long have you lived here?"

"I moved in right after graduate school, so I guess that makes it six years."

Stuart nodded. "I figured that you had been here a while. I notice that you've been watching the kids playing at the daycare center across the street. I get the impression from the emotions crossing your face that you know some of them. Am I right?"

Stuart was an observant one, Cassi thought. Perhaps he really was an avid photographer. She nodded abstractly to buy herself some time. She did not feel like revealing anything about herself to this guy. On the other hand she did not want the conversation to lapse back into politics either. After pondering her options for a moment, she decided to risk exposing a bit of her soul to Stuart in order to see what Wiley's reaction would be to her discussion of kids. "Actually I do know them. The red haired one with boots is David. He likes pretending to be tough although he's really a coward. The girl with the pink glasses on the swing next to him is Rita. She falls down a lot but never cries. The little cutie in the yellow coat hanging from the jungle gym is Sammy. He's the clown. He uses humor to hide the insecurity he feels because he still wets his pants. The girl by herself on the bench is Sara. She's not interested in their games. It's because she's smarter than the others but the ironic result is that she feels inadequate." Cassi saw Wiley looking at her with wide eyes and stopped.

"How do you know them?" He asked.

She shrugged. "They're out there every weekend. Sometimes I sit and watch them as I drink my morning tea."

"So how did you learn their names?" Stuart asked.

"Oh, those aren't their real names—just the ones I use."

"Cassi was a child psychologist before joining the Behavioral Sciences Unit," Wiley added.

Cassi faked a sip of champagne to occupy her mouth. When her former career came up, people usually wanted to know why she switched. It was a story she did not like to tell. Stuart seemed to sense that, and did not ask. Instead he inclined his head toward the daycare center and said, "It's kind of sad if you think about it. They should be spending their weekends with their parents."

It was a much more sensitive comment than she would have expected from him, Cassi thought. Perhaps there was a heart beneath Stuart Slider's dark veneer. As she contemplated that unexpected twist, he refilled their champagne flutes.

"Speaking of morning tea," she said, "I'll go brew some." Standing, she followed Stuart's gaze. He was looking at her hand as she reached for her flute and nodding to himself almost imperceptibly. He looked up suddenly to catch her expression. She felt the lining drop out of her stomach as their eyes locked. The flute slipped from her grasp but Cassi instantly forgot it. Stuart knew.

Chapter 10

Tafriz, Iran

FEELING HUMILIATED and infuriated, Odi watched from behind a sandy knoll as his team disappeared into the inky Iranian night. For a second he considered tracking their progress further with the assistance of his Urtel sniper scope, but the thought of having to look in from the outside like a wannabe voyeur just rubbed salt in his wounds. He shook his head. What had Potchak gained by relieving him of command? He asked himself for the dozenth time. A lousy ten minutes? Ten minutes that might have made the difference between eliminating terrorists and murdering kids? Was it extreme urgency that drove Potchak's severe reaction? Or was Odi missing something? He could not get his head around the incredible stupidity required to make a decision like that. It just did not compute. Potchak was a hard-ass, but he was no fool.

Odi had no idea why Potchak had been so quick to strip him of power. Aside from the occasional disagreement—like the one where Potchak prohibited him from informing his men about their mission— their relationship had been smooth enough. It was not a particularly warm relationship, but then The Bulldog was not a warm-and-fuzzy kind of guy. Again Odi came to the conclusion that there were forces at work about which he had no knowledge. He hoped that once the dust settled, one of those forces would get him off the hook. As it was, Odi did not know what to hope for as he listened for the gunshot that would begin the questionable attack. His was a damned-if-you're-right, damned-if-you're-wrong situation. Either innocents were about to die, or his career was over.

Odi also worried about his team. They were doing as demanded, following orders. That was rigidly expected of course. In fact, command repeatedly drilled in that very response in the course of some of the world's most grueling military training. But every man still had to take responsibility for his own actions, and they knew that. The guilt resultant from pointlessly killing scores of innocents could not later be ordered away—not when they had been fairly warned.

As Odi pondered that, his earphone cracked to life. Waslager's oily voice said, "All teams report."

"Red team's a go." "White team's a go." "Blue team's a go." Derek, Adam, and Flint replied in sequence.

Odi ripped off his headset and threw it to the ground. He told himself that he did not want to hear anything that might later legally jeopardize his men—like them conspiring to frag Waslager for example —but in fact he simply could not stand to listen. If the hospital did turn out to be legitimate and an investigation ensued, he would tell internal affairs that he removed his headset for tactical reasons, to better detect potential threats among the ambient noise.

It began.

The explosions reverberated like a giant's footfalls across the sleepy land. Every ten seconds there was another six-point bang as the next salvo of explosive grenades brought the suspect buildings closer to the ground. Just like clockwork. He was proud of their precision if not their mission.

Odi watched plumes of dusty smoke billow toward the inky sky, reflecting starlight back in a ghastly dance. Air that only moments ago was arid and crisp was now filled with an ominous cordite stench. He waited for the sounds of tortured screams and imploring pleas, but nothing rose above the deafening echoes of so many grenades. So much the better, he thought.

He began counting down salvos, working backward with the knowledge that there would be ten. Ten ... nine ... eight ... At two he found himself rolling across the ground with a sharp pain pulsing lighting through his left shoulder. One way or another, he had been hit. Was it shrapnel? A bullet? Divine intervention? He twisted his neck and shoulder, provoking more pain as he tried to get a look at the mysterious wound. All he could see was blood pumping through the sleeve of his shirt.

He strained to compress the wound with his chin while struggling to remove his belt with his one working hand. If only he hadn't taken his radio off, he cursed himself. Stupid, stupid, stupid. With effort he got his belt noosed around his left arm and a heartbeat later he cinched it down half an inch above the pulsing stream. He saw the flow ebb to a trickle, but it did not stop. Gritting his teeth, he cinched it further, ratcheting down until the pain was almost too much to bear. Finally the bleeding stopped. His makeshift tourniquet would be safe for a minute or two. He only needed something to keep him conscious until his team returned. Then Adam could apply a pressure bandage and achieve hemostasis without cutting off the blood-flow to his hand. He hoped he would still have enough juice in his system to run. The guys would give him grief for the rest of his career if they had to carry him to the extraction site.

Odi began laughing at the irony despite the intermittent jolts of searing pain. He could not help it. Realizing that his boisterous laughter was both dangerous and an indication of the onset of shock, he forced himself to stop. That was when he noticed the eerie silence. It would only be a few seconds now.

He pictured his teammates emerging like demons from the dark and smoke and strained to see them. He anticipated the wry smiles and jibes he would get when they saw his wound. "Can't we leave you alone for a minute, Carr?" "We should have hired a babysitter." "I think he's really a Marine."

No one came.

That was strange, Odi thought. He wondered if the loss of blood had warped his sense of time. He checked his stopwatch. Four minutes and ten seconds had passed since the first salvo. They were seventy seconds overdue.

Odi waited another fifteen seconds, but no one appeared. "The radio," Odi said, cursing himself again. He looked over to the left where he had thrown down his headset and saw a broken mess. Whatever had hit his arm had obviously demolished his headset too. The sight made him think of the magic Kennedy bullet.

Glad to have a backup he patted his breast pocket. It was empty.

Empty? Then he remembered Waslager commandeering his sat-phone. "Great. Just great."

Odi was seriously worried now. If grenades were still exploding or bullets were still whizzing he would understand the delay. They would signal that his team had encountered unexpected resistance. But all was quiet. Wounded or not, Odi knew that he had to investigate. Someone might need his help.

Getting to his feet, he wondered how long it would take for local law enforcement to arrive. The complex enjoyed a peripheral location and the village itself was remote, but capture was not the only concern. He replayed the Commander's incessant order that they not allow themselves to be identified.

The protest emanating from his left fingers became unbearable. He eased the pressure off his improvised tourniquet and craned his neck to observe the sight of the wound. Crimson began to gurgle forth. He was still losing arterial blood.

He ripped his compression bandage from his pack and slapped it down directly atop his pulsing wound. The position was awkward and neck-cramping, but he still managed to hold the wad of gauze in place with his chin. Wishing he had a spent bullet to bite he cinched his belt down directly over the wound. Judging by the pain, the shrapnel was still inside. He screamed "Waslager, you bastard!" and then made for the rubble.

Odi needed only a minute to find the first man. O'Brian. He lay in a crumpled mass and was already covered with course gray soot. Although Odi could not see the entry wound, the expansive pool of blood beneath his body indicated that he had been hit in the head or neck. Odi felt his own pain give way to a flood of rage. Then the implications registered and he felt a chill of fear followed by a wave of guilt. Hospitals did not employ snipers.

He had been wrong.

His doubt had diminished the team's strength by nearly fifteen percent—easily enough to cost O'Brian his life.

Percolating with self-loathing, Odi began cursing himself but stopped abruptly. There was no time for that selfish sentiment now. He had to investigate. He had to see if anyone from his team was still alive.

He knew that investigating would become ever more dangerous as seconds passed and smoke cleared. Visibility was still next to nothing with the smoke blocking out the stars, but that would change with dawn's first rays. Come daybreak he would be as visible as a pimple on the prom queen's nose.

As he mentally mapped out the most efficient way to canvass the complex, he realized that there was a quicker way. He muttered a fast

"Forgive me brother," as he rolled O'Brian over to remove his radio. The sight that met his eyes was striking enough to give him pause. O'Brian's headset had also been hit. It was useless.

As alarm bells went off in his mind, Odi wondered if the al-Qaeda sniper had some new high-tech equipment that allowed him to hone in on a target using radio waves. He would report that possibility—if he ever got home.

Without giving further thought to his own safety, Odi set off following a parallel trail of tracks. Twenty yards from O'Brian, Odi found Adam. His best friend also had a savage head wound, but miraculously he was still alive. Adam was just lying there, stoically silent, looking wide-eyed up at the sky as though searching for distant stars. He grew a feeble grin and groaned, "The weasel," when he caught sight of Odi.

Odi was afraid to touch his friend, afraid to make his condition worse, but as his eyes focused he realized that worse was not possible. Extreme adrenaline was the only thing keeping Adam alive.

"Swear, Odi. Swear you'll—"Adam sucked in a long, ragged breath "—get the weasel for me."

"I swear," Odi vowed perfunctorily, bending to cradle Adam's head.

"Don't let him get away," Adam gasped. Then he died.

As Odi stared down at his friend a fetid stew of surprises swirled around his faltering mind. His sudden loss of command, his shoulder wound, the mysterious death of his friends, the solicited vow of revenge—everything collided as it tried to congeal. Something about this mission was terribly wrong.

As he tried to grasp the conclusion that was hovering at the outskirts of his conscious mind, Odi realized that his head was spinning from more than just the confluence of radical events. His vision was now blurred and the ground seemed unstable. He turned his head and strained to focus on his left shoulder. His belt had fallen to his elbow. His bandage had slipped. Before he could react his world turned gray, and then, slowly, silently, it faded to black.

Chapter 11

FBI Headquarters, Washington, D.C.

WILEY DUCKED into his private bath and closed the door to his office. He bent over the sink and splashed cold water on his face. After a couple of good dowsings he straightened up and studied his reflection in the mirror. "You can do this," he said aloud. "This is nothing but a warm-up pitch. When you're in the Oval Office you will be called upon to send thousands of the nation's sons and daughters into battles where they will lose lives and limbs, serenity and sanity, innocence and affluence. Keep your focus on the big picture. This is nothing."

He patted his face with a thick white towel embroidered with the seal of the FBI. After placing it back on the rack he took a step back and adjusted the knot in his emerald tie, using more force than was necessary. Stuart had made it clear as they left yesterday's brunch, accenting his speech with pictures: Cassi had to go. Wiley did not agree with his campaign manager's judgment, but he accepted the wisdom of deferring to it. Stuart was the pro. He was ice-cold and impartial. Like him or not, Wiley could not deny that the invisible man was good.

For a second or two Wiley had toyed with the thought of defying Stuart, but he knew rebellion was out of the question. If Stuart became convinced that Wiley's campaign was a loser, he could probably still convince The Three Marks to back one of the other two contenders. Wiley had to avoid that at all costs. Someday soon his campaign would cross a mutual point of no return, and then he would tell Stuart off. At least that was what Wiley told himself this morning.

The intercom on his desk beeped and his assistant's squeaky soprano shattered the silence. "Agent Carr is here, Director."

Wiley zipped over to his desk and keyed his response, noting that the knot in his throat was now as tight as the one on his tie. "Send her in, Kate."

Cassi was beaming as she walked through the door, causing Wiley to swallow hard. She really could brighten a room. She paused halfway to his desk to look around. "You know I've never been inside this office before. It looks bigger than my loft. What do you have back there?" She nodded to the door he had just come through. "The secret files, or a private bath?"

"Have a seat," Wiley said, gesturing to the chair before his desk rather than the suite of armchairs by the window to the left. He knew that it was best to be quick and clean in situations like this. Delivering bad news was like ripping off a Band-Aid.

A cloud dimmed Cassi's radiant face, but she complied without comment, sitting with her hands in her lap.

"Cassi, I—"

The intercom cut Wiley off. "Excuse me, Director. I've got Commander Potchak here at my desk. He says it's urgent."

Wiley gave Cassi an apologetic shrug. "Send him in."

As the commander of the Counterterrorism Response Team marched into the office, Wiley could not help picturing General Patton's bull terrier. There was just something about Potchak's dull eyes and long flat nose that always invoked that particular canine image. Potchak, usually unflappable as a manhole cover, did a double take when his eyes landed on Cassi.

She stood and said, "I'll leave you two."

Wiley nodded but Potchak said, "Actually, it's expedient to have you here, Agent Carr. This concerns you as well." Potchak reached out to hold the back of Cassi's chair. She sat back down and he took a seat himself.

Wiley felt his mouth go dry. He had been dreading the breakup moment, but now that it had arrived he was anxious to plow through. Furthermore, Potchak's news was bound to be bad. Urgent news always was. He wanted to skip any further pleasantries and get this over with. "What's on your mind, Commander?"

Potchak looked uncharacteristically uncomfortable, but he nodded once and commenced. "Counterterrorism Response Team Echo was ambushed last night during a reconnaissance mission in Iran."

Wiley nodded, wearing his best poker face and keeping his gaze on Potchak to avoid Cassi's eye. "Do we know who ambushed them?"

"The details are still coming in, but since they were investigating a potential al-Qaeda training camp, our working assumption is that it was terrorists." Potchak paused as Wiley and Cassi both frowned in silence, then he pivoted to face Cassi with guilt writ large on his bellicose face. "As you must know, Echo's Team Leader was your brother, Odysseus, Agent Carr."

Cassi nodded.

"I'm afraid there were no survivors."

Chapter 12

Alexandria, Virginia

EVEN AS SHE STOOD teary-eyed before the cold oak casket and scores of familiar mourners, Cassi could not convince her psyche that she had been forever cleaved from her twin. She took a deep breath. The aromas of white lilies and freshly turned earth took her tumbling back to her parents' funeral. It seemed at once like only yesterday and yet so long ago. As then, today felt neither real nor right.

A tremble began to overtake her. She closed her eyes for a moment to calm herself before attempting to speak. She held her hand to her belly and thought of the circle of life. Odi's essence would live on—in Wiley's child.

"My brother—" Cassi choked up. She paused and readjusted her grip on the edges of the Lucite lectern. She tried to look over the crowd and block everyone out, but a small group to the far left kept drawing her eye. She wondered who they were. She thought she knew all of Odi's friends. They were not with the bomb technicians or the counterterrorism crowd. She began to take a mental tally of the other groups affected by Odi's life and the identity of the mysterious guests came to her in a flash. She smiled.

"My brother—" Cassi paused again, but this time it was for a different reason. Suddenly her speech did not feel right. Odi had lived his life unscripted. His funeral was no place to start. She reached out and tore up the sheet of ivory paper. "I can't do it," she said. "You already know all this." She shook the shreds of paper and then let them flutter to the ground. "You know Odi was nationally renowned as a bomb technician, and considered the best in the FBI. You know he switched to the FBI's elite Counterterrorism Response Team after our parents died on Flight Ninety-Three because he felt that a reactionary job was not enough anymore. What most of you do not know is the remarkable man behind those accomplishments I think I owe it to Odi in this final hour to tear down his modest façade.

"The real Odysseus Carr is well represented by the five mourners off to my left." Cassi gestured with her arm as she looked out to a crowd of confused faces and a subset of approving nods. "Odi was not truly a bomb technician or a professional at counterterrorist assault—any more than he was a dishwasher or a cook. Those were just functions he performed. In his heart, Odi was a scientist, a peacemaker, a humanitarian." Cassi saw more confused faces, more approving nods.

"My brother invented Divinylpolystyrene, a compound more commonly known by its trade name: ArmoWrap." Cassi saw about half the mourners' faces light up with shock and surprise. "For those of you who don't have experience disarming bombs, ArmoWrap is a quick-setting Styrofoam-like spray that encases pipe bombs in a highly-adhesive shock-absorbing shield. Sixty seconds after it is sprayed onto an improvised explosive device, ArmoWrap will have cut its destructive power by an average of seventy-three percent. Every Humvee and police car operating beneath the American and NATO flags now carries a can of ArmoWrap in the trunk beside the spare, and Odi's invention is already credited with saving hundreds of lives.

"Odi developed ArmoWrap when he was just twenty-three and still working at Johns Hopkins on his first PhD. Although he never spoke of them—when was the last time one of you referred to Odi as Doctor Carr—he had PhD's in chemistry and biomolecular engineering. He could have retired on his royalty checks to a yacht or a beach to live the rest of his life in luxury and peace. But being the scholar that he was Odi chose to heed the lesson of his hero Alfred Nobel instead. He donated the ArmoWrap patent to the International Association for the Assistance of Victims of Landmines. Then he one-upped Nobel by insisting that the IAAVL keep his name out of the news. The Board of the IAAVL kept that promise, but obviously they did not forget. They are here today." Cassi nodded toward the small group as a murmur broke out in the crowd.

"I'm glad that my parents got to see Odi's triumph while they were still alive. They were very proud of him for what he did. To be honest, my reaction at the time could best be described as confused. I would never have given up a life of luxury in lieu of a dangerous job and government pay the way he did. Even though he had a twin, Odi truly was unique.

"Eventually I did figure it out, although it took me years. You see, despite his contrary outward appearance, Odi was an extraordinarily peaceful man.

"I see your skeptical faces. You're wondering if grief has somehow affected my mind. The key to understanding Odi was this: He was aggressively peaceful. Wanton violence caused him such moral outrage that he felt compelled to fight back. He did not fight for glory or medals or even the adrenaline rush. He fought for peace. Like Mother Teresa who condemned herself to living among the wretched of

Calcutta, Odi condemned himself to a violent life so that others could live in peace. And he was very good at what he did.

"I will miss my brother in ways that I can only begin to express. I know that you will too."

She abandoned the lectern to stand beside the casket. Others closed in around her in a show of support. After a moment of silence, she placed a single red rose on the polished oak. "I love you brother."

Cassi wanted to walk into the crowd and fall into Wiley's arms, but such a public display was out of the question. Oddly enough, Odi's death had pulled them apart more than it had drawn them together. Perhaps since Wiley was the ultimate man in charge of that fateful mission, she held him vaguely responsible for Odi's death. Likewise he probably felt a little guilty.

Cassi heard a chorus of distant beeps as she backed away from Odi's grave. She looked up to see a few of her HRT colleagues gathering around Jack to talk in familiar animation. Inappropriate though it might be, she felt a strong urge to throw herself back into work.

Cassi accepted a few "beautiful-eulogy"s and a dozen encouraging arm pats, hugs, and nods as she made her way toward the dispersing hostage-rescue team. "Jack, hold on. What's up?"

Her boss stopped the beeline he was making toward his car and turned. "We've got an incident, Cassi. Nothing for you to worry about."

"But I want to worry. I think the distraction would be the best thing for me."

"Not today," Jack said, compassion in his eyes. "You go home and get some rest. Really, that's the best thing for you. Trust me."

Cassi had half a mind to just hop in her Toyota and follow them wherever they went, but she had parked two hundred yards away by the chapel. She would never catch up. She was wearing a long dress and, on this rare occasion, heels.

So what was she going to do then? Cassi wondered. She had not thought past the funeral. Wiley had told her that he had to spend the day in the office. The last thing she wanted to do was watch the minimum-wage ditch diggers plant Odi's casket in the ground. Nor was she in the mood for more "I'll-miss-him"s and "I'm-sorry"s and condoling pats on the back. She could call Quantico to find out where the current crisis was, but that would probably be a waste of time. The crime scene was likely a helicopter-ride away. She decided to take Jack's advice and go home.

Cassi arrived at her block twenty minutes later to find a police barricade and crowded sidewalks. She felt a lump growing in her throat as she pulled out her gold shield and asked the beat cop what was up.

"We got an anonymous tip that a man was trying to break into the art-restoration workshop over the daycare center. Dispatch sent two units, code two, but the perp saw them coming in time to take hostages. He's got a bomb and a couple of kids."

Chapter 13

Orumiyeh, Iran

ODI HEARD SCREAMS and moans and strange voices muttering all around him. He could not understand a word and he could not see a thing. Panic tried to seize him but he fought its grip. Was he in hell? He tried to think of the last thing he could remember. His mind was operating excruciatingly slowly, as though his synapses were sopped in molasses. He remembered the ground-shaking explosions ... and being hit in the shoulder ... and then he found Adam. He had a very clear recollection of the look in Adam's eyes as he died in his arms ... and then ... nothing else. That was all he could remember.

Odi began to scream. He did not know why. There in the dark with those voices all around it was a primordial reflex. He screamed and gasped, gasped and screamed. Finally he felt a demon claw at his arm until the voices faded away.

~ ~ ~

Odi heard, "Wake up," and felt something moving around his head and face. "Wake up. You have to leave the hospital right away." Now someone was shaking his arm. Had it all been a dream? He wondered. Oh please, let Adam be alive.

Odi slowly opened his eyes. The light was painful, although once his eyes adjusted he saw that the room was relatively dim. Looking off to the side as he lay on his back, he saw an old rolling partition to the left of his bed, a white sheet strung in a chrome frame. It had grown gray and frayed with service and age. As he studied it a face moved in above his and Odi thought for a minute that he had been rescued by Tom Selleck—Tom Selleck holding a big wad of dirty gauze.

The face towering above him was kind and intelligent and aged about forty years—with curly dark hair, blue eyes, and a thick mustache. The only thing he needed to look like "Magnum P.I." was a Tigers baseball cap. Although Odi did not have a mustache, he too was often compared to Selleck. They shared a tall athletic frame, lively eyes, and mischievous grin. For a freaky second Odi thought that maybe he was looking in the mirror. Maybe he had been asleep for years and Cassi had asked the nurse not to shave his mustache. She had always encouraged him to grow one. That ridiculous notion vanished as quickly as it appeared. The face above him was not that similar.

It dawned on Odi that the wad of dirty gauze Tom was holding had just come from around his face.

"I know you've got a lot of questions," his new friend whispered in English, "but there's no time for them now. I dyed the skin of your hands with iodine and have been keeping your white face hidden, but yesterday you began screaming in English. Word leaked quickly about an American's presence. They will be coming soon. We have to get you out." Tom withdrew a pair of sandals and a well-worn dishdasha from a cellophane bag. "Put these on. And hurry."

As Odi exchanged his hospital gown for the traditional Arab robe, he whispered, "Are you American?"

"Californian, born and raised. Now hurry up."

A lightning bolt shot through Odi's left shoulder as he pushed his left arm through. He winced without crying out. He had forgotten about his wound. Judging by the acute pain, he would not be forgetting again anytime soon.

"Ah, I almost forgot." Tom said, withdrawing a syringe from his doctor's bag.

Odi endured a flash of panic before realizing the obvious. If Tom intended to give him a lethal injection, he would have done so already.

Tom injected a clear serum above the wound.

Odi felt a warm sensation and the throbbing began to fade away. "Thanks."

Tom ignored the words of appreciation and ushered him toward the door near the right foot of Odi's bed. Odi glanced over the partition before ducking through the doorway. He had been recuperating at the far end of a long hospital ward. There must have been two dozen other beds lined up in the same room with barely enough space for a thin nurse to squeeze through between them. All were occupied, Odi had obviously been enjoying what amounted to the corner suite.

In the stairwell, Tom handed him a keffiyeh and without question Odi draped it around his head, being careful to cover all his wavy brown hair. He did not know who they were running from, but given the circumstances he was willing to accept Tom's judgment that he did not want to meet them.

They exited the hospital three stories down at ground level and walked quickly along a busy street that stank of stale urine. They turned left half way down the block into a dusty alley and then zigzagged through a series of short and narrow backstreets for about fifteen minutes. Odi could not tell if his savior had a specific destination in mind or if he was just trying to put a labyrinth of distance between them and the hospital. He decided not to ask.

After about fifteen minutes of dusty twists and turns, Tom became particularly watchful again. Odi observed him checking over his shoulder frequently and even scanning the rooftops. A minute later they entered an apartment building. It was old but solid. Judging by the condition of the other buildings they had passed. Odi decided that this was probably one of the most desirable addresses around. In the US it would have been condemned.

Tom led him up a dim staircase littered with trash. Odi tried to ignore the olfactory assault from rotting garbage and harsh tobacco smoke. On the fifth floor they entered a hallway. A single bare bulb of not more than fifteen watts cast dim light on four hodgepodge doors. Tom stopped before one that had the number 53 stenciled on it with a ballpoint pen. He withdrew two long, double-sided keys from a deep pocket and turned each in sequence through several revolutions to unlock the door. They had not spoken since leaving the hospital and Tom did not break the silence now. He just gestured for Odi to step inside. Odi said a silent prayer and took a leap of faith.

Once Tom had shut and locked the heavy door from within, he put his hands on his knees and let out a long breath. "I've lived here for five years now, but this is the first time I have ever had to do anything like that. I hope it was the last." He held out a sweaty hand. "Ayden Archer."

Odi gave him as firm a pump as he could muster. He was winded from the walk, and really wanted to sit down. "Odi Carr. I suspect that I'm very glad to meet you. And I certainly don't want to put you to any more trouble. If you have a phone, I'll call—" Odi hesitated. He was not sure how much he should reveal.

"A friendly embassy? Your unit?"

Odi nodded without clarifying. Actually, he planned to call his sister first. He knew that Cassi would be worried sick.

"I have something to show you before you do that," Ayden said. "But first, we should get some food and drink into you. Your brain needs food. Please, come into the kitchen."

Odi realized that he was in fact ravenous. "Thank you. That would be great. You are very kind and I certainly appreciate your trouble."

They moved down a short hall past what Odi assumed was the bath to a modest kitchen with a balcony. "It's probably a good idea for you to stay inside," Ayden said, canting his head toward the balcony door. "Although you must know more about hiding out than I. The only thing I know about cloak-and-dagger stuff comes from movies and books." He let out a little nervous laugh.

Odi sat on a stool watching Ayden fill a teapot from a Brita filtering jug and then use a wooden match to ignite the stove's gas burner with a shaking hand. Once Ayden was satisfied with the level of flame, he pulled a second stool for himself from beneath the breakfast table and took a seat across from Odi. His hands were still fidgeting with the yellow box of matches.

"Are we in danger here?" Odi asked.

Ayden brought his hands together and looked at Odi with twitchy eyes. "Yes."

Chapter 14

PoliTalk Studio, Washington, D.C.

WILEY STUDIED the image in the studio mirror as he perfected the knot of his silver tie. Appearances were not particularly important to him on a personal level, but professionally he knew never to underestimate the impact of the right look. He liked what he saw. The Hickey-Freeman suit fit him like a cashmere glove, accenting the breadth of his shoulders, while power radiated from his ice-blue eyes. He knew that those beamers would serve him well in the coming months as he sought to captivate, romance, and cajole. Today his favorite blue shirt augmented their flair while his tie amplified their twinkle.

"Two minutes, Director Proffitt."

Wiley looked over his left shoulder and practiced his most charming gaze as "Thank you, Maxine" rolled off his tongue like warm butterscotch over a sundae. He immediately turned his head back to the mirror but watched her reaction from the corner of his eye. Bingo. It did not matter how old they were, Wiley J. Proffitt could always make the ladies blush.

~ ~ ~

"We're back with our special Terror-Strikes edition of *PoliTalk*," Jim Fitzpatrick's Irish face greeted the television crowd. "Joining us now is *PoliTalk* regular Wiley Proffitt, Director of the FBI. Good morning Wiley."

"Good morning, Jim."

"Two weeks ago you were on our show discussing terrorism and you predicted that our number was almost up. As everyone in America now knows, one week later it was. Last Saturday, for the first time since 9/11, Americans were victims of multiple simultaneous terrorist attacks. The offices of the US Chamber of Commerce were bombed in Belgium. An American school—empty thank God—was bombed in France. And a hospital was bombed in Iran while an American delegation was present. Of the twelve Americans killed, eight were members of your Bureau, all victims of the hospital attack. Your prediction appears startlingly accurate, especially when viewed against the background of America's intelligence failures. Do you care to comment?"

"To be honest, Jim, I've been doing everything in my power to prove myself wrong. I have one of the few jobs around that rewards you for doing exactly that." Wiley looked down for a moment as if to compose himself. "The loss of those eight agents was, well, personal. The FBI is one big family, and now eight of our sons have been slaughtered. I knew several of them personally. Those fine young men were serving our country on a fact-finding mission, covertly inspecting areas we had identified as potential al-Qaeda bases. Obviously our assumption was correct. As you and your viewers know, that particular site was ostensibly a hospital. In truth it was an al-Qaeda training camp. Unfortunately, the terrorists somehow learned that my men were coming and they lay in wait.

"The FBI's takeaway lesson is to anticipate similar future leaks.

"The lesson for the American people is harsher still.

"Considering the calculated nature of that attack, it should now be clear to every red-blooded American that our enemies are willing to murder dozens of their own compatriots and even destroy their own infrastructure if in so doing they can also terminate a few American lives. The conventional rules of engagement no longer apply. These terrorists are not trying to win, per se. They just want us to lose."

Fitzpatrick began to comment but Wiley held up his hand. "I should add that I hope the members of the Congressional Budgeting Committee are paying attention to that particular fact. We are living in a new paradigm now. If we aim to continue the American way of life, Congress is going to have to release the purse strings. I know that the cost of protection may seem daunting at first, but I can assure you that defense is a bargain compared to the alternative. Prevention only costs an ounce."

"Reading between the lines, I take it that you're expecting more attacks?" Jim asked.

Wiley nodded somberly. "You take it right."

"Anytime soon?"

"Every-time soon, Jim. We need to remain constantly vigilant and keep striving to become ever better prepared. Tragic though they were, last week's attacks were a far cry from 9/11. By my reckoning, that trifecta was just a practice swing."

Fitzpatrick seemed taken aback. "Let me make sure that I'm getting this right," he said. "In your professional opinion al-Qaeda is just warming up?"

"I am afraid so."

Fitzpatrick let the air go silent for a moment to emphasize the gravity of that revelation. "I suspect that if you get it right again the Press will start spelling your last name P-r-o-p-h-e-t."

Wiley struggled to keep his face as stern as a battleship prow while Fitzpatrick's comment sent a surge of elation flooding through his veins. Tomorrow, Proffitt or Prophet? would garner many a headline. He said, "Let's hope I've got it wrong."

Fitzpatrick nodded and looked down at his notes. "Now that you've warmed up, let me hit you with one from left field. There is a rumor circulating around the Beltway that Dish may not be on the reelection ticket. Another correlative rumor says that President Carver is considering you for the Vice Presidential slot. Care to comment?"

"Jim, you're the Washington expert, so let me ask you this. Would you be a wealthier man if you had a nickel for every cup of coffee drunk within the Beltway, or a penny for each of Washington's whispered rumors?"

Fitzpatrick smiled, treating the home audience to a thick helping of his Irish charm. "You've got me there, but tell me this: would the job of Vice President appeal to you?"

Wiley turned toward the active camera. "I've already got my dream job. I'm honored, thrilled, and blissfully happy to be defending America from the helm of the FBI." He stopped there, even though he had more to say. He had hinted during the booking interview that

Fitzpatrick should probe deeply on this issue.

Fitzpatrick's eyes twinkled. "I'm happy for you Director, but please, tell me this: Would you accept the Vice Presidency if President Carver were to offer it?"

"It's not Carver's to offer. Only the citizens of America can do that."

"With Carver's sixty-six percent approval rating, most experts would assert that there's no difference."

"No one likes dealing with hypotheticals, Jim."

Fitzpatrick grunted knowingly.

"—But then no one likes slippery answers either," Wiley continued. "So let me say this. I will answer any call to service that the people of this great nation care to place."

~ ~ ~

Wiley found Stuart waiting for him back in the *PoliTalk* dressing room. Usually the sight of his campaign manager bristled the hairs on the back of Wiley's neck. But not today. Today Stuart actually seemed pleased.

"He called you a prophet. That's gold in itself, Wiley, political gold. But then he went on to link you with the Vice-Presidency. Congratulations. I feel like I should write him a check."

Riding the adrenaline high and hearing Stuart's words, Wiley felt a tide of courage swell within his breast. He made the split-second decision to ride it. "Thank you. Actually, I've got a little announcement of my own."

As Stuart's features snapped back to their black-granite norm, Wiley felt a wave of trepidation, but he did not falter. He knew that if he did not stand up to Stuart now, he probably never would. Since Stuart was forcing Wiley to make him his chief of staff, the least Wiley could do was teach Stuart his place. He plowed on. "I have decided to stick with Cassi. If you still think she's a liability, you will just have to find a way to make her an asset. Understood?"

Wiley thought he saw a shadow pass behind Stuart's already dark eyes, but his expression did not change. He just nodded.

Wiley continued to hold Stuart's gaze for another moment. His poker instincts were kicking in. As absurd as it seemed, he was getting the distinct impression that Stuart had not only seen this little rebellion coming, but was also somehow prepared ...

Chapter 15

Alexandria, Virginia

"YOU'VE GOT to let me have this one Jack," Cassi said, lowering her voice. "It's too important to leave to Ralph."

Jack pursed his lips, trying to ignore the last part of her comment, she supposed. "You above all people should understand that you're in no condition to be negotiating today, Cassi. Ralph will do just fine."

Cassi wanted to scream but that would just make her boss's point. She slipped into negotiations mode instead. "Forget about politics for a minute. What if they were your kids? What if that was Bobby and Becky up there? Can you honestly tell me that you would want Ralph as your point man?"

Jack shrugged. "Ralph has four times your experience, Cassi."

"Yeah, and despite that he's got triple my failure rate."

"I gave the case to Ralph. I can't take it away now—especially in order to give it to you. Go get some rest. By the time you wake up, everything will be fine."

Cassi knew that Jack was doing his best to be objective and kind. She could also sense that his magnanimity was wearing thin. She knew she should back off now and do as he asked, but the image of two little caskets pushed her on. She decided to try a different tack. "How about a deal then? I get this negotiation; Ralph gets the promotion. Just let me save those kids."

She saw surprise cross Jack's face and a flash of something else, but he just shook his head. "The job is neither yours to barter, nor mine to give away."

Cassi shot her last arrow. "Women have a thirty-percent advantage over men in negotiations where child hostages are involved. You've got a female negotiator on the scene asking to do the job. If you say no and this goes south, some ambitious reporter is going to dig that statistic up. Your judgment will be called into question, both in private with the parents of those children, and in public as the mayor conducts damage control."

Jack gave her a long icy stare. Cassi understood in that moment that she had done their relationship irreparable damage. But for better or worse, she was too spent emotionally to care.

Finally he said, "Don't fuck up."

~ ~ ~

As the other agents disappeared down the stairs, Cassi looked at the photos ripped from the children's locker doors. The hostages' real names were Masha and Zeke, not even close to the Sara and Sammy she had guessed. She hoped that was not a bad omen. With two of her kids hanging in the balance and her own unborn child along for the ride, this was going to be the most important negotiation of her life.

Cassi took a visual sweep of the empty brick hallway and then brought her focus to rest on the metal door. She closed her eyes, let out a slow breath, and willed her mind to drift down through the clouds into The Zone. The Zone was a mental room with a chessboard floor and black walls. This was where she studied her opponent and calculated her moves. Once in The Zone she blocked out every sound, every smell, every extraneous tick and tock. She only allowed the players in The Zone—just she, the perp, and the hostages. The hostages. She hated to see those two small pieces on the board. It took a real sonofabitch to use children as pawns.

Back in the real world Cassi pressed herself against the brick wall of the corridor. She spoke loudly enough to be heard through the metal door but in a tone that was still conversational and polite. "Good morning. It's just the negotiator, as you requested. Everyone else is gone. I've got two cups of coffee here, in case you would like one. My name's Cassandra by the way, Cassi for short. What can I call you?"

"What you can call me is a fucking helicopter if you don't want to lose these two kids."

He was talking, Cassi thought. That was a good sign. She began her mental tally of notes. The man had gone straight to his central demand and his ultimate threat. That meant he was both impatient and scared. Both could work in her favor if she played them right. Both could get everyone killed if she played them wrong. In either case, his condition was not conducive to the standard tire-him-out routine.

Her first objective was to establish herself as his friend. The constant repetition of his name would work wonders in that area, but she sensed that he would not be inclined to give it. Perhaps she could guess. His voice was mid-thirties Italian with a Brooklyn accent. She decided to play the percentages. "You having a bad day, Nik?"

There was a long pause.

Cassi kept her focus on the chessboard, preparing the various countermoves she would use for different reactions.

"Nice try, lady. There were three Niks on my block growing up, but I ain't one of 'em. I do respect a woman who isn't afraid of taking a chance, though. You can call me Sal."

Yes! Cassi felt the juices pumping. She was in her groove. Everything was going to fall into place. She could feel it. "You having a bad day, Sal?"

"You shouldn't be concerned with what kind of a day I'm having. I can take care of myself. You should be concerned about the kids locked in here with a bomb."

The kids were all that she cared about, but she knew that they were okay for now. She could hear their muffled sobs. Her goal was to keep them that way. She would use all her skill and experience to keep Masha and Zeke out of play for as long as Sal was in play. Her primary means of doing that would be to keep the negotiation focused on Sal until they reached agreement or it was time for HRT to intervene. "But I do worry about you, Sal. Surely, you didn't want it to come to this. Did you?"

"You got that right. This was supposed to be a quick in and out job."

"So what went wrong?"

"Humph. You showed up." He paused.

Cassi waited.

Finally he asked, "How'd you know?"

"Somebody saw you. We got a call. It happens all the time. Too many eyes in this big city. Tell me, Sal, how do you see this working out?"

"I'll tell you exactly how this is going to work out. You're going to land a helicopter in the schoolyard. I'm going to climb onboard—just me, the pilot, and the two kids. We're going to take off. Once I'm sure I'm in the clear, I'll have the pilot set me down someplace I can disappear. Then he brings you back the kids and it's like this never happened. Nobody gets hurt."

"Sounds good to me," Cassi said. She put conviction in her tone, but knew that Sal's request was a fantasy. In her business someone always got hurt.

Chapter 16

Orumiyeh, Iran

"WHO ARE WE IN DANGER FROM?" Odi asked Ayden.

"I don't know."

"Then how do you know that we're in danger?"

"It's a long story."

Odi did not understand why his rescuer was being so evasive. He was obviously nervous and uncomfortable. Perhaps evasion was his default defense mechanism. Odi decided to try a different tack. "Does anybody know where we are?"

"I don't think so, but I'm not sure. I rent this place from an old lady who doesn't even know my name. Still, I'm readily identified as the tall American. It would be easy to find me by asking around."

"And who would be asking?"

"I don't know."

Odi thought about that for a moment, trying to cut through the circular logic. He did not know what was going on, so he could hardly formulate hypotheses. He decided to calm Ayden down while taking a mental inventory of things he could use as improvised weapons—kitchen knives, a broomstick, a wine bottle filled with sand. "How did I end up in that hospital? The last thing I remember was bleeding to death on a battlefield."

"Battlefield, huh?"

Odi understood he had made a faux pas but the words were out. He just shrugged.

Ayden said, "Forget it. To answer your question, I took you to the hospital. We're in Orumiyeh, by the way. It's twenty kilometers south of Tafriz—the site of the battle."

"So, are you a doctor?" Odi asked, steering the conversation toward a non-controversial subject.

"Yes. I studied at Berkley."

"Really, Berkley. Great school. What's your connection to Iran?"

"My father was Iranian."

Odi must have shown his surprise on his face because Ayden continued. "I know, I don't look it. I take after my mother's father, and my parents gave me her last name."

Odi nodded. "Are you here with the Red Crescent or Doctors Without Borders?"

"Close. I came here with the Peace Corps. They pulled out a few years back but I didn't want to leave. Too much work to do. Too many children left to save. So now I'm working on my own."

"Who's footing the bills?"

Ayden blushed.

"I'm sorry," Odi continued. "That just slipped out. It's none of my business. Must be the drugs."

"No. That's okay. Actually I get by on an inheritance."

The kettle whistled. Ayden poured tea. Then he pulled a sleeve of Fig Newtons from the white chipboard cupboard hanging over the sink and set it down. "I don't eat many meals here. I hope this will do."

Odi said, "Thanks," before tucking in. After swallowing three he asked his host, "How did I end up in a hospital in … "

"Orumiyeh," Ayden repeated. "Last weekend I happened to be doing aid work in Tafriz when a couple I had helped a few times before awakened me in the middle of the night. Their boy had just gotten his foot blown off by a landmine. I stabilized the wound and directed his parents to the local clinic you know so well. About twenty minutes after they left I remembered that Bahir, the boy, was allergic to penicillin. I went chasing after. The rest you can guess."

"What was the boy doing that he got his foot blown off in the middle of the night?"

"A lot of kids work in the fields at night to help support their families. It's cooler and that way they don't miss school. Bahir was taking a shortcut home through the woods."

Odi nodded. One more life his team was responsible for losing. "So you found me near the clinic while returning for the boy?"

"That's right. I took you back to the hut I was working from to patch you up. Your wound was not life threatening in itself, but you had lost a lot of blood. I had some to spare."

Odi tilted his head inquisitively.

Ayden nodded. "I'm O negative, a universal donor."

Odi's head began to reel from all the implications surrounding his predicament. If any of the locals learned that he was a member of the team that blew up their clinic and killed … how many Iranians? He was afraid to ask. He had other questions that he wanted Ayden to answer as well, lots of them, but he feared that time might be short.

Since the US did not maintain an embassy in Iran, he figured that he had two options. Either he could approach a friendly embassy as Ayden had suggested earlier, presumably the British or the Canadians.

Perhaps the Aussies. Unfortunately, Tehran was over five hundred miles away. He could call and try to get someone to send a car. Or perhaps there was a major Western corporation that had an office near his current location. Any embassy would know. But how would he manage that without compromising the mission? He was not naïve enough to believe that any phone communication to a Western establishment would be secure. And now that the mission had gone to shit, maintaining deniability would be the prime American objective. Potchak would have a fit if he placed an unsecure call.

The alternative was to wait until nightfall and head for Turkey on foot. Since Orumiyeh was twenty kilometers from Tafriz, and Tafriz was twenty kilometers from the border, he had to be within forty kilometers of the Turkish border. Just a marathon.

"I can't tell you how grateful I am," Odi said. "Forgive me if I'm being rude, but I would hate to let someone interrupt us and spoil your work." He glanced over at his bandaged arm. "What was it that you wanted to show me?"

"Yes, of course." Ayden disappeared into a room off the entryway and returned a moment later with a burlap sack labeled "Brown Rice." He cleared the mugs and empty cellophane wrapper from the table. Then he upturned the bag. The remnant parts of eight military headsets clattered onto the Formica table. Obviously they had come from his team. This was the last thing Odi had expected.

"Do you know how your teammates died?" Ayden asked.

"I only saw two of them. Both were shot in the head."

"I'm no expert in forensics, Odi, but I had a look at the bodies and then consulted with a friend. Your teammates were not shot. All seven were assassinated by tiny bombs. Check out the headsets." Ayden held up the remnants of an earpiece. "I found bits of this same plastic lodged in all seven head-wounds."

Odi felt his skepticism kicking in. "How did you end up with the headsets?"

"I got them from the boy who scavenged them. He was playing with one while I examined him. I had already examined the bodies by then and found the strange shrapnel. When I saw the bloody headsets, I put two and two together."

Odi did not want to think about the implications of that revelation. Instead he began to examine the pieces one after the other. They had not been tampered with, that much was clear. They were still covered with streaks of blood and bits of gore. It did not require his expert eyes to see that Ayden's conclusion was correct—although he had missed it on the battlefield. Each headset had exploded from within. A tiny charge had been cleverly directed by the speaker dish into the wearer's ear.

Odi put a residual piece to his nose and recognized the distinct scent of RDX. He knew that a drop of RDX the size of an eraser head would take a human head clean off. Given the location of the explosive, just millimeters from the ear, the charge would not have had to be any larger than a match head to be lethal.

Odi set the evidence back down on the table as his head began to spin.

His teammates were not the victims of war.

They had died from assassination.

He felt the walls closing in.

Ayden bobbed nervously in his chair as Odi took a long moment of contemplative silence. Then Odi brushed the broken bits off the table with a single sweep of his good arm. He looked up at his new friend. "Why would someone rig our headsets to explode? Why would someone back at Quantico want to kill my team?"

"If yours had been the only incident," Ayden said, "I would say that someone on your team posed a serious threat to the person behind this—as in knowing something that would send him to jail—so he killed everyone to cover his tracks. But—"

"Hold on a minute," Odi interrupted. "There were other incidents? Other attacks?"

"Oh yeah. There were two. The AmCham office was bombed in Belgium, and an American School was bombed in Paris."

"When?"

"Both attacks took place the night your team was assassinated."

Odi leaned back in his chair and let out a long breath. His life was getting more complicated by the minute. Now he understood why Ayden had discouraged his making a call, but that was about all he understood.

He needed more information.

"I interrupted you," Odi said. "You were going to tell me why you thought someone had done this."

"Yes, well, I think the core reason is obvious. Why do people do anything?"

"Money?"

Ayden nodded.

"How does killing my team make anybody money?" Odi asked.

Ayden answered him with a question. A surprising question. "Do you know what the biggest industry in the world is?"

"Oil?"

Ayden shook his head.

Odi raised his brows.

"Fear," Ayden said.

"Fear?"

"Yes, fear. At the individual level, fear is sold in many forms, the most common of which is insurance: health, life, accident, theft. People are afraid that something big will go wrong, so they put their money down. At the collective level, fear is sold in the form of defense—against fire, flood, famine, and crime. Of course the granddaddy of these is national defense. Mention the word terrorism and people trip over themselves to hand you blank checks."

"You're losing me. What does—" Odi cut himself off. "I'm beginning to see where you're going with this, but I'm not there yet. Keep talking."

"America's War on Terror was worth around three billion dollars a week to the defense industry. Think about it, three billion dollars a week. That's greater than the GDP of many nations. Surely you don't think the guys who were pocketing that kind of cash were happy when the gravy train stopped rolling. So why would you assume that they would just mothball the mint and walk away once the attacks lightened up?"

Odi had to accept the logic, but something still bugged him. It only took a moment for him to figure out what it was. "Ayden, with all due respect. If the defense contractors were secretly sponsoring attacks to spur demand and keep that gravy train rolling, you wouldn't be the only person to figure it out."

Ayden shook his head sagely. "Nobody else knows that someone inside the FBI planned the murder of your team. The world thinks your team was killed when you uncovered a secret al-Qaeda training camp. And even if someone suspected the truth, so what? He would have no proof. If he spoke up, nobody would listen. If he persisted loudly despite the skepticism, he would just be labeled a nut."

"But we have proof, Ayden. These headsets ... my testimony as a Federal Agent ... those are proof."

"Right," Ayden said, looking up from the floor. "Now do you understand why I'm so afraid? Now do you comprehend just how much danger we're in?"

Chapter 17

Alexandria, Virginia

STUART LISTENED INTENTLY to the complementary voice streams coming from the two speakers. Timing was everything in an operation like this, so he was glad to have bugs both inside the daycare-center office and out in the hall.

Both were quiet now. Cassi had just finagled Sal's name. She was a clever one. Stuart had to give her that. If she were just three inches shorter she would be a valuable asset rather than a critical liability. Wiley had that right. Unfortunately, those three inches meant everything. It was just one more way Washington politics resembled professional sports. The difference between winning and losing often came down to fractions and milliseconds. In this case, three inches meant that he had to cut Cassi from the team—the only way that he could.

Stuart wished that there were another way. Wiley would not cooperate. Violence was never his first choice. It was too primitive. But he had no other. Cassi should not have gone and gotten herself pregnant. She had painted him into a corner and this was his only way out.

Wiley would go berserk, of course, but that would change nothing. No spark of vengeance could outshine the luster of the Oval Office. Truth be told, Stuart had been secretly pleased to see Wiley show a little spine and stand up to him on Cassi's account. The edge he displayed would serve them well in the campaign. Of course, Stuart had to ensure that Wiley never forgot his place again. Today, he would solve both issues—with the simple push of a button ...

Chapter 18

Alexandria, Virginia

CASSI FELT A JOLT of excitement run through her as she considered Sal's nobody-gets-hurt proposal. Cracking a hostage situation was not unlike cracking a safe. You had to find the right combination. As soon as he said the word helicopter, she felt the first tumbler fall squarely into place. "You seem to have thought this through," she said, keeping the dial turning.

"Damn straight," Sal replied.

Giving a hostage-taker a helicopter was out of the question, but she could not let Sal know that. "If you want me to consider releasing you, Sal, you're going to have to convince me that you're a small fish. No danger to society."

"You want a reference? A note from my guidance counselor?"

Cassi was pleased to hear Sal exercising his sense of humor. That meant both that he was looking for approval and that he was not freaking out. "Tell me about this job. It was obviously well planned and highly sophisticated. Who set it up? What was the plan? Stuff like that. We've already caught you red-handed, so you've nothing to lose—except this last chance to get your freedom back. Don't try to bullshit me though. If I think you're lying, I certainly won't trust you with a helicopter, a pilot, and two kids."

Sal met her request with silence. Either he was thinking, or she had pushed too hard. "I'm throwing you a lifeline, Sal. You'll be regretting it for twenty-to-life if you don't grab on with both hands.

Finally Sal replied, his tone softer than before. "I'm just a wrench."

"A wrench?"

"A tool. Hired help. It wasn't my idea. He called me."

"What did he say?"

"He said he'd give me a million cash if I could get him the Vermeer."

"What Vermeer?"

"The one undergoing restoration on the other side of this brick wall."

"What else did he tell you?"

"Everything. He planned it out for me. Told me about a gap in the security system I could use."

"And what gap was that?"

"What's it matter? Didn't work."

"I'm trying to work with you here, Sal. You've got to work with me back. Give me the details."

Sal sighed loud enough for Cassi to hear through the door. "The art restorer uses a hyper-sophisticated security system. Detects vibration, body heat, shit like that. I can't disable it locally because it arms and disarms according to a remote timer. On at eight every night. Off at eight every morning. Every morning. Since they open late on Sundays, there's a ninety-minute window before anyone shows up. Nothing to worry 'bout from eight to nine-thirty but the normal door and window whistles. The brick wall the studio shares with the daycare center gave me a foolproof way to get around them."

"Go on."

"I broke into the daycare center last night and hid in the storage room, that's where the shared wall is. Eight-fifteen I start drillin' brick, knowing that all them kids running and screaming below will cover up the muffled noise. I'd almost got a hole big enough to wriggle through when I sees colored lights reflecting off the wall. I go to look and see the pigs pulling into the yard. There's nowhere to run so I snatch a couple kids. The rest you know."

Cassi did know. Sal had been set up. There was no Vermeer. There was no sophisticated alarm. There was definitely more to this than met the eye, and she wanted to know what it was. "Now for the most important question, Sal, the one your future rides upon. Who gave you the contract?"

"I knew you was going to ask that. I don't know."

"You know more than you think," Cassi said. "What did he call himself?"

"X."

"X?"

"Yep."

"What else can you tell me about X? Was he working from the inside?"

"I'd say so. He had everything: blueprints, details of the security system, and, of course, he knew 'bout the painting."

Cassi saw a picture rapidly taking shape. "Did he mention the kids?"

"Yeah. He said their screams would cover up the noise. Also suggested that if the shit hit the fan they'd make good insurance."

"He said that?" Cassi asked, filling in the final strokes.

"Yeah. See. Takin' hostages wasn't even my idea. I'm no threat to nobody."

"And how did he get you the blueprints?"

"Mail."

"And how were you going to get him the painting and collect your cash?"

"He was going to call me once the job was done to work that out."

The results of her interrogation were not perfect, Cassi thought, but the police were still going to be pleased. More importantly, Sal was now convinced that she was receptive to his escape plan. It was time for her to rescue the kids.

From his explanation of the job, she knew that Sal was quick on his feet. From his vocabulary and syntax, she knew that he was intelligent but not formally educated. From his escape plan, she gathered that he was meticulous. She had to assume that Sal had studied hostage-negotiation techniques. That made her job more complicated, if not more difficult.

Given his current state of mind, Cassi knew that Sal might react violently if he caught her manipulating him with standard procedure. That meant she would not be able to play this one by the book. Still, she could not abandon negotiation's central tenets. She would still keep him off balance, but in an unorthodox way.

"You know what I'm supposed to do now, right Sal? You've seen the cop shows. I'm supposed to tell you that you that you can't take the kids. Make you release one now. Tire you out. But I can tell that you're too smart for that. So here's what I'm going to do … Oh, hold on a second, I almost forgot. You said you have a bomb, right? What kind is it?"

"What's it matter?"

I want to make sure that it won't go off when we shoot you, she thought. "I need to make sure there are no electronics around that might accidentally trigger it."

"It's plastique—not military grade, the homemade stuff. X sent it to me in case the drill wasn't enough for the wall or I couldn't crack the restorer's safe."

"How much?"

"Enough to do the kids is all you need to know."

"Don't talk like that, Sal. Don't blow it now. I can tell that you're a reasonable man at heart, not some violent psychopath. I am prepared to get you what you want. I'm going to call for your helicopter now. All you have to do for me is put the kids in the bathroom to keep them quiet and out of the way while we wait."

"These kids are staying right next to me. If you're worried about them, you'll get the helicopter here that much faster. Meanwhile they're going to make sure that you don't get any bright ideas. I do like the idea of keeping them quiet though. Hold on a minute."

Cassi felt spiders in her stomach as she heard the screech-rip sound of duct tape. Once. Twice. Then the soprano sobbing peaked and stopped. Her nerves began to kick in, yanking her out of The Zone. Suddenly she was acutely aware that two beautiful kids, her unborn child, and her career were riding on the next sixty seconds of her performance.

"Okay, Sal. I've put in the request for the helicopter. It won't be long. Now, convince me that you're not going to harm those kids."

"What can I say? I was just trying to steal a painting. That's just larceny, not a violent crime. It ain't a big deal to have me out on the streets. I'm a teddy bear. And like any bear, I'm no threat if nobody spooks or threatens me."

Cassi noted that a desperate twang had crept into Sal's voice. She kept quiet, pressuring him to continue.

He did. "I don't want to harm these kids. But if you threaten me, then that's what I'm going to do. I'm sure you agree it would be much better to let me fly out of here than to let it come down to that."

"Absolutely, I see your point. Oh, hold on ... It's here, Sal. Your helicopter is here."

"In the yard?"

"No, there wasn't room with the telephone wires and the jungle gyms. It's up on the roof. You're going to have to use the fire escape." This was all bullshit, of course. As soon as Sal put his head above the roof he would get a bullet between the eyes. Cassi could not let herself think about that, however. She could not let treachery tweak her voice.

"Okay, here's the deal," Sal commanded. "Everybody clears out. Everybody but you. Nobody is in the yard. Nobody but the pilot is on the roof. When you've made it that way, you let me know."

Cassi felt the warm glow of approaching victory when her ears seemed to erupt inside her head. Before the sound could register she found herself flying backwards through the air, borne toward the bricks with great force by a giant bubble of heat.

Chapter 19

Lake Maroo, Virginia

ODI BOLTED UP IN BED, awakened by chirping birds. He had slept well, even with his ears perked like a German shepherd's.

Two weeks had passed since his auspicious awakening in the Iranian hospital ward, and in that time his outlook on life had swung one-hundred-and-eighty degrees. Betrayal changes a man. Betrayal makes him worry about things he never worried about before. It makes him worry about things like self-preservation. Ponder motives. And plan his revenge.

Realizing that going public with their knowledge would put them squarely in the assassins' sights, he and Ayden had inevitably settled on the only course of action that was both honorable and expedient. They had chosen to hunt the killers down. Actually "they" was a generous term. Odi was the soldier. He was going after them alone.

He had entered the US using Ayden's passport in order to preserve his greatest tactical advantage: the fact that everyone still believed him dead. He had used discretion and disguise to keep it that way, and he would continue to do so for as long as it took to neutralize all the people who conspired to murder his team. Once his mission was complete, he would just wake up in Iran. A coma was an airtight alibi. And he had a credible doctor to corroborate.

Slipping out of bed fully dressed, he pulled on his hiking boots and looked out the bedroom window. Dawn's first light was just breaking over the lake. The water took on a golden shimmer and seemed to summon all living creatures to come forth for a dip. Lake Maroo was a pristine paradise. He could see why Commander Potchak spent virtually every weekend here in his cabin. It was just what one needed to balance out a Quantico workweek. At least it would have been for Odi. Obviously Maroo's charms were insufficient to stifle Potchak's ravenous greed.

Odi emerged from the cabin's only bedroom to inspect the status of his project. Potchak was still there, of course. He was standing exactly as Odi had left him eight hours earlier—suspended on his tiptoes by the noose around his neck.

Odi walked to the center of the room to appraise the condemned man. The fact that this was the traditional time for military hangings had not been lost on his prisoner. Potchak's face was beaded with sweat despite the morning chill and he had dark bags beneath his bloodshot eyes. Physically, Odi thought, he looked just about right.

Odi stretched his arms over his head and let out a contented yawn as he studied Potchak's eyes. It was a tactical ploy, designed to stress the contrast of their relative positions while simultaneously giving Odi time to evaluate his opponent. Odi liked what he saw. He could begin—but he wouldn't. Not just yet.

Odi had not said a word to his former boss since capturing him at dusk. He would say nothing now. Better to let him stew a few minutes more. He took a moment to reflect on the events that had transpired, letting tension mount.

Capturing Potchak had been surprisingly easy. When the commander returned to the rustic cabin from a day of bow hunting, Odi was waiting, hidden behind the dense foliage of a Fraser Fir. The moment his boss turned his back to un-strap the buck from the hood of his Jeep, Odi Tasered him in the back. As Adam would have said, it was a piece of pumpkin pie.

~ ~ ~

When Potchak awoke to a choking sensation his first crazy thought was that the deer had somehow turned the tables on him, for he was the one who had been strung up. He had no idea how he had gotten there, but there he was, hanging by his neck at the end of a rope in the main room of his cabin. He reached for the noose around his throat as his feet sought the floor but found his arms bound tightly behind his back. His toes made blessed contact and he pressed down vigorously and managed to ease some tension out of the rope. Potchak gasped a few breaths and sought to maintain his balance. A few seconds in that position were all it took to realize that remaining elevated and balanced enough to breathe was going to inflict a constant mental and physical strain.

He immediately recognized this as a stress position. The kind often used in interrogations. But his mind did not dwell on that. For as surprising as his new predicament was, the next sight that met his eyes as he glanced around was even more so. He found himself looking at a ghost.

Odysseus Carr was dead. Yet there Odi was, sitting beside him in an armchair, casually reading a book. Was this hell? Was this to be his special torment? Was he doomed to spend eternity struggling to breath while his victims looked on in peace?

Potchak groaned through the duct-tape that gagged his mouth.

Odi continued to read in silence without looking up.

~ ~ ~

After finishing Follett's latest thriller and breaking for a dinner he did not share—fresh venison steak—Odi retired to Potchak's bedroom without a word. He was anxious to get started but knew that the interrogation was more likely to succeed if he gave his captive's fears a chance to percolate. He wanted Potchak to contemplate the reversal of their positions as his terror fermented and his physical strength dwindled away.

Appraising the situation anew that morning, Odi found himself intrigued by the thoughts that must be going through Potchak's mind. He reasoned that his boss must have spent much of his tiptoe time trying to guess the angle that would give him the best chance of saving his own neck—praying all the while that Odi would give him a chance to speak before he hoisted him up that last lethal inch. Odi was curious to learn what strategy Potchak chose, what ploy he would invoke. Potchak's choice would tell Odi a lot about how he was perceived.

Would Potchak attempt to sway him through pity, through fear, or through greed? Would he offer Odi money? Apologies? Information? Sex? Would he try a power play and issue threats? Would he claim to be a victim himself? Or would he just beg?

Appraising his captive, Odi decided that it was time to find out. He grasped the rope that ran upwards from Potchak's neck over the central rafter and down to a cleat that Odi had screwed to the far wall. He twanged it as though the rope were the string of a giant guitar. Potchak's heels lifted further off the floor. Twelve hours of stretching had made no difference to the rope. It was still taut as a Sumo's loincloth.

Odi walked over to the cleat and partially unwrapped the end—just enough for it to slip. He added enough slack to let Potchak slump from his tiptoes onto the balls of his feet and then re-secured the rope. Satisfied that Potchak remained utterly helpless but would now have the mental bandwidth to focus on something other than balance, he spoke for the first time since the capture. "Lest you get any bright ideas, the noose is tied so that it cannot be loosened or removed."

Potchak grunted. Odi took this as a submissive sign. He untied Potchak's left hand and used the extra rope to secure his right hand to the back of his leather belt. Then he ripped the duct tape from Potchak's mouth in one swift move. It left a nasty red rash, but Potchak still looked relieved. Odi smiled with satisfaction. Then he walked behind Potchak and into the kitchen without another word, no doubt leaving his prisoner even further confused.

He watched Potchak through the doorway as he brewed a pot of strong coffee. Potchak did not try to turn around or speak. The former did not surprise Odi. His prisoner had no doubt suffered from a misstep or two during the night and learned to leave well-enough alone, even now that he was down on the balls of his feet. As for the latter, the silence, that, Odi was sure, was about to change.

When he returned with two large steaming mugs, Odi found Potchak looking much better. The smell of fresh brew, the glimmer of hope, the setting and the free hand were all having their effect—exactly as planned. He handed Potchak a mug and said "Lots of milk, lots of sugar."

Odi's knowledge of how the commander liked his coffee was a poignant reminder that, according to the soldiers' code, Potchak was guilty of worse than murder. He was guilty of betrayal.

Odi thought he saw a streak of guilt cross Potchak's face as he mumbled "Thanks." But before he could be sure Potchak dove into his mug. Odi positioned a worn old leather armchair to Potchak's left and plopped down, sending stuffing sprouting out a slit in the side like hair from an old man's ear. After settling in comfortably, he took a sip of his own black brew and began. "So, after eighteen years with the FBI you suddenly quit to work for Armed Services Industrial Supply. What was that I read in the paper, you start Monday as Vice President of Government Relations? That plum assignment must be worth quite a bump in pay. I'm curious, what were the lives of my team worth? Three-hundred grand? Half a mil?"

"I didn't know anyone was going to get killed," Potchak said.

As an opening line, Odi thought it wasn't bad, but he was still ready with a retort. "Other than the doctors, nurses, and patients at the hospital, of course. But they were Iranian civilians, so I suppose they don't count. We killed more people liberating Iraq than we lost in Vietnam, and nobody seemed to notice, so you figured, what the hell…"

Potchak closed his eyes for a long second, then continued. "When they gave me the headsets, they said they were just so they could listen in, so they'd know if you suspected anything and could decide if it was necessary to pull the plug."

"And once we were all dead, well, you were already in too deep."

"Exactly," Potchak said. Then he finished off his coffee as though the meeting were over.

Odi looked at him and thought, if you only knew … He took back the mug and grew a broad smile for what must have appeared to be no apparent reason. Potchak smiled back, trying to act chummy—for the first time in two years. He did not even resist when Odi rebound his hand.

"Do you remember what I used to do before joining CRT?" Odi asked.

Potchak's face registered the odd combination of panic and relief. He was wary about being let off the hook. As an avid fisherman, he knew that this was often the last thing that happened before the man who caught you cut off your head. "Yeah, of course. You were with the bomb squad. You shocked us when you requested a transfer to CRT because you were EOD's golden child."

Odi did not comment immediately. Instead he walked to the closet and withdrew a tripod and a video camera. He began setting them up as he spoke. "I've been fascinated by explosives ever since I got my first firecracker as a kid. Long story short—we don't have much time—before I was done at Johns Hopkins, that fascination led to PhDs in Chemistry and Biomolecular Engineering. But you know that.

"What you don't know is that I did a lot of research, a lot of tinkering in the lab during graduate school. I even came up with a couple of groundbreaking inventions." Odi spoke calmly, his tone dispassionate, very matter-of-fact. "The first invention you may have heard about. The trade name is ArmoWrap. It's a defensive tool, kind of like a fire extinguisher for bombs. The second invention is at the opposite end of the spectrum. It is a devious weapon. I call it Creamer, although since I am the only person on the planet who knows about it, the name has the irrelevance of a tree falling in an empty wood. Anyhow, sparing you the technospeak, Creamer is a bio-reactive explosive." Odi paused to study Potchak's face. His expression did not change. The words Bio-reactive explosive had not tipped him off. That was just as well, Odi thought. He wanted to capture Potchak's initial comprehension on tape.

Now that he was done revealing personal information, Odi stood up and turned on the video camera. He pointed it directly at Potchak's strung-up head while making sure that his own chair was nowhere in the frame. Then he did a test with the microphone to make sure that the oscillating sound filter he had attached over the mike sufficiently altered his voice. Satisfied with the arrangement, Odi hit the record button and continued where he left off. "Aside from a slightly oily sheen, my creamer looks like ordinary coffee creamer. Thus the name. Mix it in equal parts with Half-n-Half, add a little artificial flavoring, and it tastes that way too."

Odi licked his lips as he watched Potchak's face contort into a mask of terror. Then he continued in the same, soft pedagogical monotone. "Creamer is a stable, inert liquid until it is placed in an environment with a low pH—like your stomach for instance. Once swallowed, the hydrochloric acid in your stomach catalyzes radical hemophilic adhesion. In other words, the liquid explosive draws together as though magnetized to form an ever-denser solid. It is kind of like milk curdling, but in the extreme." Odi stood up, careful to keep out of the video, and began to pace as he continued the lesson with the aid of his hands. "Once the Creamer compacts sufficiently, it begins to sweat a polymer. That polymer further interacts with the hydrochloric acid, encasing the explosive in a tough shell. Picture a loaf of baking bread, only with a crust as tough as iron. And that's only the half of it. To continue the analogy, the yeast in the batter continues to rise long after the solid crust forms, increasing the pressure within that shell. As the pressure of that confined space rises, so does the heat—that's the first law of thermodynamics, you may recall. The pressure keeps building and the temperature keeps rising until it reaches one-hundred-ten degrees centigrade. That's the tipping point where the internal pressure becomes too great for the shell to withstand. Wanna guess what happens then?"

Potchak mouthed, "It explodes," but no sound came out.

"That's right. The explosive self-detonates."

Odi smiled at Potchak. "The whole reaction takes about thirty minutes in pigs. As for humans, well, you'll be the first to know."

Whatever psychological ploy Potchak had been planning as he stood there on tiptoe through the night, a revelation like this had not factored into the equation. He began to shake.

"We'll know that you have about ten minutes left when your breathing becomes rapid and shallow and your lips and fingernails begin turning blue. That's on account of the polymer the explosive sweats—it's extremely destructive to hemoglobin."

Potchak was writhing like a worm on a hook, Odi noted with satisfaction. When Odi finished speaking, Potchak made a visible effort to bring his body under control.

Odi waited.

When the condemned man finally opened his mouth again, his voice was surprisingly stable. "Is there an antidote?"

Odi cocked his head to the side and winked. "Who asked you to do it?"

Chapter 20

The Mall, Washington, D.C.

WILEY STUDIED his own reflection in the black rain-streaked granite as he walked the length of the Vietnam Memorial. He was not satisfied with the countenance staring back. It did not look tough enough for the meeting he was headed for. Nor did it exude his usual fire. He held out his right arm as he approached the memorial's western end and ran his fingers along the cold chiseled surface, attempting to leach courage from the hallowed stone.

"You called," Stuart said, appearing beneath Wiley's umbrella as if conjured from the wind.

Wiley stopped walking and turned toward his campaign manager, angling his body to force Stuart to face into the gusting drizzle. "I know it was you. Cassi's accident. I don't know how you did it—and I probably never will—but I know it was you."

Stuart removed his misted silver spectacles once Wiley had finished. He stared back at him eyeball-to-eyeball with those cold reptilian eyes. "If you know so much, then you're also aware that her misfortune is your blessing. The albatross has been blown off your neck. With Cassi out of the picture, Carver doesn't have a single objection to inviting you to join his ticket. I know. I asked. I have also been getting great traction off Fitzpatrick's Prophet quote. The media are eating it up. Everything is coming together for the Antiterrorist Czar. And I'm glad you know whom to thank."

Wiley felt conflicting emotions churn. He was thrilled with the career news but was not yet done lashing out. "What if I was to tell you that I'm sticking with her?"

Stuart scoffed. "I'd say that you might as well keep walking—right past the Lincoln Memorial and into the Potomac. After blackmailing her boss, breaking protocol, and costing two children their lives, your girlfriend is political cyanide."

During the half-second it took Wiley to compose his barbed retort, his cell phone began to ring. He knew by the tone that it was Carl Jenkins, his Deputy Director for Operations and second in command. He hated to see Stuart saved by the bell, but he had to take the call.

"Good evening, Carl."

"I'm calling with bad news, Wiley. Former CRT Commander Potchak is dead."

Wiley felt his stomach shrink to the size of a walnut. "Potchak is dead?" He repeated the words back to Carl while activating the cellphone's speaker for Stuart's benefit. "He just retired to work for ASIS last Friday. That can hardly be a coincidence. What do you know?"

"ASIS called us when Potchak failed to show up for his first day of work this morning, thinking that maybe old habits were hard to break and he'd driven to Quantico instead. He didn't, of course. He was not at home or reachable on his mobile phone, so Agent Dobrinovitch drove out to his hunting cabin. It's way out in rural Virginia on Lake Maroo."

"I know it."

"Yes, well, Potchak was there, in his cabin. Or at least that's what we think."

"I don't follow."

"The remains we found were severely scattered. The victim, who we're assuming was Potchak for now, was either hit center-of-mass by the equivalent of an antitank weapon or he was forced to swallow something akin to a hand grenade."

Wiley stared blankly at the leaden clouds streaking across the sky, trying to grasp the implications. Finally he asked, "Was there anything like a Mafia signature in the room? A dead fish, a horse's head, a black spot, a white rose … ?"

"If there was, it wasn't prominently displayed. At the time of the explosion, however, Potchak had a noose about his neck. Maybe that's the same thing. I'll run the MO past Edwards in Organized Crime."

"I take it we don't have any leads on the killer yet?"

"Actually we do. We know from splatter voids on the wall and footprints that a six-foot-one male with an athletic build and size eleven shoes was present with Potchak in the room. He arrived and left on a cross-country motorcycle. Our preliminary analysis indicates that he was not injured in the blast, although he must have been drenched in Potchak juice. We'll know for certain once we get the blood-work back."

"No other clues to the killer's identity?"

"None. All the windows and doors were left open, and it was a windy, rainy weekend, so we've got a highly contaminated scene. The place was wiped clean of prints. Osborn says the guy was a pro so forensics is not expecting much."

"Thank you for giving it to me straight."

"There's one other thing," Jenkins said. "The killer was using a tripod for something. We're guessing it was either to support the weapon or to capture the explosion on video. Winslow in Behavioral Sciences says that in the latter case there's even money that the killer will send us a copy as a gauntlet of sorts—either in the mail or over the web."

Wiley considered that. "As long as we don't see it on the news first."

"There's no way any public network could show this."

Wiley cringed. "Keep me posted on every significant development, as soon as you have it, day or night. The word on the street needs to be clear: the FBI takes care of its own."

"Of course."

Wiley closed the clamshell phone with a trembling hand and studied Stuart. They were obviously thinking the same thing. One way or another, this was related to Wiley's campaign. Not only was someone aware of their conspiracy, but he was out to stop it, to stop them. Potchak's death might be just the beginning.

Chapter 21

Alexandria, Virginia

CASSI OPENED HER EYES to an unfamiliar face: mid-forties female, thin to borderline-gaunt, scraggly black hair, boring brown eyes, white smock. She was looking at either a mortician's assistant or an unfortunate nurse. "What happened?"

The nurse bent over and used icy fingers to pry her left eye further open. "Follow my flashlight," she said, moving the light back and forth, up and down.

"What happened, Gretchen?" Cassi repeated, once her eyes had recovered enough to read the nurse's nametag."

"You were in an explosion. You suffered multiple abrasions and a serious blow to the back of your head, but—"

The hallway scene came back in a flash the moment Gretchen said explosion. "What about the children?" Cassi interrupted, trying to sit up.

Gretchen pushed her firmly back and then shook her index finger in silent warning. She was not to move. "I can't discuss other patients."

Cassi was about to make the request in an official capacity when she was struck by another thought and her whole body went cold. "What about my baby?"

Gretchen gave a compassionate frown and shook her head. "I'm sorry, dear. You miscarried."

As Cassi's head reeled, Gretchen placed one cold hand on her arm while reaching for the IV with the other. Using her thumb to crank up the sedative drip, she said, "You need to get your rest."

~ ~ ~

Cassi drifted back into consciousness as a nurse rolled a noisy patient past her room. Her throat felt like sandpaper and she could swear that someone had used her head to break bricks while she was asleep. She opened her eyes to see that Gretchen was there, poised like a sentry. In reaction to Cassi's movement, Gretchen shoved a straw into her mouth. Cassi drew in a sip of warm water and her throat immediately felt a little better. She spent the next thirty seconds clearing her head and draining the cup.

"Is it true? Is my baby really gone?"

"I'm afraid so, dear. But there's no reason you can't have another. You're still healthy and young."

Cassi was not so sure.

Where was Wiley? She wondered. More than anything, she needed him with her at that moment. There were flowers all over her room, and no doubt some were from him, but those were hardly consolation. She needed flesh and blood to cuddle and hold. She needed reassurance, support, and consolation. She understood that he could not possibly afford to sit watch at the foot of her bed, but she felt that he had slighted her all the same. Her and their baby.

"How do you feel?" Gretchen asked, nudging the discussion in a different direction.

Cassi decided that a change of subject probably was for the best. "Like I was hit by a truck."

Gretchen nodded. "In a Newtonian sense, you were."

Cassi wasn't sure what that meant. It sounded like something Odi would say. "What time is it?" She asked.

"Six o'clock, Monday evening. You've been asleep for nearly twenty-four hours. Are you hungry? I've got orange Jell-O and some tasty applesauce that will both go down nicely."

Cassi was not in the mood to eat, but she knew she should build up her strength. "That would be nice. I would also appreciate whatever you can give me for my headache."

Gretchen mumbled something in response as she walked out the door.

Cassi was anxious to learn about Masha and Zeke. She would watch the news during dinner. If she could not find coverage of the explosion, then she would find a phone and call over to the pediatric wing. Meanwhile, she tried to recall the details of what happened.

She remembered blackmailing Higgins into giving her the reigns of the daycare center negotiation. She remembered Sal's explanation of the job and her conclusion that he had been set up. She remembered convincing Sal that a helicopter was waiting for him up on the roof. She remembered being certain that Sal would have to expose himself to HRT sniper fire as he climbed the fire escape to the roof. She had effectively saved the children. Then, for some unforeseeable reason, the explosives he had brought for the safe exploded. One of the kids or even Sal himself must have accidentally triggered the detonator.

Gretchen returned with a plastic tray and set it on the table beside her bed. Cassi looked over to see a mushy meal and a little paper cup with two Tylenol. Gretchen refilled her water from a plastic pitcher and handed Cassi the cup. Once Cassi swallowed the pills, Gretchen said, "Your boss is here."

Cassi perked up. Jack was there. That was good news. He would tell her about the kids. She felt a wave of nervous tension run up her spine. What would she do if they were not okay? She had a sudden urge to look in the mirror, but realized that was silly. She had a thick cap of gauze wrapped around her head. Besides, how she looked was the least of her problems. "Has he been waiting long?"

"No. He called earlier and we told him when the medication was likely to wear off. He has been here about fifteen minutes. You don't have to see him if you don't want."

Cassi got the impression that Gretchen enjoyed sending people away. "No, that's okay. Please send him in."

It was not Jack Higgins who walked through her door. It was Wiley. Wiley was there!

"It's great to see you," she said, accepting a mixed rose bouquet and a kiss on the cheek. The cheek. That was disappointing. Perhaps her lips looked like an old hen's.

"I'm glad to see you too."

"When the nurse said that my boss was here, I was expecting to see Jack Higgins."

"Actually that's part of what I needed to talk to you about," Wiley said, pulling the chair up beside the bed.

"I owe him an apology. I know. But—"

"Jack's not your boss anymore," Wiley interrupted. "He had to resign. Ralph Unger is the new head of Hostage Negotiations."

Cassi felt the blood draining from her face. "Is that ... Is that my fault?"

Wiley nodded. "Jack took your bullet. But as you know, he was about to retire anyway."

"And thanks to me, after thirty years of distinguished service he went out under a cloud." Cassi bowed her head as tears swelled in her eyes. That was a double blow, straight to the heart. She needed some good news. "What happened to the children, to Masha and Zeke?"

As Wiley shook his head, Cassi thought she would faint. She was already numb when he spoke the dreaded words. "They didn't make it."

She gripped the rails of her bed like lifelines as Wiley continued. "As you might guess, their deaths have been all over the news."

Grasping for straws, Cassi asked, "Do we know what happened yet? Why the bomb went off?"

"We don't. The forensics team thinks it was an accident— homemade plastique is notoriously unstable—but that's almost irrelevant. This is a political football now, so it's sensation not science that counts.

"Look, Cassi, I'm sorry to hit you with this first thing after waking up. I thought it was important that you understand what's going on. The minute word gets out that you are awake, the press are going to be trying to get to you, and they can be pretty slippery. I wanted to make sure that you were forearmed."

"Thank you," Cassi mumbled. "So what is going to happen to me?"

"Ralph's first act in his new role was to place you on thirty-days medical leave and suspend your negotiator status—indefinitely."

Cassi felt the world closing in on her. The injustice of it all was overwhelming. It was not her fault that an unstable bomb had exploded. She had successfully negotiated Sal out of the room with the children unharmed. Ralph, on the other hand, had blown dozens of cases. This was so unfair. She had—

"Cassi, there's more."

"More?"

"I don't know how to say this other than to come right out with it." Wiley stood up and began to pace. "Vice President Dish has an inoperable aneurism. He can't stand with Carver for reelection, and it's looking like I have a serious shot at his slot." Wiley bowed his head and spoke with a soft voice. "It's an opportunity I can't let sail past."

Cassi felt the floor giving way, but she managed to hold on. She knew that this discussion, in fact this whole chapter of her life, would only last a few seconds more. Wiley was going to make a run for the White House—and she was now too heavy to carry along. Part of her wanted to scream at him and make him feel bad, but after a moment's repose she realized that that was the smaller part. In her heart of hearts she hoped he would succeed. She decided to make it easier for him. She said, "I understand. Air Force Two is like the Concorde—you have to check your baggage at the door."

Chapter 22

Wilmington, Delaware

AVAILING HIMSELF of the bridging cover provided by his chauffeur's upheld umbrella, Defcon4 CEO Mark Drake stepped quickly from the portico of his Delaware mansion into the back of his custom Bentley limousine. He had a meeting with the Italian Ambassador that morning and did not want a single drop of October rain to blemish his dove-gray Versace suit.

As he settled into the buttery black leather, the chauffeur pulled the limousine around the circle and headed down the gravel drive. Mark listened to the bulletproof tires crunching out the sound of wealth on the tiny stones. It was music to his ears. The drive to work was often his favorite part of the day. It was forty-five minutes of refined luxury and productive peace.

He plucked the steaming latte from the heated cup-holder in his armrest and savored the day's first sip. He loved the nutty warmth and the ensuing rush, the more so on dreary mornings like these. He smacked his tongue. Today's brew left a funny aftertaste. Had William used his own off-the-shelf grounds, rather than the custom order Blue Mountain beans? Drake wondered. He was about to buzz William to lodge a complaint when his eye fell upon a headline on the front page of The Wall Street Journal: Pentagon Budget Woes. He unfolded the crisp paper, swallowed another sip of latte, and began to read.

Some twenty minutes later Mark heard a television monitor spring to life. He looked up to see the limo's large central screen glowing blue.

He reached for the remote control but found the holder empty. Vexed, he pressed a burlwood button and activated the intercom. "I say, William, the tele has just come on and I'm missing the remote."

William did not reply. That was the problem with these high-technology cars, Mark thought. A twenty-five cent fuse could bring them to their knees. For three hundred thousand you expected better. That thought made him smile proudly. For that amount of money a government did get absolute reliability, in the form of one of his FreedomSeeker missiles.

Only when he glanced out the window to find an unfamiliar road did he get the feeling that something more serious than a technical glitch might be afoot. As if in answer to his unvoiced question, a video began to play. If he'd had any latte left, he would have choked. The screen showed a bulldog of a man hanging on to life at the end of a rope. His toes were barely touching the floor and his hands appeared to be bound behind his back. The man was looking at someone whom Mark guessed to be seated below the camera, although no part of him could be seen. The narrator could, however, be heard. "Aside from a slightly oily sheen, it looks like coffee creamer. Mix it in equal parts with Half-n-Half, add a little artificial flavoring, and it tastes that way too."

Mark watched the hanging man's face contort as he reacted to the words. Then Mark heard the narrator describe the chemistry of an explosive he called Creamer. When the description was over, the video paused. Mark wondered if this was some strange form of marketing video, a new explosive for Defcon4 to manufacture. Slipping it into his limo's DVD was a bit aggressive, but then his was an aggressive business.

Engrossed as he was by the morbid show and tell, Mark had not noticed that his limo had parked. Looking out the window he was surprised to see the Delaware valley below. They were at one of those scenic pull-offs beside a hillside road. It was not very scenic now, however, on account of the rain.

Mark tried the door but it was locked. He pushed the unlock button and found that it had no effect.

Panic seized him.

He pushed the intercom button frantically but received no response. He began screaming William's name. Nothing. The inescapable conclusion hit him like a punch in the gut. He was a captive, albeit in a burlwood and leather prison.

The video monitor came back to life and Mark refocused his attention on the pitiful wretch hanging by his neck. "Who asked you to do it," the unseen narrator asked.

The wretch shook his head a few times as though coming to accept his fate. That action must have caused him considerable pain, though he seemed beyond the point of noticing anymore. His neck was already rubbed raw and blood had discolored the bottom of the coarse noose. Finally, the man grew a resigned grimace and looked directly into the lens.

The camera zoomed in.

Mark began to tremble.

The shaking started deep in his bones and worked its way out through his limbs in an uncontrollable spasm. He recognized the face.

The death mask before him belonged to the FBI Commander he had to hire as part of his contribution to Stuart Slider's scheme. It was the man Wiley had given them to work the inside angle. Potchak.

"Who asked you to do it?" The narrator repeated.

Potchak spoke just two words, but they came out clear and strong. "Mark Drake."

~ ~ ~

Odi stopped the video. He wished he could have seen Drake's face at the moment Potchak pronounced his name, but his hidden camera only provided a profile view. He turned to face the rear of the car and lowered the partition half way. The pallid CEO of Defcon4 stared back at him, a look of absolute horror on his aquiline face.

"You're not William."

All things considered, Odi found that a ridiculous thing to say. "No, I'm not. Care to guess who I am?"

"No, I don't care to guess. Now let me out of my car."

"Let you out? Do you know how many lives were sacrificed to provide you with this opulent ride? The least you can do to respect their memory is to enjoy it."

"God damn it, I said let me out! I insist that you let me out of here —right now."

Odi said, "If you don't adjust your attitude, Drake, you may never leave." He raised the partition to cut off further protest.

Odi fast forwarded the DVD to the climactic scene and pushed play. The explosion happened so fast that you missed it if you blinked. One second Potchak was there, then you heard a sickening ka-woomf, and the next second you found yourself looking through a misted red lens at an empty pair of boots. After enough time passed for your mind to register what your eyes had not seen, a cloth wiped the lens, providing a clear view of the grisly remains and the blood-drenched, gore-splattered room. The video showed that medieval picture for a full thirty seconds before it stopped.

Odi gave Drake a minute of silence before flicking the intercom switch with his leather-gloved hand. "Potchak got testy too. He didn't have your advantage though. He didn't have the visual of what happens to people who don't fully cooperate. Tell me, Drake, are your fingernails turning blue?"

Again Odi wished he could see Drake's face, but he did not dare to lower the partition a second time.

"Oh my God. You've got to give me the antidote." His voice was no longer the haughty drone of a faux-British aristocrat. It was a nasal whine born of horrified desperation.

Odi let him dangle for a moment longer at the end of his metaphorical rope and then asked, "Does that mean you're willing to cooperate fully?"

"Yes, yes, of course I'm willing to cooperate. Just hurry. My fingers. My fingers are already blue."

Odi smiled. He was not enjoying the violence. He wasn't the sadistic type. But he loved it when everything went precisely according to plan.

"Who are you working with?"

"Mark Abrams, Mark Rollins, and Wiley Proffitt." Drake spit out the words as if they were poison.

The first two names Odi had expected. Together with Drake they rounded out the Wall Street darlings known collectively as The Three Marks. The third name stole Odi's breath away. He was glad that the partition was raised so Drake could not see him shake. Wiley Proffitt was seriously involved with his sister. In fact, if her prediction was correct they were already engaged. What possible motivation could Wiley have for getting in bed with Defense? He had his own island for chrissake, and was the Director of the FBI. What could The Three Marks possibly offer him that he did not already have? "Tell me why," Odi commanded.

Odi listened to Drake's panicked account of the defense contractors' plight, of how the river of cash from the War on Terror was drying up, and they were desperate for another Iraq. It was precisely as Ayden had hypothesized, but Odi still found himself amazed at both the brashness of their plan and the depth of their greed. He was also stunned by the personal connection. The fact that the consortium had selected Wiley for its White-House puppet was an amazing coincidence, and Odi did not believe in those. Drake, however, knew nothing about Cassi. Nor did he recognize Odi's face or name. The investigation of that coincidence would have to wait.

"Now give me the antidote," Drake implored, his voice accented by an adolescent crack.

"Coming right up."

Odi scanned the scenic pull-off again to ensure that they were in fact as alone as you would expect at a location like this come seven A.M. in the rain. They were. He opened the driver's door and went around to the trunk. He pulled wet-weather clothes on over his chauffer suit and then pulled a small motor scooter from the trunk as Drake pounded away at the windows.

He spoke into the intercom before riding the scooter away with the limo's keys, leaving Drake locked inside.

"Drake?"

"Yes!"

"Adam Brazer, Flint Mulder, Jeremy Jones, Mitch O'Brian, Derek Doogan, Tony Oritz, and William Waslager."

"What?!"

"Those are the names of my teammates. Those are the names of the men you killed."

Drake could not get any paler. He just looked up with pleading eyes, and said, "The antidote ... you promised."

"There is only one antidote for Creamer ... and that antidote is death."

Chapter 23

The Horus Club, Washington, D.C.

AS THE GRISLY IMAGE of Potchak's boots faded to black, the four men stared silently at the blank screen. They did not know Potchak personally, but they knew Drake. Now they also knew the circumstances of their friend's grisly end. Now they also understood the true horror of the threat. And so they sat there, motionless, silent. None wanting to meet another's eye. None wanting confirmation that the nightmare was real.

Wiley was not surprised that it was Stuart who eventually broke the silence, but nonetheless his words left Wiley choking on his Dalwhinnie.

"It must be Odi Carr," Stuart said.

Every time, Wiley thought, wiping his chin. He does it to me every frigging time. "Why do you say that?"

"Yes, why?" Abrams echoed, incredulity in his voice. "Carr is dead."

Nestled amidst the sea of embassies in Dumbarton Oaks, the exclusive club Wiley had selected for their meeting was a flashback to a time when men of extraordinary privilege and means routinely gathered to exchange news and talk business at the end of the day over grossly priced brandy, the very best imported cigars, and whatever else men of unlimited means might desire. The only indulgence not offered at The Horus Club was whores. The deficiency was not a morality statement. It was just their stubborn adherence to a policy maintained for over two-hundred years. Horus was for gentlemen only. As General Manager Oliver Appleton loved to point out whenever he could do so with discretion, even Supreme Court Justice Sandra Day O'Conner's application had been denied.

Abrams turned to Wiley. "You're sure we can talk here?"

Wiley took a long, contemplative puff on his cigar. He wanted to present himself as cool and composed while his friends were still reeling from the shock of the video. "Absolutely," he replied, blowing out a long stream of smoke. "The waiters, you know, are all deaf."

"That's ridiculous," Rollins chuffed.

"Not at all," Wiley said, teasing out the moment by pretending to study his cigar. "They read lips."

Rollins and Abrams both raised their brows and nodded.

Wiley savored the moment before continuing. "Still, given this day and age, I brought in the Bureau's best technician one evening to perform a surreptitious electronic sweep. Rives declared the club to be clean as a virgin's sheets." The men nodded their approval, teeing up the kicker. "On the way out that evening, Oliver Appleton pulled me aside. Despite Rives' expertise, his actions had not gone undetected. Oliver told me that he recognized what my guest was doing because he did it himself—twice a day."

Wiley accepted another round of kudos, noting that even Stuart actually looked impressed for once. "So yes, I am sure that we can talk. Stuart, you were going to tell us why you think our troublemaker is a dead man."

Stuart took a sip of his twelve-dollar club soda. "Whoever killed Potchak and Drake was obviously very familiar with explosives. I'm no expert, but I work in defense and I've never heard of anything like the device that was used. Yet the killer was familiar enough with the explosive to stay in the room. That requires both intimate knowledge and humungous balls."

"Like the balls of a CRT leader," Abrams added.

Stuart nodded and continued. "Odi Carr not only has every reason in the world to kill those two men, but he is also one of the world's leading explosive ordnance technicians. Furthermore, only seven bodies came back from Iran. Potchak assumed that Carr's body was incinerated in the explosion, given that there were no reports of survivors. In retrospect, I concede that perhaps that was wishful thinking. At the time it seemed the most reasonable conclusion."

"It still seems a stretch," Abrams said.

"Perhaps," Stuart agreed. "But there's more. I didn't mention this before, but Potchak actually had to remove Carr from command mid-mission."

"What?" Wiley asked.

"Apparently Carr figured out that it really was a clinic and not a training camp. When planning the attack, we figured that there would be no activity in the middle of the night, but were unlucky. A peasant boy got his foot blown off harvesting at night and showed up in an ambulance just as Echo Team was prepping for the attack. Anyhow, when Carr's body was not with the others and not a peep was heard from him, Potchak assumed that he must have tried to rescue some locals and either succumbed to the smoke or got caught up in the blast."

"That's a lot of assumptions," Rollins said.

"He has paid for his mistake," Wiley replied.

Everyone nodded somberly.

"What about the letter?" Abrams asked after another protracted silence.

"Read it again," Stuart said. "Aloud."

Abrams picked up the note that he and Rollins had each received with their copy of the Potchak execution video and read its single sentence. "Come forward, confess all, and resign within twenty-four hours of receiving this, of share the same fate as Potchak and Drake." Abrams put down the note as everyone pictured the smoking stumps. Then he said, "I don't see any clues to the author's identity."

Wiley was most curious about that himself.

Stuart said, "Carr was the leader of Counterterrorism Response Team Echo. Consider what that tells you in terms of character profile. He is a man of action, violent and intense. You are all defense guys. You know that Special Forces soldiers tend to be men of few words. I'm sure that is exactly the kind of letter that an FBI profiler would expect Odi Carr to write."

Wiley nodded in response to the other men's inquisitive looks.

"So what do we do?" Abrams said. "I sure as shit am not going to resign and turn myself in."

"Nor I," Rollins said. "But I'm not going to be fatally egotistical about this either. If he could get to Potchak and Drake, we should assume that he could get to us too."

"You have several advantages they did not have," Stuart said. "First of all, you know that someone is after you. Potchak and Drake were caught unaware. Secondly, you know your stalker's identity. That means that we can launch both offensive and defensive countermeasures."

"I've got no problem with that," Rollins said. "Defense is what I do. But I don't want to have to hide out forever. Bunkers are boring."

"I second that thought." Abrams said. "I don't know if Hitler gave up or he just needed a change of scenery."

"What do you suggest?" Wiley asked Stuart.

Stuart told them.

When he finished, Abrams said, "I like your approach, Stuart, especially your clever use of that secret weapon. If you are confident that it will work, we are willing to go along—but only as long as Rollins and I are not the only ones with skin in the game."

Wiley met Abrams' eye with a calm gaze, although he knew the coming words would shake him to the core.

Abrams continued. "We won't be organizing any more terrorist attacks until you take Odi Carr out of play—and put him in a box. Consider your campaign on ice."

Chapter 24

Alexandria, Virginia

AN ADRENALINE SURGE accompanied the doorbell's chime, making Cassi feel an odd mixture of longing and fear. She missed Wiley dearly despite his decision to sacrifice their relationship for his political ambition. She got up from the sofa, set down the latest issue of *The Journal of Child Psychology*, and walked to the door.

The last time she had seen Wiley she was still in the hospital, confined to a bed and sporting an inch-thick cap of gauze on her head. He had left her after saying that he needed to let things cool down before he would attempt to salvage her career, and she had not seen him since. Then out of the blue he had called an hour ago to say that he was coming over with news. Did that mean she was in the clear? Or declared radioactive?

Cassi had struggled to get through the job suspension with her sanity intact. With no Wiley or work to distract her, she had been alone with the demons of her mind—and the ghosts of two dead kids. Every time she looked out her window, she only saw what wasn't there. She loved her loft, but she was going to have to move. Her family, her career, and now her home—she had lost them all. Yet as depressing as her situation was, when she thought of Masha and Zeke, Cassi knew that she was better off than she deserved.

She opened the door to find Wiley wearing what she had come to know as his politician's face. That was not a good sign. With little else to do but sleep-in, read books, and watch the news, she had been following the rumors of his impending campaign—rumors that she knew to be true. She still had mixed thoughts.

In her heart Cassi hoped that Wiley would not get the job. She wanted him for herself. She acknowledged that this was selfish, but knew better than to try to deny her own emotions. It did not look like she was going to get him, however. Since the recent round of terrorist attacks—the same blitz that took her brother—Wiley's name recognition and public opinion ratings had soared. She tried to be happy for Wiley, but it was no use. For a six-foot-one over-thirty female with a PhD and a badge, finding a meaningful match was a next to impossible task. This was a once-in-a-lifetime opportunity for Wiley, no doubt about that, but it might be for her as well. "Are you alone, or did you bring the Secret Service?"

Wiley chortled as he stepped through the doorway. Then he gave her a single, soft kiss on the cheek. He never did that when they were dating, she noted, kiss her while they were standing up. She figured it was his subconscious aversion to having to tilt up his head.

Cassi procrastinated receiving news of her own fate by preemptively asking about Wiley's. "So, is it going to happen? Will President Carver offer you the job?"

"I have no idea what the President intends," Wiley said dismissively. "Mind if I take a seat?"

"Of course," she said, leading him to the armchairs she had repositioned before her indoor waterfall. This was her new favorite sitting spot, now that the view of the playground was out.

She had a bottle of Chablis cooling in an ice bucket. She wished she had thought to turn on music as she poured them each a glass. The silence was awkward. "Cheers."

"I've come with good news," Wiley said without taking a sip. "The FBI is not going to force you out. In fact, I've already got your new assignment."

Wiley's words seemed to open a curtain, and Cassi felt sunshine come streaming into her dark world. "Oh, Wiley, that's wonderful. Thank you. Thank you so much."

Wiley spread his arms and bowed. "Anything for you."

Oh, if only that were true, Cassi thought. "What's the assignment?"

"Well, it's an unconventional role—for political reasons—but I'm sure you're going to like it."

"An unconventional role," Cassi repeated, not liking the sound of that. "What does that mean, exactly?"

"Two children died, Cassi, so it's going to have to look like you're being punished. Officially you're going to be swept aside into a back-office research role."

Cassi wanted to protest that it wasn't fair, that Masha and Zeke's deaths were not her fault. But to be honest she could not even convince herself. She had to consider herself lucky to be getting anything but sacked. In fact, she realized, lucky probably wasn't the appropriate word. Wiley must have gone to bat for her big time. "And unofficially?"

Wiley brightened. "I know your passion lies in counterterrorism, so that's what you'll be doing. In fact, you'll be in charge of a very important case."

Cassi felt a surge of warmth growing in her belly. That sounded wonderful—too good to be true. Alarm bells started to sound but she stifled them. "A terrorist case?"

Wiley nodded and dove in. "A terrorist case. And a highly classified one at that."

"And I'll be in charge."

"You will, although it's just going to be a one-woman team."

Cassi bit her lower lip and considered this. Although physically surrounded by others while working, she had always managed her negotiations alone. "I'm okay with that. Tell me about it."

"In a nutshell, a terrorist has begun assassinating US Defense Contractors. Your job is to catch him."

"How can that be a one-person task? Is this just a theory I'm to prove?"

Wiley shook his head gravely. "Last Friday the CEO of Defcon4, Mark Drake, was murdered."

Cassi nodded. "I saw that on the news. Someone put a bomb under his car. They said a major investigation was underway by both the local police and the FBI, on account of his being a prominent British citizen." Cassi read Wiley's expression and her mind raced ahead. "But that's not what's really going on, is it?"

"It is as far as the public, the police force, and even the FBI are concerned. But no, it's not. Believe it or not, I got a call from the director of the CIA. It seems they have a mole highly placed within al-Qaeda who says that Drake's death was an al-Qaeda hit. In fact, that mole told us that Drake is just the first of many. Apparently al-Qaeda has hired a professional assassin, and they've given him a list."

"A hired assassin," Cassi interrupted. "Why would al-Qaeda hire an assassin?"

"You're the profiler. At least you used to be. Consider the profile of the average assassin, and then compare it to the average al-Qaeda operative. I'm sure you'll see there's quite a difference."

"A difference that circumvents half our screening and security measures," Cassi thought out loud while nodding appreciatively.

"The CIA mole has no idea who the assassin is, but he was able to get us the names of his next two targets."

Cassi's adrenaline continued to surge as issues and ideas began colliding in her head. This was getting very deep very fast.

"Here's the rub," Wiley continued. "The CIA is desperate to protect the fact that they have a mole. In fact, sacrificing the next two victims is a price that they are willing to pay. They need their source in place to give them notice of the next mass attack, the next 9/11."

Cassi was beginning to understand. "So you can't let the public know that you know Drake's death was the first in a series of planned terrorist assassinations."

"Correct. And it gets even more complicated than that. The CIA mole says al-Qaeda has a highly placed source within the FBI, although again he doesn't know who it is. That leak led to the ambush that killed your brother. Al-Qaeda knew that Team Echo was coming.

"Needless to say, I can't let anyone in the agency know what I've just told you. Furthermore, whoever the mole is, he is willing to kill to protect his identity. Commander Potchak was murdered by the same means as Drake, presumably because he saw or heard something that made the mole uncomfortable." Wiley stopped talking and raised his eyebrows, waiting for her reaction.

Cassi struggled to separate the flood of emotion from the wave of information. She would digest the facts later. For now, she was just pleased to understand her new role. "Thus you need a low-profile, one-person team. Someone you know you can trust. Someone you can reassign without raising any alarms."

"Precisely."

"So what, exactly, am I to do."

"The first thing you have to do is meet with the next two people on the assassin's list and make them hard targets. They, like Drake, are both defense-corporation CEOs. One is Mark Rollins, CEO of Rollins, and the other is Mark Abrams, CEO of ASIS. Wall Street knows them collectively as The Three Marks."

The irony of the moniker was not lost on Cassi. She nodded. Her task sounded simple enough.

Reading her mind, Wiley said, "It's not going to be an easy sale. First of all, I can only send you, which implies that the FBI is not overly serious. And of course you can't let them know that they're on a list or even that we have inside knowledge, for the reasons already mentioned. But at the same time you have to get them to take this seriously enough to agree to some highly inconvenient lifestyle changes."

"So basically, you're placing their lives in my hands, but they're not allowed to know it."

"Precisely."

Cassi thought about what that would mean in practical terms. She did not know anything about Rollins or Abrams, but she could guess that billionaire CEO's would be arrogant and cocky and would have a child's immortality complex. Her assignment was not going to be easy. Then she thought of Masha and Zeke and decided that saving these two might be her best chance to begin making amends. She drew her gaze from the slate waterfall back to Wiley. "I'll get the job done."

"I know you will, Cassi. That's why I was thrilled to come by the opportunity to give you this job. I think it's a perfect fit, given our circumstances."

"Any suggestions on where I should start?"

Wiley opened his briefcase and withdrew five thick folders. "This is everything we have from Potchak's and Drake's murder scenes, as well as background information on Drake, Rollins, Abrams, and their companies. You are to use this to create a profile on the assassin and then use that profile to make specific security suggestions to Rollins and Abrams—all the while being careful not to betray the fact that we have a source."

Cassi nodded. She understood. "Thank you Wiley. I'm your Agent. What's the timeframe for the profile and plan?"

Wiley flashed her a guilty look. "I hope this leave has given you a chance to catch up on your sleep, because you may not be getting much until you catch the assassin. You're presenting to Rollins and Abrams in Wilmington—tomorrow afternoon."

Cassi grimaced. Profiles usually took weeks to compile and then got sent off in the mail. She would be hopping on an airplane to present hers in less than twenty-four hours. "Tomorrow afternoon. Great."

"That's not all," Wiley continued. "Once you've gotten Rollins and Abrams squared away, your real job begins—"

Cassi raised her chin.

"You're to use that profile to anticipate the assassin's moves ... and lure him into a trap."

Chapter 25

Chesapeake Beach, Maryland

SITTING ON A DARK PORCH in a white wooden rocker, Odi nursed a beer and stared at the glow of his laptop computer screen. He hoped Ayden would come on line as promised. He had a lot to get off his chest.

He was holed-up in his Aunt Charlotte's summerhouse. He found it the perfect place to plan his moves and hide out between hits. There were few residents on her stretch of the Chesapeake Shore this time of year. Most sought warmer climes, including Charlotte herself. She was in Phoenix.

He drew comfort from the surroundings. Their familiarity was a soothing balm, given that everything else in his life had changed. His family had enjoyed many a summer there with Charlotte when he and Cassi were kids. Her cottage was a modest, wooden structure built largely by his uncle in the mid-sixties. Odi had not noticed back then just how modest it was. He reflected on how wonderful it was to be an unspoiled kid. He closed his eyes, leaned back in the rocker, and listened to the rhythmic clang of a neighboring warning buoy. As a kid he had fallen asleep to that sound a hundred times.

A different sound interrupted his reverie. His computer had chimed ta-dong, indicating that Ayden had arrived on line. Odi leaned forward and pressed send, dispatching the message he had prepared.

Two minutes later, he heard a friendly zzhing announcing the arrival of an instant message. He looked down and read Ayden's reply. "Saw your video. Unbelievable. That Creamer of yours is powerful stuff!"

Odi gathered that the gory shots had not repulsed his friend. That was no surprise, his being a doctor in a violent region, but it was still a relief. Ayden had helped to put together the general plan, but Odi had not decided on his tactics before leaving Iran. His e-mail package to Ayden contained a brief explanation of the Creamer along with ten seconds of highlights from the Potchak video clip. "So you approve?" He typed.

"Sure. Where did you get the explosive?"

"I made it," Odi typed with some pride. "I went back to Johns Hopkins and used the same lab where I invented the stuff—working at night, of course."

"No risk of getting caught?"

"Naw. I'm still young enough to be mistaken for a graduate student if someone sees me, and the graduate chemistry lab has used the same formula for their door code for years."

"Formula?"

"It's the square of the numeric value of the month converted from Centigrade to Fahrenheit."

"Pardon?"

"This is October, the 10th month. So the code's 212. That's 10 squared times 9 divided by 5 plus 32."

"Okay ... Anyway, your explosive is brilliant. Brilliant and chilling."

"Thanks. Let's hope that it's chilling enough to catalyze the desired reaction." Odi leaned back from the keyboard feeling better for having shared his experiences. His newfound sense of relaxation and relief made Ayden's next message all the more disturbing.

"You're going to have to kill them all. It's naïve to think that those kings are going to walk away from their thrones. That isn't the way of the world. Never has been. Never will be."

Odi tried to think of a clever retort. It only took him a second. "Attorneys make deals every day for the sentence of life behind bars when the alternative is the electric chair or the needle."

"Nice analogy," Ayden replied. "But it only applies to people who have been caught. These guys don't consider themselves caught yet. Your proposition is nothing to them but an invitation to a game of cat and mouse."

"I've got claws."

"Maybe, but kings like these are going to consider you a mouse."

Odi felt his excitement deflating. He thought he had found a way to render true justice, to get the truth out and put the bad guys behind bars. In fact, judging by the rich-and-famous cases that had made it to court in recent years, he considered his solution to be the only way that an American billionaire would ever be exposed to justice. He owed his fallen comrades that justice. He pounded his response into the keys. "One way or another I am going to dethrone those kings—starting tomorrow night."

Chapter 26

The White House

"THANK YOU, GENTLEMEN," President Carver said, rising from his chair.

As Wiley filed out of the Roosevelt Room with the other members of the committee, the president's Aide took hold of his elbow. Jerome Murphy would normally have been one of those guys you loved to hate. He had a brilliant mind, a Herculean build, and exceptional good looks. But he was so unassuming and nice that you could not help liking him instead. Still, Wiley had no doubt that Murphy had his eye on the boss's office, so he was ever on guard. Vigilance was Wiley's watchword around men of ambition.

Wiley allowed Murphy to escort him silently through a couple sets of guarded doors and the chief of staff's office into the president's private study. "Please have a seat," Murphy said. Then he walked out and closed the door.

Wiley had grown up wealthy among men of power, so titles and architecture did little to impress him. He knew that the president pissed yellow just like everyone else, and he saw the Oval Office as nothing more than a famous arrangement of bricks and mortar. Still, he got a thrill out of this first visit to the president's private study. Rumor had it that this was where presidents conducted much of the business unsuitable for the official record. Had Marilyn Monroe waited here as he did now? Naked?

As he sat down to wait, Wiley felt butterflies begin to dance. His subconscious was voicing the words his conscious did not want to hear. Whatever happened next would be either very good, or very bad.

President Carver entered the study almost immediately through another door. Wiley caught a quick glimpse of the Oval before it closed. "Thank you for staying, Wiley. Please, remain in your seat."

The windowless study had royal blue carpet and white plaster walls.

The furnishings were handmade from gold upholstery and rich mahogany wood. Wiley was pleasantly surprised to detect the scent of cigar smoke, though the cleaners clearly tried to overpower it with room freshener and furniture polish. He always found deep satisfaction in the discovery of another man's peccadilloes.

As Carver sat opposite him in a matching chair, Murphy entered with two glasses of freshly squeezed orange juice. Wiley would have preferred another cup of Joe to the president's favorite drink—the only C Wiley ever craved was caffeine—but he accepted it with a grateful smile, saying, "Perfect," after savoring a sip. He set down the glass, smiled at Carver, and tried to relax.

"A privilege of the office," Carver concurred. Then he hardened his features and cut to the chase.

"We didn't predict the fall of the Berlin Wall or the collapse of the Soviet Union. We didn't foresee 9/11 or Hamas. Yet even with all that precedent, I'm going to look like one of history's greatest fools if al-Qaeda pulls off something major on US soil after my own FBI Director has spent the year blasting the airwaves and editorials with predictions of an impending attack."

"With all due respect, Mr. President, that's not necessarily true," Wiley interrupted. "You just need to be seen taking a firm and active stand."

Carver paused to consider Wiley's words, but then forged ahead on a predetermined course. "I trust you didn't hold anything back earlier in your briefing. You really have no idea when or where the next attack will come?"

"I could give you the techno-fluff we feed the media about increased chatter and prime targets of attack," Wiley said, "but that won't get you further in practical terms than a little common sense."

"Still, you're predicting that the next attack is coming soon, say within a few months?"

"I am, Mr. President."

"Please elaborate."

Wiley knew that he was on dangerous ground. He had to remain vague yet valuable, coy yet credible. "I wish I could, but all I have is intuition—the confluence of thousands of subliminal clues gleaned from the endless stream of reports crossing my desk." With someone else, Wiley would have repeated the same statement another way, adding no facts while making his answer seem more complete. But he knew that tactic would not fool Carver, so he stopped.

Carver stared at him, and then seemed to make a decision. His stern look evaporated into his trademark smile and he said, "Well, it's good to have a prophet on my team."

"Thank you, Mr. President," Wiley replied, struggling to suppress the glee erupting within at Carver's choice of adjectives.

Wiley thought that was the end of the meeting, but then Carver continued. "If there's one thing the base likes, one thing that will drive them to the polls next November, it's a hellfire-and-brimstone prophet —assuming, of course, that terrorism still piques their interest."

With that repetition and embellishment, Wiley felt a hot surge of adrenaline rush from his heart to the far ends of his body. Carver had said it. He had actually said it. Only thanks to a lifetime of practice was Wiley able to keep his poker face un-cracked.

Carver seemed to be reading his expression anyway. The president flashed him an amused smile. "I understand Stuart Slider is consulting for you now."

Wiley was shocked. Carver was throwing all subtlety aside. This was unbelievable.

"You're not my only source of information," the president continued. "Anyway, I was glad to hear that. Stuart is very, very good."

"Thank you," was all Wiley could think of to say. He was elated beyond words, at least until his eyes drifted to the doorway of the chief of staff and remembered the price he had to pay.

Chapter 27

Annapolis, Maryland

STANDING THERE in the ASIS boardroom, Cassi could not shake the feeling that the two CEOs had something dubious to hide— especially Rollins. He looked positively evil. She could tell that both men were a lot more scared than they were letting on and her instincts were screaming that that was important. But she had yet to pinpoint why. Were they just being coy because they were mighty captains of the defense industry and she was a woman? That was possible, but Cassi did not find it likely. Given the context, she felt that the very fact that they were trying hard not to betray their fear indicated a sense of guilt. Still, she was not there to investigate collusion, be it with Drake or against him. She was there to salvage her career and save two lives.

So far Cassi did not have the impression that she was doing well on either account. She would know for certain soon enough. She concluded the formal portion of her virtually impromptu presentation with what she hoped would be a provocative line. "One thing we do know for certain is the nature of the beast. Mark Drake was killed by a professional."

Abrams and Rollins both continued to lean back in their leather chairs as she finished. Cassi felt a chill of disappointment. Her lure had not brought them forward. "But you don't know which professional," Abrams said after an uncomfortable silence. It was a statement of fact by a man unimpressed. "Nor do you know whom he was working for."

"Or why," Rollins added. "Yet you chose to warn us. That's quite a leap."

"Might even border on harassment," Abrams said.

Cassi bit her tongue, reminding herself to stay on target even as she felt her FBI career slipping from her grasp. Their skepticism might not be personal. Perhaps these guys had endured a recent proctologic exam courtesy of another federal agency, perhaps the IRS. In any case, she had to deduct that her feed-them-the-facts approach had failed to light their fires. The fact that she'd had only hours to prepare it would not buy her any slack in Quantico. Whatever goodwill she had previously enjoyed, the daycare disaster had destroyed.

She weighed her options and decided to regroup to launch a second offensive from more familiar ground. She closed her eyes for a second, just long enough to slip into The Zone. She pictured Rollins and Abrams on her chessboard, looking like Laurel and Hardy. She leaned forward toward the obese Abrams as the fire reignited in her eyes. "You're right," she said. "There are dozens of reasons why someone might want to kill your colleague that have nothing to do with either of you. Why, there could be a hundred. So for the sake of argument, let us suppose that there is only a one-in-a-hundred chance that Drake's killer is planning to shove a grenade up your ass. Are you willing to accept those odds, gentlemen? Are you willing to risk everything on a single roll of the dice? Or would you rather work with me to keep your proctologist happy?"

Rollins' gaunt cheeks assumed a lemon-like pucker. He turned to Abrams, who shrugged his fleshy shoulders. "What do you know about the assassin, Agent Carr?"

That was more like it, she thought. She decided to skip the usual statistical qualifiers and give it to them with both barrels. She needed to make the assassin's threat seem credible. To do that she needed to make the assassin feel real to them. Besides, if she got something wrong, nobody would know it until she caught him, and then no one would care. This time she leaned toward Rollins. "We're looking for a white male in his thirties. He is a large man, about six foot one inches tall, with an athletic build. He keeps his hair short and does not wear glasses. He is skilled as an actor, and capable of convincingly altering both his appearance and his voice. He works alone on the basis of meticulous advance planning. He is highly disciplined, highly educated, and exceptionally creative. He is a techie, comfortable with everything from digital cameras to laptop computers. And he is a chemist, capable of brewing sophisticated original ordnance. He is knowledgeable of investigative procedures and forensics. He is passionate about his work and yet coldly detached. In short, gentleman, he is as serious as the death he deals. Of all the profiles I've worked over the years, this is the man I would fear the most if he was after me."

During her speech, Cassi was delighted to see both faces begin to crack. Now she leaned back in the plush chair and hoped for an inviting fissure.

Abrams offered one. "What are you asking of us?"

"I want free reign to work with the heads of your corporate security to augment your personal protection. I want them and everyone working for them to know that my orders are to be accepted without pushback."

"We're a defense contractor," Rollins said. "Our security is already top notch. You must be aware of that." Then he walked right into her trap. It couldn't have happened to a nicer guy, she thought. "I'm sure that even with your gold shield you didn't get your gun past my men."

Cassi smiled and opened her purse. "You're right. They asked me to leave my firearm at the door." She withdrew three lipstick tubes from a side zipper pocket. Then she added, "Hexamine, nitric acid, and ammonium nitrate," as she set each down like a missile on Rollins' precious table. "I may as well be packing a rectal grenade."

Rollins grew a shade paler, but he was not finished yet. "Do I understand that it's our personal safety rather than our companies' security that you are worried about?"

"That's correct."

"Well, then you needn't worry about me. I'm scheduled for two-weeks of annual leave starting Monday. There's no reason I can't start a few days early. I will be staying at my Florida beach house, which may as well be Fort Knox. It's built to withstand category-five-hurricane winds, and the security system is state of the art."

"That sounds like a promising start," Cassi said. "The important thing in the short term is to get you out of your usual routine. Do you have room at your beach house for a contingent of guards?"

"As many as you'd like."

"Tell me about the place."

"I've got two acres of oceanfront property on a semi-private beach."

"Semi-private?"

"Velveteen Beach is a three-mile-long, one-bridge island separated from the Florida mainland by the intracoastal waterway. The houses on Velveteen are few and far between, numbering only eighteen in total."

Cassi nodded. "Very well. I'd guess six guards should be able to secure a location like that around the clock. With your permission, I'll ask your Director of Security to make those arrangements."

Rollins nodded.

Cassi turned to the larger CEO. "What about you, Mister Abrams? Do you have any vacation coming?"

"No, and I'm afraid that taking leave is out of the question at the moment. But I can confine myself to my home and the office, with a short helicopter ride in between."

"I'll need to inspect both sites. Will you be flying home tonight?"

"Yes."

"May I join you?"

Abrams stroked his chin between a pork-chop thumb and two sausage fingers.

"I'll only need a couple of hours if your majordomo will cooperate," Cassi added.

"All right."

"So we're agreed then," Rollins said. "I'll leave immediately on vacation in the company of the dirty half-dozen. And Miss Carr will accompany Abrams home tonight to help wall him in."

As Cassi concurred, Abrams asked, "Agent Carr. I'm assuming that you will be able to wrap this up in a week or so. Is that correct?"

Cassi attempted to give a nod that conveyed more confidence than she felt.

"Then I'll give you my full cooperation—until a week from this Friday," Abrams said. "If I haven't heard the all-clear by then, I'm going to make a call to your boss."

As he spoke those closing words an odd look passed between Abrams and Rollins. Cassi did not know what it meant, but she left the meeting with an unsettling impression. It was almost like she was being used ...

Chapter 28

Velveteen Beach, Florida

ODI PAUSED with his finger on the trigger. Something did not feel right. He squirmed to adjust the pile of sand beneath his chest and then added a few scoops. He wanted to take more weight off his elbows, leaving his arms completely relaxed. Satisfied with his position, he closed his eyes and focused on the ocean's swishy roar as he slowly inhaled and exhaled a deep breath of salty air. It was time.

He refocused his gaze on the laptop lying before him on the dune and squeezed the joystick's trigger. Four yards to his left the rotor of a remote-controlled helicopter spun to life, kicking up a cloud of fine white sand. Odi squeezed harder and the craft began to rise. He took it straight up, easing off on the trigger only when the altimeter display on his computer screen indicated a height of forty feet. Forty was what he needed to clear the neighboring rooftops with a margin of safety.

Focusing on the screen's main display, he watched his own prone form come into focus as the helicopter leveled off. There between the rolling dunes of Velveteen Beech he looked like a single hotdog in a sea of buns. He smiled, pleased that the hobby-shop salesman had not talked him out of an extra four-hundred bucks in vain. Even at night the picture quality transmitted from above was remarkably clear. He could trace the individual camouflage splotches on his desert BDUs.

He used the joystick's thumb lever to orient the helicopter due south and then pushed the handgrip forward. The bird responded like a dream. It was both nimble and quick.

Odi had positioned himself three houses down from Rollins' place where he still had line-of-sight to the CEO's third floor across half a mile of sea-oat-covered dune. He had reconned the beach from Charlotte's cottage using Google's keyhole satellite shots. With those photos, it took him just ten minutes to find what looked from above like the perfect spot, and the reality on the ground had not disappointed him.

He had exercised extreme caution getting to Velveteen, especially for the last few miles. Odi reasoned that if he were in charge of Rollins's security, he would have a man watching the bridge through a long-distance lens. So he parked his rental car at a motel on the mainland and crossed the river on the bridge's scaffolding just as the sun was going down. It was the time of day when everyone's eyes played tricks and the ground was still hot enough from the Florida sun to make infrared binoculars worthless.

Once on the island, he low-crawled sniper style most of the way from the bridge to his chosen location, taking his time, moving bush to bush when no one was around. The size of the pack he had carried would have earned him a kick in the balls from every drill sergeant he ever knew, but for this operation he needed every bit of the bulky cargo stored therein so he had risked it. If detected, he had planned to pretend to be the nephew of a local resident, a soldier on leave preparing for upcoming Special Forces training. But he made it to the beach without incident or challenge. Once settled into his pre-selected spot on the dunes, he had spent six virtually motionless hours studying his target through a telescope lens while struggling to ignore the constant nipping of sand fleas.

The presence of attentive guards working three-man shifts bothered Odi. It was not that they posed any particular threat or challenge. He had built his plan around them. Rather, he was irked because their presence reconfirmed that neither Rollins nor Abrams intended to come forward and confess. That was a disappointment if not a surprise. Ayden had predicted as much, but it still blew Odi's mind. How could the condemned men ignore him once they had seen the explosive video of their lackey and the encore with their colleague? Odi retained hope that Abrams would come forward tomorrow after Rollins's death, but he would not hold his breath.

Odi tracked the helicopter's position by comparing what he saw on the laptop screen to the printout he had made from the Google satellite shot. As the neighbor's swimming pool disappeared from the screen, he felt the thrill of the end game kicking in. A moment later the helicopter was over the target.

Rollins' beach house was a beautiful three-story white structure, with multiple balconies and lots of floor-to-ceiling tinted glass. Looking at it from his flea-ridden dugout in the sand, Odi could not help remembering that he had passed up the opportunity to spend his life in one of those. He had passed on the beach to work for Potchak. The thought set his blood aboil. Only with effort was he able to push his feelings of betrayal aside and refocus his attention completely on the mission at hand.

He could see the whole oceanfront side of the mansion from his position in the dunes. When the guards were out of sight, it looked more like the setting of a romance novel than a thriller. "Except for the damn fleas," he added aloud, swatting for the thousandth time. Once the sun had set and the lights had gone on, it had not taken him much time with the telescope to figure out which balcony belonged to the master bedroom. Now that the lights were out, he steered the helicopter to where they had been.

He tried to position the helicopter directly over the master balcony, but gusting winds were creating a dangerous stability challenge. For this to work he had to align it midway between roof and rail and perpendicular to the master bedroom's sliding glass door. He cursed himself for forgetting to factor wind into the equation when designing the payload. If, after all he had gone through to get here he had to abort his beautiful plan on account of something as mundane as wind, he would go berserk. That would be like scrapping the moon shot for a flat tire.

Three minutes and five aborted attempts later sweat was rolling down his face despite the evening chill. After six he began to worry about running out of fuel. After seven he was weighing the risks of a frontal assault. On the eighth he managed to hold the bird in place just long enough. The instant he had the position right, he brought the bird straight down. Given the position of the camera on the belly of the craft, all Odi saw for the last couple of feet of descent was a quickly rising floor and then a close-up still shot of tile grout. Tactically, the landing was perfect. He hoped it had not made too much noise. That was another oversight, Odi realized with a groan—not installing sound. For all he knew, a guard could be studying the helicopter right now, asking his boss via radio what he should do. Live and learn.

He pushed the silver button on the joystick's base, causing the cargo clamps beneath the helicopter to disengage. The camera jiggled a bit and Odi let out a sigh of relief. He had successfully separated the cargo from the bird that had delivered it.

Odi lifted his night vision binoculars, located the porch, and felt a wave of relief. No guard. No lights. Time for stage two.

He fine-tuned the focus on the binoculars and then, still holding them in his left hand, squeezed the joystick trigger again with his right. He watched with satisfaction as the helicopter rose straight up into the air above the roof while the image transmitted to his computer screen remained unchanged.

He continued to take the unburdened helicopter up to a height of fifty feet where, using the binoculars and joystick's thumb toggle, he pointed its nose out to sea. He pushed forward fully on the stick, sending the helicopter racing out over the water. Without any cargo, it streaked like a missile across the sky. He let it fly until it was little more than a dot on the horizon. Then he released the trigger. The rotor stopped, and the helicopter dropped like a bagged duck into the waves. Speaking to no one but the sea, he said, "Stage two, complete."

Odi withdrew a second remote from his backpack and lay back down between the dunes. Once settled, he returned his attention to the computer screen. He had custom built the robot that now graced Rollins' balcony using a remote-controlled toy jeep as a base. It rolled on four suction-cup covered wheels and had lots of sophisticated robotic equipment attached. He turned on the joystick and gave it a short forward nudge to confirm that it was operational, sighing with satisfaction when the camera image moved. So far, so good, Odi thought, knowing that the real tests of his engineering prowess still lay ahead.

He used the run of the grout to position the robot so that it was perfectly perpendicular to the sliding door. Then he drove it forward. The image shook back and forth after a couple of feet and then the view jumped to show the weak reflection of moonlight off heavy glass. Odi felt the thrill of the hunt coursing through his veins. He was almost there.

He propelled the robot up the sliding-glass door to a height of six feet and then released the joystick with a silent prayer. From his practice sessions on Charlotte's door he knew that this was a tender moment, but the technology did not fail. The robot stuck.

He toyed with the focus, trying to get a good look inside the bedroom. With the helicopter gone, there was not much he would be able to do if the robot was in the wrong place. Odi was sure that he had the master bedroom, but there was still the chance that Rollins had swapped rooms with a guard as a security measure. All Odi could do about that was hope that Rollins was too stubborn or the guards were not that good.

He adjusted the focus, taking the image a couple of turns in the wrong direction before finally getting it right. Once the image crystallized he felt another satisfying surge. Mark Rollins was sleeping beneath a white duvet on a raised platform bed. Odi used the computer to zoom in on the face just to be sure. The meticulously-parted dark hair and long patrician nose of the master of the house greeted him. "Bingo."

He pressed a black button on the joystick, engaging the robot's auxiliary suction cups. Now even with the activities to follow, the robot would not slip.

Panning back out to a wider view, he saw something that made his heart skip a beat. There was a brassiere on the floor. Unless Rollins had a habit of cross-dressing, he was not alone in that big platform bed.

Odi would not allow collateral casualties to taint what Ayden had facetiously dubbed Operation Just Revenge. He would not be able to live with himself after that. He also felt certain that his fallen comrades would not want their revenge at that price. If the woman buried beneath that king-sized duvet did not remain motionless during the next few minutes, Odi would have to abort. To minimize the chances of that happening, he decided to sacrifice caution for speed.

He pushed a yellow button on the remote control, spraying concentrated hydrofluoric acid onto the glass a couple of inches below the anchoring suction cups. Hydrofluoric acid was especially potent on glass. It would dissolve a baseball-sized hole in less than a minute, even in Rollins' hurricane glass. The hole would both help to direct the explosion and make the entire window weak.

Odi watched the duvet while he worked. Nobody stirred. Full speed ahead. He pressed the orange button exactly sixty seconds after the yellow, holding it down. He smiled with satisfaction as the camera began to respond with a slight, rhythmic shake. The orange button controlled a pecking device, which was now double-tapping every other second against the glass. Tap-tap ... tap-tap ... tap-tap ... After half a dozen pecks, the duvet began to stir.

"Attaboy."

After a few more taps, Rollins rolled cautiously out of bed.

Odi let off on the button and the pecking stopped.

As Mark Rollins stood up and looked around, Odi's eyes were drawn to the gun in his hand. "Excellent," he mumbled. "With a nine-millimeter Beretta in your hand, you're not feeling the need to call for help."

Odi glued his eyes to the screen as Mark surveyed his room. Each time Mark turned his head from the balcony, Odi gave the button another quick press. After the third salvo Mark raised his gun and walked directly toward the camera, tilting his head from one side to the other as though trying to focus. He was probably wondering if it was possible for a seagull to fly fast enough to imbed itself in hurricane-proof glass.

Odi would have enjoyed watching the doomed man's confused face, but he forced himself to keep his focus on the duvet. He prayed the owner of the brassiere would stay fully covered for another two seconds. She did.

Pictures of Odi's fallen friends flashed through his mind: Adam, Derek, Flint, Jeremy, Mitch, and Tony. Finally Rollins' inquisitive face got so close that Odi could see nothing else. He said, "You should have confessed," and then pressed the red button.

Chapter 29

FBI Headquarters, Washington, D.C.

WILEY LOOKED OVER at Stuart, pleased to have his campaign manager's company for once. Stuart seemed to sense Wiley's gaze even with his back turned. When he looked over his shoulder, Wiley said, "I've finished with London Heathrow. A dozen were close, but none were close enough. I've got nothing."

With Drake and Rollins now dead, Abrams was the only defense CEO they had left. That made Wiley nervous. Though Stuart would not show it, Wiley was convinced that his campaign manager was feeling the butterflies. While the CEOs replacing Drake and Rollins would surely give Wiley's campaign their financial support, agreeing to stage terrorist attacks was an entirely different matter. Abrams insisted that he would be able to bring the new CEOs on board with the plan, but he refused to make a move until Odi Carr was on a coroner's slab. The man was adamant. "No toe tag, no dice."

Wiley silently cursed his partner in crime although he could hardly blame Abrams. The man's ass was now squarely in a clever assassin's sights. Of course Abrams wanted the Director of the FBI fully focused on catching the bastard. Who wouldn't? As part of that focus, Wiley had broken with discretion and brought Stuart to the Hoover Building to help him scan immigration videos. Misery loves company, and Wiley could think of little that was more miserable than spending midnight to dawn studying an endless stream of faces.

Video of every passenger arriving to the US from Europe and the Middle East during the four weeks between the Iranian mission and Potchak's death was queuing up to parade past their tired eyes. It was a monstrous task. Even with the aid of the FBI's sophisticated software, which Wiley had programmed to fast forward the video past women and children and men too short or tall, they still had tens of thousands of faces to study. They were dredging in an ocean rife with weeds but containing only one fish. And the election clock was ticking.

Given the time pressure presented by the election cycle, Wiley was thrilled to have devised a two-pronged approach to killing Odi. While he and Stuart chased Odi from behind, Cassi was out in front of him ready to intercept. Talk about a secret weapon. Whatever disguise Odi chose to use to try to get close to Abrams, there was little chance that Cassi would not recognize him—even though she did not know that it was Odi she was looking for. Yes, Wiley thought, they would get him. The question was, would they get him soon enough?

"What country's next?" Stuart asked.

"I'm thinking Germany. How much Turkey do you have left?"

"I've got sixteen more flights," he replied, stretching his arms over his head.

"Can you believe that there are people who do this all day, every day? You'd think they'd go nuts."

"Or blind.

"What if we can't find Odi before he gets to Abrams?" Wiley asked, noting that his use of we left a bitter taste in his mouth. "You helped plan the first series of attacks. Could you do it again without a CEO's help?"

Stuart shook his head. "I was able to set that up because I had cushy jobs to offer our coconspirators. Without the defense contractors backing us, I don't have anything to offer besides cabinet posts, and that would be too risky."

"But we're so close. You should have heard the president. It was as though Carver took the words right out of your mouth. He said, quote, 'It would be good to have a prophet on my team, assuming terrorism still piques the voters' interest come Election Day.'"

"Well then let's hope your ex comes through," Stuart said, adding: "I'd love to be a fly on the wall at that reunion."

Wiley imagined that scene—Cassi learning that her twin was alive but a terrorist assassin. Talk about a double-edged sword. He wondered if it was possible to feel like even more of a shit.

"I've got him!" Stuart said, shooting out of his chair.

"Odi?"

"Odi!"

"What name did he use?"

"Hold on. It will take a moment for me to query using the time and station code."

"He flew in from Turkey?"

"Yep. And the name on the passport he used is ... Ayden Archer."

Chapter 30

Annapolis, Maryland

CASSI WAS BACK in the ASIS boardroom, bracing for another fight. As she sat there on eggshells she found herself feeling woozy. Her head had not seen a pillow since Wiley visited her apartment two days before, but she knew that a lack of sleep was only marginally responsible for her imbalance. Her incompetence was the real problem. She had lost yet another life entrusted to her care. Wiley and the FBI had given her a second chance, a shot at redemption—and now Rollins was dead. The fact that she was one person assigned to protect two people would be but a footnote beneath that glaring headline. All her excuses, legitimate though they might be, were not going to keep Rollins' corpse off her performance record. Her only chance of salvation now would be to catch the assassin—while Abrams was still alive.

As she struggled to force her latest failure from her mind, Wilbanks and Abrams entered the boardroom and took their seats without a word. She had spent every minute since their last meeting on plans to enhance Abrams' security. It was time for her report.

Wilbanks, ASIS's chief of security, opened the dialogue. "So you've completed your appraisal?" He asked, leaning back with his arms folded defiantly across his chest. "I trust my men were helpful."

"I have and they were." Cassi replied, understanding at once that there would be no mention of Rollins today. His death was still too fresh, their emotions too raw.

Cassi studied her fencing partner. He had thick white hair which he wore cropped short like a general. Normally this made him look fierce, but today it just presented a strong contrast to the dark bags beneath his eyes. Cassi found herself feeling for the man despite finding him to be a self-promoting prick. Nobody liked an outsider poking around in his affairs, especially when that outsider's job was to tell your boss everything you were doing wrong. She surely wouldn't.

Last night while weighing her options on how to proceed after what was probably the worst first-day on FBI record, Cassi realized that the potential longevity of her relationship with Wilbanks added constraint to complication. She was going to be working closely with him until she caught the assassin. That meant she had to avoid alienating him as she ripped his organization to shreds. She knew that in similar circumstance most people would say, "Screw it," and then blast the guy. But the psychological nuances of daunting situations like these actually fired her up. They also played to her strengths. So she had formulated a teardown-buildup plan.

"Tell me, Special Agent Carr," Abrams said, joining the row, "what exactly did you find?"

"Your complex is a fortress," she said, watching from the corner of her eye for Wilbanks to give Abrams an I-told-you-so nod. He did not disappoint her.

"Wonderful," Abrams said.

"No, it isn't. Not really."

On cue, Wilbanks fired back a petulant, "What's wrong with a fortress?"

Cassi stood and leaned forward, bracing her palms on the gleaming table. "Fortresses are essentially walls meant to keep people out. They will intimidate some, but in fact they are useless once someone gets in."

Wilbanks waved a hand dismissively, though his body language showed that he was worried. "That's like saying a safe is no good if someone opens the door."

"Perhaps, except that in your case tens of thousands of people have the combination." Cassi held up her temporary identity card. Then she withdrew a stack of two-dozen duplicate cards and slid them onto the table where they scattered across the polished surface like a plague. "I made these while I was at lunch."

Wilbanks' face dropped, but his response remained aggressive. "We can't run a company if nobody can come to work."

Now for the build-up, she thought, retaking her seat. "No, you can't. For that reason, security at ASIS is similar to what you find at most major corporations. In fact, you've done a better job than most."

Wilbanks' posture relaxed a hair.

"Tell me what needs to be done to make it better," Abrams said.

"To continue the analogy I started earlier, what you've got now with your electronic card-key system is the equivalent of a computerized wall. It's good at fending off a straightforward frontal assault, but like a brick-and-mortar wall, a computerized wall is useless if the enemy can find a way to open the gate or walk around."

"Or tunnel under," Abrams added. "Yes, I got your point. Tell me about our holes."

"Every card key is a hole, and there's little you can do to make it difficult for an assassin to obtain one of those. All he has to do is snatch a purse or break into a house. If he's clever about it, he'll duplicate the card key and return it without the owner ever noticing that it was gone."

Abrams sighed. Cassi continued. "Then of course there's hacking. Someone could break into your system and authorize his own card. Theft and hacking are just a couple of the many electronic means available. A less sophisticated assassin could simply apply for a job on your maintenance or security staff, or with of one of your subcontractors."

Cassi paused to study Abrams. "I can see by the look on your face that you're beginning to understand the problem."

"What am I going to do?" He asked. "I can't raise the drawbridge."

"For starters, you need to put humans in place at all entrances to compare photos to faces."

Abrams looked at Wilbanks who nodded. "Done."

"Next, you need a redundant procedure at the entrance to the executive tower. That guard will also verify everyone's business. Furthermore, you need to make the tower off-limits to all subcontractors and anyone with less than a year on your payroll, including maintenance. Don't allow any service people into the tower, including deliverymen, exterminators, or gardeners. Bring those functions in-house. Even emergency-service personnel like police, firemen, and paramedics need to be held at bay until their identities can be verified. In essence, you're only to allow known people through that door."

"HR will have a fit, but I can live with that. Anything else?"

"Yes," Cassi pressed. "I know you like to mingle with the troops, but that's going to have to stop. Until we catch this guy, everyone comes to you, here on the twelfth floor. We'll put a guard in each elevator and only allow people on your appointment schedule to access the twelfth floor."

As she finished she saw Abrams preparing to object when a shadow suddenly crossed his face and he gave a single nod. He had obviously remembered Rollins. Cassi continued. "Other than the two glass elevators, the service elevator, the stairway, and the helipad on the roof, is there any other way to access the twelfth floor?"

Abrams and Wilbanks both shook their heads.

"I'll have the stairway and the service elevator locked," Wilbanks added. "Fuck the fire inspector. And I'll let my men know that we're not expecting any window cleaners."

"Excellent ideas," Cassi said. "And you might want to put steel bars over any large ventilation ducts."

"Agent Carr?"

"Yes, Mister Abrams."

"While everything you're suggesting makes sense, I have to wonder if any of these measures would have helped Mark Drake?"

Cassi felt her stomach drop. "I don't know," she answered honestly. "We still don't know the exact nature of the device used to kill him. The current theory is that the assassin waited in an offshore boat for Rollins to approach his bedroom window and then fired a Light Antitank Weapon, but that's just a preliminary analysis. The guards swear that they kept watch on the ocean and saw nothing. But the fact is Mark's dead. And you're right, nothing I've suggested thus far would protect you from a LAW. Are you sure you won't reconsider taking a secret vacation?"

Abrams shook his head. "I'm in the defense business, and as with every business, image is crucial. I can't be seen running with my tail between my legs."

"Well then, I'll work with Wilbanks to get spotters in place by both helipads, and I'll talk with your pilot about varying your route. Other than that, you'll need to keep clear of windows."

"What's to keep the assassin from firing a dozen LAWs into my office?"

Cassi cocked her head. "Two things come to mind. First of all, there's practicality. The odds are slim that he's got that many LAWs. But more importantly, there's his modus operandi. All of the killings thus far have been surgical affairs with no collateral damage. He didn't kill Drake's chauffeur in order to replace him. He just knocked the man out. And he didn't kill Rollins' girlfriend despite the nature of the method. That indicates highly discriminatory behavior."

"In other words, I should keep my assistant close."

"So long as you make me your assistant," Cassi said.

Abrams smiled weakly and then said to Wilbanks, "Why don't you take Agent Carr down to the cafeteria for lunch? You can go through the details of her recommendations, and then spend the afternoon implementing. We can meet up at four o'clock for the flight back to my place. I can hardly wait to see what changes are in store for me there."

~ ~ ~

Four hours later, Cassi was feeling better. Wilbanks had proven to be cooperative, and most of her suggested security measures were already in place. The rest would be implemented by morning. She doubted that the assassin would have had time to plan and execute his next hit within twenty-four hours of the Rollins job, so she felt Abrams was reasonably safe.

Riding up to the twelfth floor in one of the glass elevators that overlooked the flower-and-fountain festooned ASIS quad, Cassi was pleased with the agreement that Abrams would no longer be riding them. If she were the assassin, her tactic would be to watch them through the business end of a sniper scope, waiting for Abrams to step aboard. Killing him here would be like shooting a big fat fish in a small glass barrel. With that thought, Cassi realized that this might be the perfect place for her to set up a trap. Her weary mind kicked back into overdrive.

She looked up at the other glass elevator as it descended a couple of yards away. There was a lone soul riding in it now. If she were the assassin, he would be toast. Surely she could make that work in reverse —if she knew what the assassin looked like. Cassi was confident that her profile was accurate, but it was not discriminate enough to be the basis of a kill shot. Statistically speaking all that she had done was whittle the US population down to about ten thousand contenders.

As though sensing her stare, the man in the other lift turned to face her. They locked eyes and stared, neither one believing. A second later the elevators' opposing movements cut their line of sight like an umbilical cord. Cassi's heart began pounding, as it never had before. She continued to stare downward in disbelief as conflicting emotions took the fight from her knees. She sank to the floor with a pathetic thud. She had just seen a ghost.

Chapter 31

Chesapeake Beach, Maryland

AS THE HANDS on Charlotte's antique clock lined up on twelve, Odi heard a friendly ta-dong from his computer. He smiled. Midnight on the Chesapeake Bay was seven-thirty A.M. in Tafriz. Ayden was now on line. He took his feet off the kitchen table, leaned forward in his chair, and typed, "I'm screwed."

A second later he heard the zzhing announcing the arrival of Ayden's reply. "What happened?"

"Abrams just beefed up his security. This morning all I had to do to get into ASIS was swipe an employee ID. This evening they had guards in place checking photos. I got out just as they were sealing the executive tower."

"So Abrams is scared, but not scared enough to come forward and confess," Ayden summarized.

"He's hiding behind an army of corporate security."

"You'll think of something."

Given a little time, Odi knew that he would think of something. Strict procedures were good for the weaker links, but they conditioned brighter people to stop using their heads. That created new opportunities and opened new gaps. It would not take him long to identify a snafu that he could exploit.

If only it were that simple.

He typed, "I was spotted."

"You know someone at ASIS?" Ayden asked.

"It was my sister. Wiley must have brought her in. The bastard. That means he's figured out it's me."

"Did you speak to her?"

"No, but that doesn't matter. She saw my eyes. In her mind, there's no question. Now my airtight alibi has a leak."

"Only if she tells someone."

That was true, Odi thought. He was not sure what Cassi would do with the news. She would certainly feel torn. "I saw her eyes too, Ayden. I saw her emotions change from shock to jubilation to horror over the course of two seconds. She thinks I'm a cold-blooded killer." His fingers trembled as he typed.

Ayden's reply was mercifully swift. "Only because she's ignorant. She doesn't know about Iran, about Adam and Flint and the others. Look, Odi, I see children stare at their parents like they're Benedict Arnold every time I pull out a needle. The kids scream of betrayal but the parents always go through with the shot. They accept the temporary emotional backlash because they know that the pain is for their child's own good."

Odi stared at the keyboard and thought about that. Ayden had a good point. Still, he was not sure he could go ahead with the Abrams execution, much less Wiley's. The danger was at a whole new level now, and with his sister aware and watching, it just did not feel right. He contemplated that for a moment longer with his fingers poised over the keys. Finally he typed, "I think I'm through."

Ayden took a long time to write back. When he did, he said, "Don't quit just because it's getting hard. You owe it to your men to see this through to the end."

Ayden's encouragement helped, but Odi needed more. He typed,

"Abrams is in a vault now, and he knows I'm coming. There's a good chance that I'll get caught, which is the same thing as being killed. Remember, since I'm already dead, they can kill me with impunity. Besides, maybe the pressure will get to Abrams and he'll come forward and confess—now that Rollins is also gone." Odi fully expected Ayden to retort with a scornful assault on his continued naïveté. Instead he got a shock.

"I can handle Abrams."

"What?"

"It turns out that I have a friend who can get close to him, close enough to slip him some Creamer. All you need to do to be rid of Abrams is get her a dose."

Odi stared at his computer screen. Tactically, that would be perfect. Strategically, it was dubious. He ran the back of his palm over his sweaty brow. Ayden's plan meant that somebody else would be involved. By involving a third person in their plans, they were multiplying the risks exponentially. What was that old saw: three people can keep a secret—as long as two of them are dead. With nervous fingers he typed, "Tell me more."

"I don't think that's a good idea. The less you know the better. Better to just leave a dose of Creamer at a drop and move on to your next target."

Odi was relieved to find Ayden half-a-step ahead of him. He asked himself what he had to lose—and came up empty. Besides, he was anxious to get back to Iran and wake up. Still, he had promised himself never to give Creamer to anyone else. It would be a disaster if his invention ever got released to the world.

He stared at the cursor for a long minute, weighing the pros and cons with a heavy heart and a troubled mind. Finally, he typed "Agreed."

Chapter 32

The Horus Club, Washington, D.C.

WILEY WAITED for the Horus Club's deaf waiter to set down their drinks and turn his back before giving Stuart the news. "Ayden Archer is a real man."

Stuart raised his eyebrows, as if to say, Is that all the Director of the FBI was able to learn in twenty-four hours. "Is that surprising?" He asked. "I assumed Odi just stole the passport, or maybe bought it. Either would be easier than trying to generate a fake."

Wiley enjoyed watching Stuart take the hook. Now he had to make him swallow. "Even overseas, in Iran? Don't forget, passports have a photo."

"That's hardly an obstacle. If I were Odi, I would find a place that serves alcohol—a five-star hotel or an expat function—and look for someone who resembled me. Then I would get him drunk discussing war stories, and pick his pocket."

Wiley had often found geniuses to be incompetent if asked to perform a hair's breadth outside their area of expertise, so he was pleased to hear that Stuart's talents extended from politics to the dark arts—not that that was much of a stretch. His campaign manager was about to need that additional competence.

Wiley pulled a photo printout from the breast pocket of his blazer and handed it to Stuart. "This is Ayden Archer."

Stuart accepted the photo and studied it under the soft light of a reading lamp. "You've just made my point. He looks like Odi would, if Odi were trying to pass as Tom Selleck."

Wiley took the printout back, crumpled it, and tossed it into the fire. "I went through Ayden's FBI and CIA files."

"Let's hear it."

Wiley savored a sip of his Dalwhinnie and began. He remembered everything without his notes. "Ayden was born in California in 1968 to an American mother and an Iranian father. Given that he had his mother's complexion and that they were both well aware of the benefits of having an Anglican name, they gave Ayden his mother's name.

"Ayden Archer lived in California until he was six, when his mother died from cancer. Then he moved with his father, Tigran Taronish, back to Iran. Tigran worked for the Shah as a royal engineer. When the Shah fell in 1979, Tigran took his son and fled to Turkey, where he got a job expanding our air base in Incirlik. He and Ayden lived there for two years until Tigran was injured in a construction accident, and died.

"Are you with me?" Wiley asked, noting that Stuart was staring into the fire.

"Ayden's Iranian father died when he was 13, orphaning him." Stuart replied without shifting his gaze.

Wiley took a second to check Stuart's math in his head and found it accurate. He was impressed, but did not show it. "Here's the rub. Tigran's accident should not have been fatal. A chunk of concrete fell on him, breaking some ribs and damaging a lung, but he could have been saved through a routine procedure. Since he was not American, however, Tigran was denied treatment at the air base's modern hospital —the very air base he had worked two years to construct. He died from internal bleeding while waiting for an operating room to open at the local Turkish hospital."

Stuart looked up from the fire with interest radiating from his eyes. "That's how terrorists are made."

Wiley nodded. "Ayden got himself arrested the day of his father's funeral for throwing rocks at the base commander's jeep.

"After being assaulted by a teary-eyed thirteen-year-old American boy, the Air Force General looked into Ayden's story and recognized a potential PR nightmare. He shipped Ayden back to California posthaste to live with his grandparents.

"Back in the US, Ayden behaved himself. The FBI stopped keeping tabs on him four years later when he entered Berkley.

"Both Ayden's grandparents died while he was at college, leaving him an estate worth a couple hundred grand. He graduated in 1989 with a philosophy major and then used half his inheritance to get a medical degree at UCLA. Instead of doing a normal residency, however, Ayden went straight into the Peace Corps. He worked for them in the Middle East for eight years and then quit to stay behind when the Ayatollah got unruly and the Peace Corps pulled his group out of Iran. He has been living in Iran doing his own thing ever since. As a low-priority case, there is not much else in his file, but there are indications that he has been acting as an international aid coordinator of sorts and running a mobile clinic."

"Who pays him?" Stuart asked.

"Good question. As far as we know, he's living off his inheritance, or rather the interest from it. That amounted to just five-hundred dollars a month, but to the best of our knowledge he managed to survive on that amount for years in Iran."

"You're speaking in the past tense," Stuart noted.

Wiley jiggled his ice cubes. "Ayden's situation has changed. About a year ago he began to draw down his capital, dipping into the original hundred grand. Since then, he has been withdrawing ever-increasing amounts. It looks like he's getting desperate. As of yesterday, his balance was down to forty-one thousand."

"But you don't know what's changed?"

Wiley shook his head.

"One man's problem is another man's opportunity," Stuart said.

"I was thinking the same thing."

"Do you think he sold Odi his passport?"

"Perhaps," Wiley said. "But I suspect that their relationship is deeper than a purely financial one. Since everyone else on Odi's team was killed, it is reasonable to assume that he was seriously injured. Given what we now know, I think our working hypothesis should be that he fell into Ayden's care."

"I think I see where you're going with this," Stuart said. "All of a sudden Odi is back in the US on a multiple-assassination mission. He's using Ayden's passport. Meanwhile we know that Ayden has reason to hate America, that he is sympathetic to Iran, and that his life has destabilized of late. You think Ayden has morphed into a terrorist mastermind, and Odi—motivated by betrayal and rage—is his gun." Stuart nodded subconsciously as he thought out loud, obviously intrigued. Perhaps even impressed.

Wiley felt an unwelcome sense of pride as he noted Stuart's reaction. "I'm not sure whether Ayden himself is the mastermind or he too is being used. It would not be unusual for terrorist recruiters to keep an eye on Americans in their midst, looking for opportunities to leverage. If such a person were monitoring Ayden's financial situation, he would have pounced. In either case, whether Ayden is master or pawn, we could probably benefit from cooperation."

Wiley could see the gears whirring behind Stuart's dark eyes. He was doing what he did best—figuring out the most productive way to use a man.

"Where is Ayden now?" Stuart asked.

"Since his passport is here, I assume that he is still in Iran …" Wiley trailed off the end of his sentence.

Light dawned in Stuart's eyes. "You want me to find him, don't you? You want to find him and recruit him to our cause. Give him some spiel about differing ends requiring common means."

Wiley shook his head and smiled inside. It felt wonderful to be in strategic control. "Not exactly. I want you to find Ayden and feel him out. If he is everything that we suspect he is, tell him that the Director of the FBI would like to meet with him. Keep it general. Just tell him that I'm interested in working with him to achieve mutual goals."

Chapter 33

Alexandria, Virginia

"FORGIVE ME FATHER for I have sinned. This is my first confession," Cassi spoke into the grate. After the first remark, she expected to have to explain that by faith she was Presbyterian. But the priest just said, "Go ahead," and she concluded that she was not the first non-Catholic to seek holy release.

"I don't really know how this works."

"Why don't you just tell me what brought you here."

"I saw you preach once. I was here with a boyfriend. He didn't stick with me, but the wisdom of your sermon did, that and the kind crinkles around your eyes."

"I see. Well, what I meant to ask was, what have you done? What do you need to confess to our Lord and Savior?"

Cassi felt her face redden and was glad to be sitting in the dark. She sat back and faced the door. "It's not so much what I've done, as what I fear I'll have to do."

"I see," the priest replied. "The confessional is not really the place for counseling. I would be happy to sit down with you for that purpose in my office."

"Thank you, Father. That's a kind offer. But I need the sanctity of the confessional."

Cassi heard rustling sounds coming through the grate. She was making the priest uncomfortable. She began to have second thoughts about coming here. Part of her wanted to flee, but she had nowhere to run. And she had to get this out.

Finally the priest said, "Go on."

Cassi had spent the last eighteen hours in agony, torn between two masters. She quickly determined that she could not share her shocking discoveries with anybody. She would never forgive herself if Odi got killed because she made a call. At the same time, the decision she now faced was too momentous for her to make alone. Around two A.M. she had been struck by the brilliant insight to consult a priest. The very thought of unburdening her soul to a wise man with whom she could speak with impunity had made her feel better and gotten her through the night. But now that she was in the confessional, she did not know what to say. Not so brilliant.

"You may proceed," the priest prompted.

As she tried to formulate her opening words, Cassi realized that describing her situation in a roundabout way was not going to be so easy. She could hardly tell the priest that she thought her twin brother was assassinating people, even though he was legally dead. The priest would be morally obliged to call either an asylum or the police.

The priest rustled some more. She concluded that what it all boiled down to was this: Someone was either going to slap the cuffs on Odi, or pull a trigger. As painful as that moment would be, and even though it would give her nightmares for the rest of her life, Cassi was damned if she was going to let it be anyone but her. At last she spoke. "I may have to betray someone I love, harm him ... severely."

"Can you tell me more?" The priest asked.

"I don't know how much more I can say."

"I'm here to save souls, not to judge,"

"I'm conflicted by clashing loyalties. I would do anything, anything to help this person, but he has done ... he is doing something terribly wrong. And it's my duty, both contractual and moral, to stop him."

"In other words, you feel that you have to betray either this person, or yourself, and you want to know what Jesus would do."

"Exactly." Cassi said.

"Are you sure there's no way to be faithful to both?"

"I fear not."

"I see ... Then my advice to you is simply this: Whatever you do, do for love. Vengeance, my dear, is the Lord's."

Chapter 34

Chesapeake Beach, Maryland

ODI WAS HUNKERED DOWN at Charlotte's cottage, again planning his fifth and final hit. "Fifth and final hit," he said out loud, his feet up on the computer desk, a cup of strong coffee in one hand and a notebook in the other. "Commander Potchak, Mark Drake, Mark Rollins, Mark Abrams, and soon ... Wiley Proffitt." His words came out as a yawn. He emptied his hands and rubbed his eyes.

He considered the list an honor roll, but it was easy to picture a prosecutor reading the names as a list of charges. That thought was undoubtedly torturing Cassi at this very moment. Odi wanted desperately to call her to explain everything and relieve her misery, but he could not permit himself that luxury. Just the sound of her voice might make him weak. He needed to be strong, he reminded himself. For just a few days more he needed to be strong.

Odi knew that security made Wiley an even harder target than Abrams, but he was undaunted. By sinking so low as to deploy his own sister against him, Wiley had Odi doubly committed. Given that they were on to him, however, he had decided to break the pattern. He would not be using slight-of-hand or remote bombs. Before he sent Wiley Proffitt to meet his maker, the two of them were going to have a long talk—man-to-man, tête-à-tête.

He stood, turned up the volume on the TV, and walked out onto the porch. There, beneath whitewashed rafters and a rusting ceiling fan, he paced in the cool sea air with one ear tuned to the news and the other to the sea.

He was expecting word of Abrams' assassination to break any minute, and the waiting was driving him nuts. He hated to have an operation so completely out of his control. Yet it wasn't relinquishing the operation that flustered him now. The fact that he had left a dose of Creamer at a dead drop for Ayden's friend was what had his nerves tied in knots. Some anonymous woman now had two ounces worth of his secret explosive, the same amount he had used on Potchak and Drake. The quantity was perfect if you wanted the deterring effect of dramatic, blood-drenching, bone-scattering explosions. But it was much more than you needed simply to kill a man. Half a cc might not completely disembowel a person like a swallowed hand grenade, but it would certainly puree his internal organs and achieve an equally lethal result.

Pacing the porch, Odi worried that Ayden's contact might figure that out and cut the dose like a cocaine dealer. It pained him to think what such a person would then do with the remainder of the dose. In the best case she would use it to kill just one other person. If she was more entrepreneurial, she might take it to a lab. Then the world would never be the same. Once released, a secret like Creamer could never be put back in the bag. It was Pandora's Box. The thought made Odi shiver.

He had taken measures to prevent exactly that. He had stressed to Ayden that Creamer became inert after twelve hours. Twelve hours did not leave enough time for a lab. Furthermore, to keep her from breaking up the dose, he had explained that the victim had to drink the full two-ounce dose because the reaction required a critical mass. Odi figured that his bluff sounded credible enough to pass muster with both laymen and chemists alike—but he could not be sure.

With those two bases covered, there was still the possibility that Ayden's friend would take the Creamer and run, planning to use it on an ex-lover or boss. But Odi reasoned that his contingencies could only go so far. At some point he had to trust the judgment of his new friend. Odi did trust Ayden. He would feel the pain in more ways than one if Abrams was not killed tonight.

He continued pacing the balcony while repeating, "Come on" to the news. After a few minutes Odi realized that he was timing his laps to coincide with the nearby warning buoy, doing exactly one length between each bong. His conformity reminded him of a scene from the movie *Dead Poets' Society*. It was odd, he thought—that innate urge to conform. He altered his pace.

Despite all his worries, Odi liked it out there on the porch. He decided that if he lived through this and kept out of jail, he would take a long vacation and come back to do some reading and make some repairs—assuming that the cottage was still standing. He had installed a sophisticated booby-trap to deal definitively with intruders. He armed it each time he left on a mission. He had enough on his mind without the added worry of returning home to a trap or leaving damning evidence behind. He did feel badly about endangering Charlotte's cottage, but as with the Creamer, there was only so much he could do. Perhaps that was why he wanted to return on vacation and fix the place up. It would be a karma-balancing act. He figured—

"This just in," the news anchor announced. Odi turned to see the red Breaking News banner filling the bottom of the screen. He ducked through the open window without taking his eyes off the TV. "While the details are still foggy, we have just learned that an explosion in an exclusive Annapolis suburb claimed two lives this evening. We take you live to the scene where Bob Kenny is standing by.

"Bob." The image cut to a man broadcasting from atop a news van parked near the lofty iron gate of an enormous estate. Red and white lights were spinning across the stone edifice of a mansion at the distant end of a long drive. Odi recognized it immediately as Abrams'. "Thank you Rita. Mark Ezekiel Abrams III, the billionaire CEO of ASIS whose Annapolis estate you see behind me, was killed here moments ago by an explosion in his bedroom. The police have yet to issue a statement, but sources say that he was in the company of a young woman whose identity is not yet known. While the possibility of an accident has not been ruled out, as our regular viewers will know, Mark Abrams is the third defense CEO to die a fiery death this month, so the authorities are approaching this as a double homicide. We go now to—"

Odi felt his stomach drop and his knees began to shake. *In the company of a young woman.* "Cassi! Oh God, no." He pulled the throwaway phone from his pocket, and dialed Cassi's mobile number with a trembling hand.

Chapter 35

Washington, D.C.

WILEY LOOKED IMPATIENTLY at his Patek Philippe and cursed under his breath before downing his last sip of Dalwhinnie 1981. He felt tense enough without being kept waiting on pins and needles. He caught movement in the corner of his eye and turned his head, pleased to have finally caught one of Stuart's approaches. Disappointment struck. It was just one of the Horus Club's observant waiters. Wiley nodded—yes, he'd like a refill—and returned his gaze to the fire.

A voice to his left broke the silence. "I'm sorry to have kept you waiting. I was just getting out of the limo from Dulles when the story hit Headline News, so I stayed in the car to watch the whole report."

Stuart must share a bloodline with Houdini, Wiley concluded, vexed at being caught yet again unawares. "What story?"

Stuart arched his eyebrows behind his rimless silver spectacles. "Abrams is dead."

The news hit Wiley like a bat to the chest. This time he didn't have a drink to spill, but he almost would have welcomed that momentary distraction. Abrams' death might mark the end of his presidential aspirations. Hell, he thought, it might even signify something worse than that. Much worse. Although he had not received a video and ultimatum like Rollins and Abrams, Wiley could not rule out the possibility that one of the victims had exposed his involvement. He knew that the wise move was to assume as much. He gulped involuntarily. With Abrams dead, the odds were fifty-fifty that his was the next name on the list. With a dry throat, he asked, "Was it another bomb?"

Stuart nodded, and then added, "There's more. An unidentified woman was also killed in the explosion."

Wiley felt an arctic chill sweep over the desert in his mouth. "Cassi?"

"It could be. I don't know."

Wiley studied Stuart's face and decided that he was telling the truth. He really did not know. "I don't think it's her," Wiley said. "Odi wouldn't kill his own sister. Of that I am totally sure. Still, accidents do happen. I better call to find out."

As Wiley reached into his breast pocket for his cell phone, Stuart's arm shot forward fast as a cobra strike to grab his wrist. "Not now. You are about to receive a very important call." Stuart stared at Wiley until he got it.

"Your meeting went well?"

"Excellent."

"Tell me."

"In a word, he's perfect."

Wiley arched his eyebrows in appreciation. Stuart was hardly predisposed to superlative compliments.

"Ayden has brains and charisma and a deep-seated hatred seething within. He could easily be the next Bin Laden—given a little guidance, and the proper financial backing."

"And he's about to call me?"

"In precisely two minutes. As you requested, I have arranged for the two of you to meet. This call is to work out the details."

Wiley felt dizzy, as though the air pressure had changed in the room. This was it, he realized, capital I, capital T. He had been committed before but this took his campaign to a whole new level. By personally conspiring with a terrorist, he would be crossing a different kind of line, entering a whole new level of the political game. There were only two doors at the end of that road. One led to the Oval Office, the other to the electric chair.

"It's the only way—now that Abrams is gone." Stuart said, reading Wiley's face.

Wiley expected Stuart to pull a voice recorder from his pocket and play his "Whatever it takes" quote. But he didn't. He just added, "Picture the plane."

Air Force One immediately popped into Wiley's head. He hated the fact that Stuart read him so well. Air Force One was the image to which he fell asleep every night—that open door and staircase with the red carpet and presidential seal. Still, he had a pretty darn good life already. Given the increasing possibility of door number two, Air Force One was no longer enough.

Before he could say no, Stuart continued. "Ayden is not only the best chance we have of catching Odi. He is also the perfect man to coordinate the future terrorist attacks. We need someone like him, now that Abrams is dead."

Wiley was about to concur when his phone began to ring. He looked down at it and then over at Stuart. "One door closes and another one opens ..."

Chapter 36

Annapolis, Maryland

CASSI POURED the last drops of Barolo into the hotel's oversized wineglass. Then she lit a fresh candle with the remains of the first and plopped back down into the tub. She knew she should have been working out rather than drinking to relieve her stress, but the room-service menu had been at hand, while both energy and willpower had seemed well beyond her reach.

She took another sip as Andrea Bocelli's *Viaggio Italiano* began its third repeat and contemplated adding more hot water to the cooling tub. Her marathon of indulgence had thus far yielded neither rest nor peace and she did not relish the thought of seeing her breasts prune, but she had neither the energy nor the desire to move.

Both of her charges were gone now. Dead. Caput. Rollins and Abrams had quite literally been blown to bits—as had her career. A week ago, she would have considered this the worst thing that could possibly happen. Now the anticipation of being fired in disgrace barely raised her pulse. Odi's bomb had done more than break bones and boil flesh; it had shattered her faith.

The ring of her mobile phone eclipsed Andrea's swooning voice, and Cassi looked over her shoulder to give the intruding device a forlorn stare. That would be Wiley, she thought, calling to inform her that she was fired. He would apologize for using the phone, explaining that the folks in public relations could not wait. For the good of the Bureau, they had to be swift and decisive and all that, blah, blah, blah. She decided to let voicemail take the call. That would make it easier on both of them. If she ever emerged from the tub, she would text message her resignation.

She drained the last sip from her glass as she waited for voicemail to kick-in. This was the first time in her life that she had drunk a whole bottle of wine. Staring at the bottom of the glass, she realized that she would be screwed if Wiley chose not to leave a message. She would never be able to get to sleep then despite the Barolo's depressive effect. She would just lie there staring at the phone, willing it to emit a dreaded ring. She decided to get it over with now, while the wine was still rendering its full numbing effect.

"Hello."

"Cassi?"

The voice was unusually weak but intimately familiar. She nearly dropped the phone in the tub. "Odi, oh my God."

"Thank God you're alive. I was so scared."

"Odi, what are you … why …how could you do this? Why are you doing this? To them, to me, oh my God, I—"

"I can't explain that now. But I can explain it later. You're just going to have to trust me on this. I'm a patriot Sis, don't doubt it. Despite all appearances I have not changed."

Cassi got out of the tub but didn't towel off. She wanted the sobering effect of the chill, and she wanted to pace. "I love you Odi, you're a good man. Fight the evil. You're sick. You need help. Let me help you. Just tell me where to meet you, one-on-one. I'll—"

"I can't do that. Not yet. There's something I need to do first."

"Odi, you mus—"

"I love you, Sis."

Chapter 37

Chesapeake Beach, Maryland

ODI PACED before his computer screen, waiting for Ayden to come online. He was in a hurry to get to the lab, but he had to get this out of the way first. Brewing Creamer safely required absolute concentration, and he knew that would not be possible until after they spoke.

During a contemplative walk, he had found a pink rubber ball on the beach. He gave it a thousandth bounce against the kitchen's linoleum floor. He was not panicked anymore, not now that he knew Cassi was alive. But he was still upset that Ayden's friend had caused collateral damage. He needed to know who the dead woman was—or more appropriately, who she had been.

His fingers flew from the ball to the keyboard the second the ta-dong announced Ayden's arrival on-line. "Your friend pulled it off, but a woman was also killed. Did she tell you what happened?"

"Abrams requested the company of an escort for the evening from his usual service."

"So the dead woman was a prostitute," Odi thought out loud, his fingers poised motionless above the keys. A desperate life had met an unfortunate end. The thought made Odi sad until he considered the caliber of woman a billionaire would choose to buy. It would not be a destitute drug addict or a white slave. She would be someone Abrams could pretend was a date. She would be a classy-looking educated girl—polished, refined ... and very highly paid. Prostitution would be the life she chose.

That deduction took the edge off Odi's pain, but he still felt terrible that a bystander was now dead. Then Ayden sent a follow-up message that stole Odi's breath.

"My friend paid the girl to take her place."

Odi stared at the last sentence. This had gone from bad to worse—with a very unexpected twist. He typed, "A suicide bomber?"

"It's not what you think. She was an old friend of mine from the Peace Corps, a beautiful, brilliant woman—with an inoperable tumor."

Ayden did not add further detail. He must have figured—correctly—that Odi could fill in the rest. As a man who had risked his life for others hundreds of times, Odi understood the oxymoronic serenity that one derived from being willing to die for a cause. He was about to ask how Ayden knew about Abram's penchant for escorts when Ayden surprised him yet again. "How do you feel?"

The question struck a chord and Odi typed an honest response without thinking. "I thought I'd feel a sense of satisfaction, accomplishment and relief once the CEOs were dead. But the truth is, I don't. I just feel dirty."

Ayden's reply came back surprisingly fast. "That's because you haven't wrought any permanent change."

Odi stared at Ayden's words, unsure how to react. Eventually he typed, "How can you say that?"

"There's an endless supply of people with equally-dismal moral fiber lined up for those CEO slots. The day after tomorrow they will be back to business as usual at Defcon4, Rollins, and ASIS. To create lasting change you have to be more creative. You have to think big picture …"

Chapter 38

Washington, D.C.

"WHERE WAS THE BLOODY ORANGE PHONE?" Wiley cursed as he inspected the hissing labyrinth. Embarrassing as it was to admit, he had never before ridden the Washington Metro. Was the Orange Phone something all regular Metro users would know, like the Green Monster at Fenway park? It was worth a try. He said "Excuse me," to a well-dressed young man walking past with a lawyer's briefcase. "Do you know where I can find the orange phone?"

The man said, "Try Toys-R-Us," without slowing his stride.

Wiley raised his arm and said, "Thanks."

The three payphones visible from the base of the F-Street escalator all appeared to be the standard stainless steel and black. Was he missing something? He repeated Ayden's order again to himself from memory. "Use the F Street entrance to Metro Center. At precisely six o'clock, approach the orange phone. I'll instruct you further on our meet."

Approach the orange phone, Wiley repeated. That seemed

unambiguous enough.

Given the simplicity of this mundane meet, he was beginning to appreciate the strain that sophisticated deep cover ops must put on his men. He was starting to lose it and he was the bloody Director of the FBI. By the same token, Ayden must be a wreck.

Looking around, Wiley concluded that Ayden had probably given the staging of this meet some serious thought. Perhaps he had just read a few John Le Carré books, watched a few James Bond videos, and worked it out from there. Or perhaps he had been coached. In either case, if Ayden knew the truth he would be much more relaxed. Despite Wiley's title, this was the first time he had donned an operative cloak, and he did not even own a dagger.

Wiley circled the station, getting increasingly flustered as he searched for a less-obvious fit—a picture, a toy, two orange-juice cans and some string. He found nothing that fit any variant of the orange phone description while circling Metro Center, so he returned to the base of the F-Street escalator. Then he saw it. While he was away, someone had placed an orange sticker on the receiver of one of the payphones he had first seen. "Of course."

Ayden must have arrived early, waited to see if Wiley was alone, and then watched to see if he spoke into his collar or anything like that as he walked around in frustration. Once Ayden was comfortable that Wiley was truly alone, he put the sticker on the payphone. He had probably hopped straight onto the up escalator from there, and was now poised to make a call from the busy bank of phones up top. Wiley looked up the tunnel just in case, but all he saw was the backside of a dozen raincoats. Ayden had set up a good meet, ideal really for one man working alone.

Wiley guarded the orange phone, waiting for it to ring. He did not have to wait long. "Hello."

"What's your favorite color?"

"Orange."

"Give the boy your cell phone battery, and put on the pink carnation." Ayden hung up.

Wiley looked around for a boy and spotted a twelve or thirteen year-old in a dirty green coat riding down the escalator and holding out a flower. Little Green Coat walked over to Wiley, and held out his empty hand. Wiley released the battery from his cell phone and handed it over. The boy said, "Thank you," and gave him the pink boutonnière. As Wiley pinned it on, the boy pulled a slip of paper from his pocket and read. "Ride the last car of the blue line to Capital South, get off, and wait right there on the end of the platform."

"Can I have the note, I might forget?" Wiley asked.

The boy said "No," and shoved it in his mouth.

Wiley was glad to see Ayden taking precautions. Ironically, Ayden's paranoia made Wiley less nervous. Still, he was glad that he had chosen to wear one of the special suits the Secret Service had tailored. It was lined with a fabric that could not be punctured by small-arms fire. A bullet fired at him could still pierce his flesh, but the fabric would catch it before it penetrated very deep. He also sported his never-walk-the-street-without-it bulletproof vest. Wiley smiled at the boy and said "Tasty?" before turning to do as he was told.

Nobody was waiting for him at the Capital South Metro stop, so he stood alone at the end of the platform and waited as instructed. He was getting tired of breathing the stale ozone air when the arrival of another train caused him to hold his breath. The last person to get off that train was another boy. This one wore a faded Mighty Ducks cap and held a yellow rose in his hand.

The Mighty Duck spotted Wiley's pink carnation and approached. "Trade you, Mister."

"Okay."

Wiley gave the boy his pink carnation and pinned on the rose boutonnière. Once he was suitably attired, the boy said. "I have a message for sale. The price is twenty bucks."

"Did the man tell you to say that?"

The boy nodded.

Wiley hated to take his wallet out in a place like this, but he and the boy were the only people at that end of the platform. He gave the Mighty Duck a twenty-dollar bill and received a horse-like flash of white teeth in return. The boy then cleared his throat, but instead of pulling a slip of paper from his pocket, he read a message off the palm of his hand. "Exit to First Street and walk north to Union Station. Enter the Metro, find the phone, and answer it before the second ring."

Wiley nodded.

The boy licked his hand and rubbed it on his jeans.

It took Wiley twenty minutes to reach Union Station by foot on a route which took him between the Capital and the Supreme Court. Even in October this really was a beautiful city, he noted, promising himself to walk more often.

This time the orange phone was ready and waiting. Two minutes later it rang. "Hello."

"What's on your lapel?"

"A yellow rose."

Ayden said, "Take the Red Line to Rockville—sit in the last car," and hung up.

Wiley was getting tired of this, but he focused on the bright side.

This experience would help him relate to his field agents. Ironically, it would also help him relate better to the men they were trying to catch. Wiley felt afraid for his life, and he was just going to a talk. Thieves and drug dealers went through this routinely to swap their duffel bags of contraband for briefcases of cash. Both parties in those transactions had to have either a gnat's brains, a shark's nerves, or a bull's balls. It was no wonder someone often freaked out during a swap and provoked everyone to empty his automatic into his neighbor.

Three stops into the trip the mechanical voice announced "Next stop, Metro Center." Only then did Wiley realize that he had completed a triangle. Now he was being sent to the suburbs, having been deemed clear.

Rockville was still thirteen stops away, so he sat back to wait. Everyone not standing was either reading, sleeping, or listening to music. He had neither book nor radio, so he tried to blend in by closing his eyes. That also made it less conspicuous for him to keep his hand in the pocket of his wool overcoat—wrapped tightly around the walnut handle of his Colt.

Wiley wondered why he had not been disarmed along the way, at least not yet. He decided that Ayden must have figured that whatever he did, the Director of the FBI would have access to enough special gadgets to get something past him. And he was right. Given that, Wiley reasoned, Ayden would just level the playing field by showing up armed as well. He might even try to tilt the odds in his favor by bringing a friend …

Wiley opened his eyes in reaction to that last thought. What if he was simply walking into the sights of Odi's next hit? He wondered, realizing that he had been so caught up in his own moves that he had not given much thought to Ayden's. It was the same amateur mistake he always made in chess.

Wiley was considering calling off the meet, just standing up and getting off the metro at the next stop, when the Rastafarian sitting across from him reached out and put his hand on Wiley's knee. Wiley pulled the trigger in shock. He heard an empty click. Thank goodness for safeties, he thought. He peered through the disguise of the man he might have killed and recognized a familiar face.

"So, what is the mutual interest your aide said you were so eager to discuss?"

Chapter 39

Annapolis, Maryland

CASSI LOOKED OVER at the bedside clock. It was two A.M. Her mind and body were exhausted but her nerves forbade sleep. She had nearly drifted off a few times only to be awakened by the annoying bing of the elevator bell. She would be sure to request a room farther down the hall next time, although that was little consolation now. Judging by the elevator traffic, there was some kind of party happening on her floor. She closed her eyes and waited for the next installment of the business-traveler's equivalent of Chinese water torture, the cursed elevator bing.

She eventually drifted off again, dreaming of endless dark hallways and brightly lit elevator doors. Then lightning struck as one door opened and she bolted upright in bed. She knew where Odi was hiding! The clue had been there in the background during his call, a very different kind of bell.

~ ~ ~

Two hours later Cassi parked her rental car at the Lever's, knowing that Thelma and Morton were always in Fort Meyers this time of year. She had driven the last quarter mile without the aid of headlights, but she still gave her eyes a few minutes to adjust to the darkness after slipping quietly from the car. The sea breeze, the pine scent, the rustling of reeds and sea grass—everything about this place was calmingly familiar. Only the man now sleeping in Aunt Charlotte's bed had changed.

She stuck to the moon's shadows as she crossed the three intervening lawns and made her way silently toward Charlotte's long front porch. She was afraid that Odi would slip away if he heard someone approach, not realizing that it was her. There were boat, truck, trail, and even hang-glider options available for escape. Odi would surely have an evasive route or four planned.

She studied the two visible sides of the cottage as she executed her silent approach. No lights were on, the shutters were closed, and nothing was parked in the drive. Cassi began to worry that she had dreamed the buoy sound. Lord knows she had been sufficiently drunk on wine. What would she do if Charlotte's cottage was undisturbed? She had not a clue, but guessed that it would involve puddles of tears.

As her spirits fell, Cassi realized just how desperate she was to see her brother. She needed him as much as he needed her. Over this past month she had endured more shock and disappointment than one person should ever have to bear. She needed this victory, this confirmation, this release. And she needed to bury herself in Odi's problems so that she could forget about her own.

Cassi bypassed the second stair knowing that it liked to squeak and stepped silently onto the wooden porch. She stood there in silence for a moment, listening to the night. She took a deep breath, and tried to steady her nerve. So far, so good. She reached behind the decorative net and red-striped buoy hanging on the wall and felt for the crevice in the cork that concealed the key to the front door. She found it. The key's presence was good news, but a bad sign.

She kissed the key before sliding it slowly into the lock. In the early-morning quiet she could hear each individual click as it displaced the five spring-loaded pins. She turned the handle slowly and then applied pressure to the door while willing the old hinges to refrain from protest. As the door cracked beneath her gentle touch, a fragrant whiff told Cassi that she had gotten it right. The garlic and sausage scents of Odi's famous spaghetti sauce greeted her nose. Another drop of adrenaline hit her blood. Despite her tension and exhaustion, she began to smile. Some things did not change.

When the opening was about a foot wide, she slid sideways through the gap and pushed the door quietly closed behind. She found the inside of the cottage darker than it was outdoors, as the hurricane shutters were closed all around, blacking out the moonlight. So she stood motionless with her heart pounding and ears peaked, waiting for her eyes to acclimate.

Aware that the information flow was still one way, Cassi moved with caution. "Odi? Odi, it's me, it's Cassi. I'm alone." She spoke softly at first and then raised her voice, not wanting to startle him awake. "Odi, it's Cassi. I just came to talk. I'm alone." Her ears strained to detect the slightest noise or pressure shift coming from the hall that led to the master bedroom, but nothing seemed to change. Keenly aware that her brother had always been the type to set booby-traps, she realized that she would be foolish to grope around blindly in the dark. She reached back slowly with her right hand and turned on the overhead light.

As the light went on, Cassi heard a scraping sound behind her and spun about only to find that nothing was there. The noise must have come from the other side of the door. She reached instinctively for her gun but found herself grabbing at air. Her mind caught up with her hand as it patted her side and she remembered that she had intentionally left her weapon in the car.

She tried to crack the door to find the source of the sound, but the door would not budge. The sound had been a bolt, a bolt that locked her inside. Cassi felt like a rat suddenly trapped in an oxygenless cage. She needed to escape.

Escape might not be easy, she realized in a panic. In response to the wild hurricane seasons of recent years, Charlotte had installed storm shutters, the tough metallic kind that roll down from above. They were designed for keeping two-hundred-mile-an-hour winds out, but they could just as effectively keep people in. She moved to the window beside the door and felt for the shutter switch without taking her eyes off the hallway to the bedroom. Cassi found the switch and slid it up. Nothing happened.

What did you expect? She wondered.

As she stood there cursing her bad luck, the sound of a computer booting up drew her gaze back to the kitchen. She began to tiptoe in that direction. "Odi, what's going on?" She asked, her voice just below a shout.

An annoying "beep ... beep ..." from the computer was the only response.

Cassi spotted a laptop sitting on the kitchen table. For some reason, the sight of it sent a chill scurrying up and down her spine. She assumed that her reaction was just the paranoia born of too many late-night movies—until she moved around the counter and got a look at the screen. Then she learned that it had been intuition.

The computer displayed the picture of an antenna with green waves radiating out. Cassi recognized the enlarged icon. A wireless network was in use. The other image on the screen indicated the reason. To the right of the icon were the cascading red digits of a large digital clock, followed by the words "Seconds until BOOM."

Cassi felt her intestines turn to water as she stared in shock and disbelief at her brother's devious work. 00:53 ... 00:52 ... 00:51 ...

Chapter 40

Baltimore, Maryland

"TWENTY-FIVE. TWENTY ... FIVE." Odi kept repeating the number to himself, shaking his head as he worked. That was a lot of senators.

Tearing a paper towel off the roll without removing his protective yellow gloves, he dabbed the sweat from his brow. Time was running short. Dawn was approaching, and he needed to be gone by first light. He wished he had not had to come to Johns Hopkins a second time. If it weren't for the need to super-cool the nitric acid, he could have used Aunt Charlotte's kitchen instead of the graduate chemistry lab.

He had perfected the Creamer's formula while preparing for the Potchak hit. He had the chemistry down cold. So aside from the potential of being blown to bits, he found no excitement in the task. Although the final product was magical, the production of Creamer felt mundane as chicken à la king. It boiled down to measuring and mixing, heating and cooling, filtering and separating—for hours on end. Because he had a lot of things to occupy his troubled mind—twenty-five to be exact—neither the tedium nor the physical danger bothered him. Still, he was afraid. He was afraid of getting caught. Although breaking into his old lab was not a serious crime, if caught he would be identified. Then his Iranian alibi would dissolve faster than the sugar he now poured, and he would go to jail for murder.

Odi tried to focus on the bright side as he stirred. The graduate lab had state-of-the-art equipment, so it was faster and easier to make Creamer here. It had temperature-controlled variable-speed mixers, electronically calibrated pipettes, and programmable centrifuges—everything required to get each stage of the twelve-step process just right. Working in a proper lab was safer than a basement too, and that was of no small concern. His perspective had been changed by his government's betrayal, but he still valued his vision and thumbs.

An added bonus of working here was that the university lab stocked many of the ingredients he needed, including distilled water, concentrated nitric acid, and acetone. He had acquired the rest for cash at area drug, hardware, and grocery stores, under the cover of a simple but effective disguise. Those purchases included hexamine, urotropine, methenamine, calcium-magnesium powder, powdered cream, sugar, and the omnipresent artificial flavoring.

He watched with satisfaction as the viscous white mass began to bubble slowly in the thick ten-liter beaker. It looked like a bleached lava lamp and it certainly was volcanic. Come to think of it, Odi thought, so was Ayden's plan.

Ayden had a sympathetic friend who was an aide to a senior member of the Senate Armed Services Committee. Sheila, he claimed, was certain that she could exchange the Half-n-Half served at a committee meeting for Creamer.

"How soon will she be able to do it?" He had asked Ayden.

"The Senate Armed Services Committee is going to be locked in conference tomorrow evening. It's a marathon effort to finalize the naval budget before recess. Everyone will be there, and unless something changes they will be alone in the building. It's perfect."

Odi thought that it sounded almost too good to be true. Still watching the bubbles, he wondered if there were video cameras in congressional meeting rooms. He had not thought to ask about that although Ayden probably would not know. He doubted that there were. Few people treasured their secrecy more than elected officials. But then, politicians also loved their security. He decided that there would likely be video surveillance, but no sound.

Waiting for stage eleven to ferment, Odi tried to picture the scene that would unfold that evening. Having been on many a stakeout, he found himself taking the security guard's point of view. The guard who drew duty the first evening of recess would be sitting with his black shoes propped up on a gray metal desk littered with Styrofoam cups containing the cold dregs of bad coffee. There would be a box of donuts somewhere off to the side. He would check it three or four times, although the last cruller would have vanished long ago. Most of the monitors before him would be devoid of life, unless you counted the drone-like cleaners vacuuming rugs and polishing floors. The exception would be the conference room with twenty-five famous faces. That was where the guard would direct the eye not tied to the *Post* crossword puzzle. If he were new he might even find it interesting, watching famous faces doling out billions to their pet constituents in the name of national defense.

About forty-five minutes into the meeting, the guard would see a pale senator pause mid-tirade to rub his stomach. If that was interesting enough to draw both eyes, he might even notice that the bellyacher's fingertips had turned blue. Then the senator would disappear in the blink of an eye. For the attentive guard it would be a perplexing version of now-you-see-him, now-you-don't.

The alarm would begin to blare a second later once the blast blew the windows out and in shock he would knock the coffee cups off the desk with his feet. Meanwhile, the senators sitting closest to the deceased would keel over, their bodies impaled by shrapnel made from splintered rib. The non-veterans would scramble up from the floor, their minds failing to comprehend the chaos that engulfed them. Then a second senator would explode in their midst and complete pandemonium would erupt. Slack-jawed but on his feet, the guard would now be struggling to make sense of the muted drama playing out before his eyes.

Seconds later the conference-room doors would crash open and other guards would rush in only to be shoved aside by terrified senators running out. As the guards looked blankly at each other, clueless about what to do, the explosions of the white-coffee drinking senators would continue in polished mahogany elevators and on stately marble stairs.

Within hours the world would begin scrutinizing how the SASC carved up the lion's share of the national budget. Would that change anything? Odi was not sure.

Although taking out The Three Marks had served justice and satisfied the debt of honor Odi owed his fallen friends, it would not create permanent change. Ayden had been right about that. But making the public aware of how they had been duped, and why ... that just might make a lasting difference.

The big beaker stopped bubbling as Odi pondered that thought, indicating that the penultimate reaction was now complete. For the final stage of the brew he had to slowly mix in a liter of super-cooled nitric acid. Very slowly. This was by far the most dangerous step. This was how many an anarchist had met his maker. He gripped a huge flask with a pair of heavy tongs and prepared to stir its acidic contents into the beaker on the hot plate. Once the two containers were mixed and cooled, he would have just over two gallons of Creamer. Eight liters.

"Why does she need two gallons?" Odi had asked. "I'd think a quart would be more than enough. Surely twenty-five Senators won't consume that much cream in their coffee?"

"She can't control which carton of Half-n-Half Senate Food Service will take from the fridge," Ayden had replied. "So she will have to replace them all."

"Tell her to find a way. I can't have six or seven unused cartons lying around. I don't want any innocents accidentally killed."

"We're lucky to have Sheila, Odi. Let's not push it. I'll get her to promise to go back to the kitchen and replace the Creamer with the original containers once the conference room is set up. That will have to suffice."

Odi saw Ayden's point, but he did not like it. "Can't she just replace the cream after it's already set up in the room?"

"I asked her that too. She said it was too risky. Compared to the kitchen, the conference room is much more secure."

Odi shook his head. "Okay. But she has to promise to pour the remaining Creamer down the drain right there in the kitchen."

"No problem."

"And Ayden, I am going to have to insist on delivering the Creamer to Sheila personally, so I can make that point."

There was a longer than usual pause before Ayden typed, "As you wish."

As Odi began pouring the large flask of super-cooled nitric acid into the beaker, the pager in his front jeans pocket began to vibrate. Maybe it was the fact that he had been up all night. Maybe it was because his nerves were already at their end. Whatever the cause, the shock of the pager was too much. Odi's hands trembled from the jolt and the liter of super-cooled nitric acid plummeted from the tongs.

Chapter 41

Baltimore, Maryland

AYDEN BOUNCED up and down on the balls of his feet, listening to the symphony of beeps and boops that indicated his international call was going through.

"Royal Falafel."

"Do you have fresh tabouleh?"

"Just a moment. Who's asking please?"

"Doctor Jones."

Ayden stopped bouncing and took a deep breath to calm his nerves. This was really intense.

"Doctor Jones, how nice to hear from you. Where are you calling from?"

"I'm at Johns Hopkins University. I ... I'm not sure I can go through with this." There, he had said it.

When Arvin's voice came back on the line half a beat later, it was calm as ever. "Of course you can Ayden. Just look at what you've already accomplished. Why, just six months ago you were a desperate doctor burning through his bank account in a noble but doomed attempt to single-handedly bailout an ocean of poverty with a leaky thimble. This evening you had a private meeting with the Director of the FBI to discuss the future of the planet. In the next twenty-four hours you will do more to alleviate world suffering than you could have done in ten lifetimes back in Iran. And that brings up a key point for you to remember, Ayden: you are no longer alone. You have friends now, comrades in arms, support."

Ayden found Arvin convincing, but he was not yet there. He decided to lay it all on the table, hoping that his sponsor would erase all his doubt. "I've gotten to know Odi over this last month. He has become a friend."

"Friends die in war, Ayden. It's sad, but true. I have lost many. Unless you can get Odi to back off his demand to meet the woman you invented—Sheila was her name as I recall—you have to go through with it. He would see through an imposter, and his Creamer is crucial to our plans. I'm sorry, but there's just no other way. I truly wish there were."

"I just don't know. I am a doctor, after all. I took an oath."

"The men whose corruption you are fighting took an oath as well. Because they have forsaken theirs for years, you must set yours aside for a day."

"I'm not sure that I can."

"Look, Ayden, I know the burden is heavy. But do not let it slip from your shoulders. By seeking to get out from under it, you will only crush yourself. Think about it. You are one of the few Western doctors who have seen the pitiful, imploring looks epidemic in Third-World children's eyes. If you turn your back on them now, you will never forgive yourself. Nor will you be able to go back to your old life. If you tried, you would be paralyzed by debilitating guilt. Every time you encountered a child suffering from preventable disease and facing a shortened life of grinding poverty, you would feel responsible. No my friend, your only real option is to move forward."

As Ayden reflected on the wisdom of Arvin's words, his sense of purpose returned like a torch reignited. "Will this really make—"

"Of course it will make a difference, Ayden. Of course it will," Arvin interrupted. "If there is one thing that Americans are good at, it's standing on a pedestal and making noise. Once you rivet the world's attention to the congressional budget for defense, there will not be a literate man, woman, or child on Earth unaware of the poverty and suffering the United States could alleviate with the resources it now dedicates to war. Public opinion will force them to beat their swords into plowshares. Unfortunately, this is the only way to usher in a peaceful new world. These are their rules, not ours."

"But it's so violent, so ... counterintuitive," Ayden pressed.

"Think of it as chemotherapy. Yes, when viewed in isolation it is caustic. But the cancers that your therapy ultimately cures will salvage countless lives. This is the day you'll paint a hundred million smiles."

"You know about that?" Ayden asked.

"Of course."

Ayden consciously recognized that the man he knew as Arvin had done a fine job of pushing his buttons, but it did not matter. Arvin had said exactly what he wanted to hear. He did not really want to back out. He just had a case of the jitters, he told himself. Like a bride on her wedding day.

He thought back to the evening when Arvin first knocked on his door. Arvin had asked him, "If you had the resources, would you be willing to do more?" With those words Arvin had given him hope, hope that kept him going while his resources diminished. And faith, faith that was rewarded when Agent Odysseus Carr landed in his lap. He remembered the pride and trepidation he felt when he used the coded exchange at Royal Falafel for the first time.

He had made his first call to Royal Falafel just seconds after treating Odi's shoulder wound and getting him stable. His initiative had paid off. Arvin's subsequent investigation had revealed circumstances that could not have been more perfectly suited to their cause. Eighteen hours after Ayden had picked up the phone, Arvin had personally delivered the telltale headsets to his door, and the recruitment of Odi Carr had begun.

Because of his courage that day, three defense industry CEOs, three men who ran cruel and exploitive companies like the one that killed his father, were no longer of this world. By contributing to their demise, Ayden had done right by his father. He had avenged Tigran Taronish. Thinking about that, Ayden realized that he felt better than he had in over twenty years. By honoring his father he had cured himself of a chronic disease. With a flash of blinding clarity he understood that he could not shy away from the opportunity Arvin now presented. This was his destiny.

"Tell me about your meeting with Director Proffitt," Arvin continued, sweeping Ayden back into their present discussion. "Was it successful? Did he get you the list?"

"Your insight proved accurate. Proffitt's approach is analogous to a pharmaceutical corporation's. He is making a career of treating the disease of terrorism. So, contrary to the FBI Director's vociferous rhetoric, the last thing he truly wants is a cure. Yes, he got me the list."

"Excellent. When you have the Creamer call me back. I'll give you instructions for meeting with my twenty-five volunteers."

"Twenty-four," Ayden corrected.

"There are twenty-five senators on the armed services committee, my friend," Arvin persisted.

"I know, but you need supply only twenty-four volunteers. I would consider it an honor to be the twenty-fifth. I will take out the chairman."

Chapter 42

Chesapeake Beach, Maryland

00:53 ... 00:52 ... 00:51 ... Cassi stared at the screen, counting in disbelief as the final seconds of her life vanished into the ether. An overload of emotions bore down on her as she stared, squelching her ability to think. She wondered how Odi managed it—working under such conditions. As a psychologist, she knew the human species to be remarkably resilient, but fifty-three seconds hardly gave you time to acclimate. Then it struck her. Perhaps Odi had not acclimated. Years of this strain could explain why he had snapped in Iran. It only took a final straw to break a camel's back.

00:50 ... 00:49 ... 00:48 ... From her discussions with Odi and the occasional glimpse over his shoulder, Cassi knew much more than most on how to disarm bombs. But this was not a bomb. This was just a computer. The bomb could be anywhere within wireless range. Forty-eight seconds was not going to cut it.

00:47 ... 00:46 ... 00:45 ... Still mesmerized by the screen, Cassi flashed through her alternatives. Her best move would be to break out of the cottage, but Odi had prevented that by disabling the shutter mechanisms. He had probably accomplished that by simply removing a fuse, or—more cleverly and thus more likely—replacing a good fuse with one that looked good but did not work. Regardless, with just forty-five seconds left on her life's clock, Cassi did not have time to run down her hunch.

00:44 ... 00:43 ... 00:42 ... Cassi recalled that the shutters could also be operated with a crank key. It was a safety precaution for times when the power was out. Cassi dashed around the cottage, scanning each window for the presence of a crank key and pummeling all the other switches just in case. Failing to produce any result, she returned to the computer cursing herself for thinking that Odi could be so easily outmaneuvered. The fanciful flight had cost her a priceless twelve seconds.

00:30 ... 00:29 ... 00:28 ... Realizing that escape was no longer an option, Cassi ran to the bedroom and pulled Charlotte's quilt off the bed along with three thick decorative pillows. She hauled them to the bathroom and leapt in the tub, burying herself like a mole beneath. Then she remembered the door. It was not solid wood or anything close—just two thin sheets of masonite—but every little bit helped. While climbing out of the tub to close it, another thought came to her. She should pull the mattress off the bed, drag it into the bathroom, and lean it over the tub. How long did she have left?

As if answering her question with "not much" the computer began an accelerated beep. Was it the final countdown, or something more? Cassi had no time to think, she could only react. She glanced fleetingly toward the mattress as though Brad Pitt lay naked there, and then ran for the kitchen.

00:08 ... 00:07 ... Cassi saw at once that something had changed. The maddening beep had ushered in a new message. Seconds until BOOM had been replaced by a trick question. She read it aloud. "What's the best size?"

Chapter 43

Baltimore, Maryland

EVEN AS THE FROSTY FLASK of acid slipped from his grasp, Odi contemplated the pager's implicit message. Someone had entered Charlotte's cottage. The bomb was now armed. In one minute the sanctuary of his youth would be reduced to matchsticks and his research would be turned to dust—along with anyone caught inside.

The heavy Pyrex flask crashed down on the desktop gas valve even as Odi lunged to catch it with gloved hands. As it shattered, he rolled to his left and dove for the floor. The reflex saved his face, but acid rain deluged the right side of his torso.

Odi heard his clothing begin to sizzle and felt his right shoulder start to burn. He scrambled to his feet and made a screaming beeline for the chemical shower by the door. Yanking on the dangling chain like Quasimodo incensed, Odi prayed that he would not emerge looking like the bell-ringer too.

He had seen acid burns before. Many times. A friend of his from this very lab referred to the cheese-grater scar on his cheek as his birth-control wound.

Twenty or thirty gallons into the drenching blast, Odi peeled off the protective goggles and heavy gloves. After a quick inspection of his hands, he tore off his shirt.

His right shoulder had borne the brunt of the splash and even it had seen worse. The blood-pocked patchwork reminded him of a gravel-slide he had suffered after falling off his dirt bike as a kid. If the acid had not been super-cooled or the shower seconds away, it might have eaten through to the bone. Still, between the shrapnel wound in his left shoulder and the acid burn on his right, he would not be breaking down doors anytime soon. Given his luck and the way things were going, that ability was probably about to become important.

He stripped off the rest of his clothes and stood there two minutes more, using one of his socks as a washcloth to scrub. He was going to be cold and conspicuous crossing campus soaking wet and shirtless in the middle of October. But that beat looking freakish for the rest of his life—assuming that the-rest-of-his-life lasted longer than a few hours.

Odi wrung out his clothes as best he could and got dressed. He tried to be mad at himself for screwing up, but found himself feeling grateful for his blessings instead. "Ten fingers and two eyes," he repeated aloud, recalling his earlier musing.

Looking over at the smoking green tile floor, Odi remembered the vibration that catalyzed the reaction and his heart sunk. He dug anxious fingers into the wet front pocket of his jeans and withdrew the little black box. The pager was dedicated to the intrusion alarm on Charlotte's cottage, so its vibration yielded only one conclusion. Boom.

"Unless someone had dialed a wrong number," Odi thought aloud. The display dashed that hope. It read 843-7448, the numeric equivalent of THE SHIT, which, as his British colleagues loved to say, he was now in. Barring a robbery or some other equally unlikely coincidence, someone was on his tail. The obvious conclusion was that Cassi had talked.

The loss of his childhood getaway was a psychological blow, but in practical terms it did not matter. Not in the short run, at least. Come this time tomorrow he would be headed for Iran where he would miraculously awake. Cassi's split-second sighting would be attributed to a grieving mind playing tricks. No jury in the world would be left without a reasonable doubt. But that was all in the distant future, Odi reminded himself. Today, he had one final but crucial stop to make.

Though the tabletop and floor were now etched with nitric acid, the big Pyrex beaker full of Creamer base sat undisturbed. He could still salvage this batch. That was important. He had a rendezvous with Sheila.

Thirty-two minutes later the recipe was complete. After curing for an hour, the Creamer would be ready. He emptied the eight liters of Creamer into two gallon-jugs and had about a pint of Creamer left over. Rather than pouring it down the drain, he emptied his sixteen-ounce bottle of Dasani into the sink and poured the remaining Creamer inside. He put the Dasani bottle back in his jacket pocket and then secured the gallon jugs in his backpack. The sound of the backpack's zipper was a welcome one. He had come close to disaster tonight, but in the end he had pulled it off.

With a spring in his step, Odi opened the laboratory door and nearly walked into the man waiting silently in the dark.

"Hello Odi."

Odi jumped. "Ayden?"

His friend's face was shadowed, but the corridor's emergency lighting reflected off the gun in his hand. The surprising scene took too long for Odi's tired mind to compute. By the time the threat had registered he was flying backwards through space as an explosion of pain ripped through his body from the center of his chest. Agony racked him with an almost physical grip until his whole world was reduced to a blinding white light. Then everything went black.

Chapter 44

Washington, D.C.

"I TOLD YOU never to call me here," Wiley said, his voice raspy from lack of sleep. "It's too dangerous."

"You're in the office at five in the morning. You didn't leave me much choice," Stuart replied. "Check your Hotmail account. I'm sending a file."

Wiley bit his lower lip and did as he was told. The subject line on the message from SSSlick1@hotmail.com was "FBI's Most Wanted." There was no text, but it contained an attachment. Wiley double clicked. A second later he was looking at a composite picture of Odi's face. "Where did you get this?"

Stuart scoffed. "The important question is why did I get this. The answer is that it's time to turn up the heat."

Wiley looked back at the message header. "You want me to make Odysseus Carr one of the FBI's most wanted?"

"Don't be daft. Odi Carr is dead. I want you to make someone who looks like Odysseus Carr—someone who is impersonating a fallen federal officer—one of the FBI's most wanted."

Wiley bristled but managed to control his temper. He knew that Stuart was up to something, and Wiley had yet to figure out what it was. "Impersonating a federal officer isn't a big enough crime to warrant that."

"No, but assassinating the CEO's of three major US defense corporations is."

"True, but what good is that going to do us?" Wiley asked.

"For starters, it's going to make it a lot harder for Odi to get to us."

Wiley smiled, pleased that Mister Slider was nervous about that too. They had not discussed it, but both men knew that they were prime candidates for Odi's next attack—and the man was batting a thousand.

"Furthermore," Stuart continued, "by proactively framing those murders as the acts of a look-alike foreign assassin—someone whose employer is intent on weakening the US defense industry—you divert the authorities from resurrecting the real Odi Carr and searching for his motive."

"But what happens if they catch him?"

"Think, Wiley, think. You don't wait around passively. You stack the deck against Odi to ensure that doesn't happen. Paint him as a treacherous enough bastard that officers will shoot first and ask questions later. Tell them he's prone to booby-trap himself, and that he has sworn to never be taken alive. Tell them not to take any chances."

"That may take care of the police, but what do I tell my own people?"

"You're not thinking," Stuart repeated, adding a soprano lilt to give his words extra dig.

Wiley still drew a painful blank.

Stuart prompted him. "How many departments do you have?"

Of course, Wiley thought. He could classify the source of the intelligence as compartmentalized information. Bob would think that it came from Bill and vice versa and so on. He could come up with an excuse to introduce the APB to the system a few layers down the chain of command so that nobody would turn to him for details. The ideas were coming fast now—thirty seconds too late. Leo Tufts would be perfect for running the look-alike-assassin case. He would run with it like the wind, assuming incorrectly that it was a test prior to promotion.

Wiley tightened his grip on the receiver. "Very well Stuart. It will be done."

Chapter 45

Chesapeake Beach, Maryland

00:08 ... 00:07 ... "What's the best size?"

The trick question struck Cassi like a balmy Hawaiian breeze on a bitter winter night. She spoke the answer aloud. "A cubic centimeter." She typed "CC" into the computer. The countdown stopped with four seconds left.

Growing up in a family of scientists, her initials had spurred both a nickname and a longstanding family joke. How could someone so big, be so small? Odi had posed a question that both she and Charlotte could instantly answer, but which would dumbfound anyone else.

Eight hours later, Wiley pulled his black Escalade into Charlotte's drive.

Cassi remained seated on the front porch, ostensibly enjoying the late afternoon sun. In truth she wanted to watch Wiley's approach. She was expert at reading body language, especially on people she knew well. Wiley, however, habitually maintained control over his face, eyes, and hands. He was a natural-born poker player. Cassi had discovered his tell, however. It was his walk.

A lump grew in her throat as Wiley trampled grass beneath a testy stride. She knew she had tried his patience by asking him to drop everything and drive out there without explanation. Apparently the drive had not mellowed his mood. "Thank you for coming. I know it's ... awkward."

"You said it was important." Wiley's words were much softer than his stance, an indication that he was trying. "What happened? You were, shall we say, uncharacteristically nebulous on the phone."

"Nebulous. I don't think anyone has called me that before," she said, trying to lighten his mood.

"So what's the urgent matter you summoned me to Crisfield for?" Wiley said. He did not alter his stance.

"Come inside," she said. "There's something I need to show you."

She led him into the kitchen and pointed at four folders she had found hidden between placemats in the credenza. She was certain that one of the reasons Odi had booby trapped the cottage was to destroy these files. No doubt he also wanted to destroy his laptop computer, but she was not about to touch that. The first thing she had done after stopping the countdown was re-enable the storm shutters. As she had guessed, Odi had disabled them with a faulty fuse. Unfortunately, she had not guessed or discovered where he had hidden the bomb. Until it was disarmed, she would treat the computer like the Ebola virus.

"What's in those?" Wiley asked.

Cassi pushed the manila stack toward him. "Take a look."

Wiley took a half step back after opening the top folder, as though he were afraid it might bite him. Staring up at him from a glossy page was Mark Drake's smiling face. The posed headshot was part of a *Car and Driver* article entitled *Drake's Gallant Steed*.

Wiley scanned the article and then read aloud the caption beneath the picture of the automobile that now occupied an FBI forensics garage. "A bulletproof chariot drawn by five hundred horses, Drake's custom Bentley is large enough to accommodate six knights and their round table." The next page showed Drake entering the Bentley before his Petite Versailles mansion. Wiley was about to flip further when the chauffeur's familiar features caught his eye. It was obvious to Cassi that that very picture had been the catalyst for Odi's assassination plan. Wiley seemed to draw the same conclusion too, as he said, "I'll be damned."

Cassi watched Wiley flip quickly through the remaining pages of the file, having already ascertained its gist. The remainder consisted of similarly laudatory stories from other distinguished periodicals. *Business Week*, *Inc.*, and *American Rifleman* each had feature articles with pictures and useful biographical details.

Wiley set the first file aside and opened the second. This one led with an *Esquire* article entitled "A King and his Castles." The title was splashed above Mark Rollins' headshot, which was flanked on four sides by four royal residences: a mansion in Suffolk County, a penthouse in Manhattan, a ranch in Montana, and a beach house on the

Virginia coast. "Son of a bitch."

Cassi did not comment. She knew that the assassin's mother was anything but a bitch.

Wiley slid the second file off the stack and then paused with his fingers on the third. He pushed it aside as well, apparently grasping the significance inherent in the quantity of folders. Only three murders had been committed thus far—aside from Potchak, whom Odi had no need to research. He looked up at her before opening the forth. Cassi clenched her jaw and nodded.

The fourth folder led with an article from the *Rappahannock Record* entitled "Celebrity Getaways." Odi had circled a paragraph in the middle with a red pen. According to Reedville Coffee Stop owner Norm Evans, Director Proffitt never misses the chance to clear his head of city smog and fill his lungs with fresh Chesapeake air. This was doubly true, Evans noted, on the weekends Proffitt was scheduled for a Sunday-morning talk show appearance. "There's nothing like a Chesapeake morning to put you at your best."

Cassi felt hot tears running down her cheeks as Wiley studied the words. When he finally looked up, she had no idea what to say.

"So I'm next?" Wiley asked.

Cassi slowly nodded.

Wiley handed her a handkerchief and she dabbed at her eyes. Up until this moment, she had been working alone, feeding off adrenaline. Now she felt like collapsing, knowing that Wiley was there to keep the world from crashing down around her. This was no time to slack off, however, so she closed her eyes and made a determined effort to pull herself together. "Fitzpatrick's website mentions that you'll be his guest on *PoliTalk* this Sunday."

Wiley nodded somberly. "So you think the assassin will come for me at Asgard?"

"Yes."

"Why me? I'm not a corporate CEO."

Cassi had spent the afternoon walking the bluff, thinking about that very question. A satisfying answer, if one could possibly be found, had eluded her grasp like a wisp of smoke. Still, she knew that her conclusion was correct, so she was going to act on it. The motivation would eventually be revealed. "I'm not sure why he's after you, but I have discovered the assassin's identity, so I'm sure that it's my fault."

Chapter 46

Baltimore, Maryland

ODI DREAMT OF SNAKES. He was trapped among them, paralyzed in their dark midst as they writhed and hissed. He had harbored an irrational fear of snakes since his eleventh year when a corn snake surreptitiously shared his sleeping bag. It had awakened him after a dormant night while slithering to escape across his naked thigh. At the time his groggy mind was unsure whether he had imagined the sensation or not. When the movement repeated he lay paralyzed with fear until the scaly head emerged an inch from the tip of his nose and broke the spell. The other Scouts found him at the base of the hill, still kicking and screaming and trying to break free of his sodden sleeping bag. Twenty years later Odi could still hear their incessant laughter.

Today his dream recycled as nightmares often do, playing over and over again accompanied by a ceaseless hiss until at last a bolt of pain lanced through his acid-burned shoulder and jolted him awake. The first thing he noticed as his mind pierced the fog was a familiar smell. Once it registered, everything became clear and his eyes shot open like blinds released. He was back in the chemistry lab. The hissing was real, but the source was not snakes. It was gas.

A sea of green met his eyes. Tile. He was on his stomach with his left cheek resting numbly on the cold laboratory floor. His arms were tied behind his back. Ayden.

Complicating his predicament, Odi did not know exactly where the truth ended and the fiction began, but one sad fact was blindingly obvious. Once again he had been betrayed. Ayden's motivation was also obvious. He wanted two gallons of Creamer. He was left feeling foolish that it took a Taser blast to bring him clarity. No doubt Ayden had invented the story about Sheila and the SASC to accomplish that end. The big question was why. Why did Ayden want an arsenal of Creamer? He had only learned of the Creamer a few days earlier. Before then nobody but Odi knew of its existence. That was hardly enough time to orchestrate a grand plan. Odi supposed that it was possible that Ayden had simply opportunistically inserted Creamer into a preexisting framework, but that seemed farfetched. Or perhaps Ayden had simply grasped the black-market demand for such a weapon and greed had overwhelmed him overnight. Two gallons was the equivalent of two-hundred-and-fifty-six invisible hand grenades. He shuddered to think what the likes of Bin Laden could do with an arsenal like that.

His thoughts returned to Ayden. There had to be more behind his actions than greed. Ayden had abandoned his values. He had turned on his friend. That did not happen in a day. Or did it? Odi asked, turning a mirror on himself.

As uncomfortable questions rolled in, Odi tried to push them aside so that he could focus on the present. Although his hands were bound behind his back, he could tell by the way his legs were sprawled that his feet remained free. Had Ayden gotten sloppy, he wondered, or did that anomaly signify something else? Perhaps Ayden was still in the room.

Wary now, Odi rolled slowly over, trying to get a better look around. As his hands rolled beneath him, he heard a soft metallic click. A shiver shot up his spine as he froze. Nothing focuses an explosive ordnance disposal technician's attention more acutely than an unexpected mechanical sound. Either he had just rolled onto something metallic that Ayden had placed on the middle of the tiled floor, or a device of some kind was strapped to his arms. Both possibilities yielded the same horrifying conclusion. The room was a gas-fueled bomb, and he was the trigger.

Filtering out the hissing of gas overhead, Odi tried to replay the sound in his mind. He had heard a hollow clack followed by a metal-on-tile scrape. It was mysterious, but mysterious was better than the all-too-familiar arming click of a pressure switch—probably.

He considered screaming for help, but given the hissing jets that might be the worst thing he could do. If Ayden had rigged him to be a trigger, he had probably rigged the door as well. If anyone barged in responding to his call before Odi evacuated the gas, both he and the Good Samaritan would go up in flames.

Odi summarized his situation. If he moved or called out for help, the gas would ignite and he would suffer an excruciating death. If he did nothing, he would suffocate once the gas filled the room. It was not going to be a feel-good day.

He raised his legs slowly until they were perpendicular with the floor. Then, clamping his eyes shut in a grimace, he brought his legs down so that their momentum sat him up without the use of his hands.

No Boom.

He looked over his shoulder to inspect the floor. He saw nothing but tile. That narrowed down the possibilities. Slowly Odi worked his feet beneath himself and stood up, being careful all the while not to move his hands. He tiptoed over to the wall mirror beside the chemical shower. He found the smell of gas much more intense while standing and his head began to swim. He knew he did not have much time before succumbing to the fumes.

The mirror revealed that Ayden had not strapped a bomb between his arms. He had, however, done the next best thing. Ayden had duct taped one arm of a gas-igniting sparker to each of Odi's wrists and used a third strip of tape to bind his wrists together, leaving the sparker cocked. If Odi pulled his hands free, he would release the tension holding the sparker's arms together. Then the flint would scrape back across the scratchpad and emit a deadly shower of sparks. Odi pictured his life ending with a sucking whoosh and a searing boom.

Perhaps that would be for the best, he thought. Poetic justice. Just what he deserved for releasing two gallons of Creamer into the world, endangering innocents and disgracing his family. A surge of emotion swept over him. He had allowed himself to be used, and in so doing he had betrayed everyone he knew. A fiery death was too good for him after that. Besides, how many times had he cheated Prometheus while working EOD? A dozen? Fifty? A hundred?

Staring into the mirror, his suicidal thoughts disappeared as quickly as they came. He was not one to take the coward's way out. Speaking of which, now that he understood his predicament, his first impulse was to open the door and run, to get the detonator strapped between his wrists well beyond the reach of the gas. But years on the bomb squad had conditioned him not to yield to rash impulses. He turned his eyes to the exit and spotted the redundant detonator at once. As predicted, Ayden had rigged another sparker over the door. Fortunately, disabling it would be simple—once Odi had the use of his hands.

His mind raced to find a solution, aware that it was competing with a hissing clock. If he passed out now he would never awake. Did he have seconds? Minutes? One? Two? Five? Ten? There was no way to tell. One moment his head would start to spin and the next he would fall. Whoosh-boom.

Although he had disarmed hundreds of bombs, Odi had never been trapped inside one before. Being part of the mechanism brought him a whole new perspective, but it did not help.

He tried to take a mental step outside the box, to approach this bomb like any other EOD problem. The objective was the same. He had to prevent the detonator, the sparker, from exploding the ordnance, the gas. The question was how. He had only very limited use of his hands, and the gas was everywhere. He could not clip a wire or divert a circuit or place a circuit breaker between the sparker and the gas.

Or could he?

Careful not to put pressure on his arms, Odi walked to the nearest lab station and squirmed onto the countertop. The noxious smell was strongest here, and he felt his dizziness begin to spike. He bit down hard on his tongue in an effort to stay awake while arching his back and lowering his hands into the sink in an attempt to engage the stopper. As he reached for the faucet, he tasted blood and his vision began to blur. The solution was in his grasp, but he was already too late.

To buy a few seconds more he pressed his leg against the nozzle of the closest jet, plugging the deadly flow. This was like playing a demented game of Twister—without the girl. Keeping pressure on his leg, he strained forward so that his bound hands could reach the faucet and turned on the cold water.

The wait for the sink to fill seemed the longest of Odi's life. His shoulder burned, his head pounded, his tongue bled, his arms cramped, and oblivion was just a spasm or twitch away. He used the time to slowly, deliberately shut off the nozzle he had been blocking with his leg. Now he only had nineteen gas jets to go.

Once the water was sufficiently deep, Odi leaned back and plunged his hands to the bottom of the sink. He yanked his wrists apart the instant the sparker was submerged. As the tape ripped, he heard the sparker's flint scrape across the scratch pad but the water rendered it impotent. It was the first time he had used that word with a smile.

With a sigh of relief contrary to the physical pain he was feeling, he rolled his wrists to peel off the tape, losing the hair on his forearms in the process. God, what was he going to look like when this was all over? He wondered. Then he laughed at himself. Anything but a cinder would do.

He tossed the sparker back into the water and sprang to the floor. He closed the remaining gas jets in less than a minute and enabled the smashed ventilation switch in a few seconds more. The noise of the overhead vent sucking gas into space was the sweetest sound he had ever heard.

After thirty seconds of breath-catching, oxygen-sucking rest, Odi sprayed the second sparker with the fire extinguisher. Then he removed it from atop the door and tossed it into the water beside its twin. He grabbed his jacket from the stool on which it was draped and was further relieved to feel some extra weight. He checked the pocket and felt a further surge of relief. The Dasani bottle full of Creamer was still there. As the sight of it registered, so did the outline of his next moves.

Chapter 47

The Grand Hyatt, Washington, D.C.

AS AYDEN WATCHED the crowd of young men growing around him, filling the suite, he felt a warm glow percolating inside. These martyrs were nothing like the barbaric, deranged, ignorant thugs the manipulating politicians and sensation-seeking press liked to finger with upturned noses. These were clean-cut, crystal-eyed, educated leaders, soberly making the ultimate sacrifice for a charitable cause. Tomorrow, the establishment's propaganda tricks would backfire. Homeland Security would never see his soldiers coming.

Before they disbursed, however, Ayden knew that such a quantity of Middle-Easterners was apt to draw attention from a wary populace. To counteract any suspicions that might arise, He had let it slip that he was auditioning to fill a dozen minor roles in a new Tom Clancy movie. The bellboy's eyes lit up as they strayed from the platter of sandwiches to the videotaping equipment. "How exciting. You know, I was once in a—"

"Well, now that I've taken you into our confidence," Ayden interrupted, brandishing a crisp Benjamin, "I'd appreciate your keeping our presence quiet. These days everyone thinks they can act, and the last thing we need is a line of Tom Cruise wannabes at our door."

The bellboy made the c-note vanish faster than a chameleon's lunch. Then he bowed and offered an obsequious "But of course."

Ayden looked out at the crowd and nodded. Arvin's twenty-four volunteers had arrived at odd intervals over the previous two hours and now they filled the two-thousand-dollar-a-night Hyatt suite. Their air was more jovial than somber, but Ayden could sense the tension percolating just below the surface. Suppressing that tension was half of today's job. The other half was locking in their resolve.

As he took a seat atop the granite counter of the sitting room bar, the chatter trailed off and the room grew silent. He rolled his shoulders once and began. "We are strangers united by our mutual commitment to a great cause. That makes us friends. Friends, please listen to me now, for I have much to reveal.

"To my left you see a stack of envelopes, to my right," he

ceremoniously lifted a black cloth, "one hundred mini-bar beverage bottles. Four for each of you." Ayden held up one of the fine linen envelopes and withdrew a 3-ounce bottle of Baileys Irish Cream from the case. "These are your mission and your means. I will begin by explaining precisely how and when the Irish Cream is to be used. Then after lunch, each of you is going to make a video, a video that will make your family proud for countless generations to come ..."

Chapter 48

Asgard Island, Chesapeake Bay

AS THE NORSE WIND approached Asgard across a choppy bay, Cassi walked out to stand by the rail. She caught some spray on her face. It tasted bitterly cold and very salty—not unlike her present predicament.

She traced the yacht's heading to the coastline ahead. She had not studied Wiley's tiny marina on her previous visits. There had been no need. For the next twenty-four hours, however, Wiley's island was going to be her battleground. She began to study it as such. "Tell me about the marina," she shouted into the cabin.

"It can handle yachts up to 120 feet in length." Wiley yelled back, his voice buffeted by the wind. "The two central lifts are powerful enough to raise sixty footers completely out of the water. That isn't usually necessary, but it's nice to have when seas get rough."

Cassi knew that they would not be using a lift now. Per their agreement, Wiley was not even going to cut the motor. He was just dropping her off.

"Is something wrong?" Wiley asked. "You seem to be staring."

"No. I'm just getting a tactical perspective. Is this the only place a boat can safely land?"

"Sure is. The rocks will shred your hull if you try to tie-up anywhere else."

Cassi realized that she had never seen the island from the eastern side. They always approached from Virginia. "So the whole circumference looks like this—rocky cliffs rising from water?"

"Yep. Geologically speaking, Asgard is a rocky mountaintop

protruding from the bay. The average drop is over thirty feet, and nowhere is it less than twenty."

"So why did you build the dock here? Why not closer to the house?"

"This is the best-protected spot on the leeward side of the island."

Cassi nodded and studied the scraggly cliffs. "When I look at it from a tactical perspective, it kind of reminds me of Alcatraz."

"My grandfather would have banished you forever if he heard you say that. We Proffitts prefer to think of our island as Valhalla."

Their banter was growing lighter as each tried to cover the growing awkwardness of their situation—the nervousness, the guilt, and yes, the sexual tension. They were not taking the familiar trip to make love in the clover on the bluff or to walk through the sculpted gardens kissing and holding hands. They were colleagues on a mission, nothing more, she realized. It hurt. "What's the circumference of your earthly heaven?" She asked.

"Just over two miles. The island covers roughly one square kilometer, although it's not square. As my grandmother used to say, Asgard is shaped like an open-mouthed smile."

Or a frown, Cassi thought, depending on your perspective. "With the marina for its front teeth?"

"And the house as a dimple."

Cassi continued to study the marina as Wiley masterfully maneuvered the forty-eight foot yacht toward an iron berth. The last time she had been here, she had been with Odi. Odi would come this time too, but this time she would be against him.

Wiley drifted in alongside the dock, gave the twin engines a second of reverse, and put the motor in neutral. The Norse Wind halted as though on wheels. "Are you sure you want me to leave, Cassi? I would much rather stay. I don't feel good about leaving you here alone."

The woman in her yearned for him to stay, but today the agent prevailed. "I am sure. I have to handle him myself, one-on-one."

Wiley shook his head. "What if he doesn't give you that chance? What if there's a bomb waiting up there, like the one he left at your aunt's cottage? Or what if he changes MO's and uses a sniper rifle?"

Cassi looked down at the sea to hide the doubt in her eyes. "I'm not just his twin sister, Wiley. I'm also a profiler. I'm convinced that Odi won't do that."

"How can you be so sure when you don't even know his motivation? He has obviously changed. Who knows what happened to him over there. Maybe he's hearing voices or taking his orders from a dog."

Wiley was playing to her emotions effectively. She knew that she had to keep it professional or she might crack. "Because whatever his reason, the first killings show that this is very personal to him."

"We don't know that," Wiley shot back. "I'm not a defense contractor. Even if the others were personal, this one could be different."

"I appreciate your concern, Wiley. Really I do. But we agreed on this hours ago, and you promised to let me do this my way. I'm getting off the boat now. I don't want to see you again until this time tomorrow."

Chapter 49

Asgard Island, Chesapeake Bay

ODI FELT AN ADRENALINE KICK as the rising sun crested the island bluff and sent rays of golden light through the bulletproof windows. He knew it would not be long now. Wiley was a creature of habit.

Odi had given up on trying to guess Ayden's intentions for the Creamer in order to focus on a sure thing. He could not allow a traitor like Wiley to assume the second highest office in the land, but he could not expect to stop him either—at least not with political or legal means. Wiley was far too rich and powerful for conventional measures like that. Fortunately, Odi was an unconventional kind of guy—and he still had a Dasani bottle full of Creamer.

He bent over to touch his toes, holding the stretch for a ten-count to warm his muscles. Wiley did not heat the manor house at night. Odi was not surprised. Despite his wealth, Wiley struck Odi as the traditionally frugal New-England flannel-pajamas-and-thick-comforter type. That really sucked when your body was as sore and cold as Odi's was after his pounding midnight Jet Ski ride. But he was not complaining. He had come a long way to reach this final phase. After weeks of struggle, he had just one battle to go.

Odi studied the room through the crack in the closet door. This was something he had not been able to do in the dark of the night. Wiley's enormous study looked exactly as it had the one time he had visited with Cassi. Windows along the east side of the room, a long aquarium along the west, with a sixty-inch screen on the far wall and a suite of matching black-leather furniture in the middle.

At the far end from where Odi hid, a bar occupied one corner and a large glass desk the other. Behind the desk a Plexiglas lectern faced out the window. Odi had asked Wiley about the lectern's odd placement. "It helps condition me to ignore diversion and distraction," Wiley had explained. "Both are key to Beltway survival."

The lectern was the focus of Odi's attention now. It was the lure that would draw his rat to the trap—sometime soon from the sound of it, he noted. The pipes had just come to life. He guessed that Wiley was taking a shower.

He caught sight of the large remote control next to the marble ashtray on the end table, the one Wiley had used during their last visit to activate the panic room. He should have hidden it as a precaution, Odi realized, but he did not want to risk retrieving it now that he knew Wiley was awake. It probably didn't matter anyway. There was no button you could push when you had a bomb in your belly—except perhaps game over.

Odi was still contemplating the irony of setting a trap in a panic room when Wiley walked in. That was quick, he thought, but then Wiley had obviously come straight from the shower. He was wearing Scottish flannel PJ's and a thick white robe with a hood that made him look like a prizefight boxer approaching the ring. He supposed the analogy was suitable. The lectern was a politician's arena.

Wiley crossed the study to his practice lectern without so much as a glance toward the closet, and began to practice for his upcoming *PoliTalk* appearance. "It's a pleasure to be back on *PoliTalk*, Jim."

Odi slipped silently out of his hiding place.

"I'd like to be the bearer of good news today," Wiley continued, "but from where I sit the situation looks bleak."

Odi raised two Berettas toward Wiley's back and said "It does indeed."

Wiley said nothing in response. He just froze.

Odi thought he detected a tremble. "Look at me," he commanded.

Slowly, very slowly Wiley turned around while using his left hand to remove his hood. First Odi saw the voice recorder, then he saw the face. The person in the bathrobe was Cassi.

Chapter 50

Asgard Island, Chesapeake Bay

"COME ON, SHOOT HIM," Stuart whispered, staring at the security monitor. "Shoot the bastard."

"You're dreaming," Wiley said without averting his eyes. "Cassi's not going to shoot her brother. There was a chance that he might have shot her in the back thinking she was me. Then we might have gotten really lucky and seen him shoot himself after discovering his mistake, à la Romeo and Juliet, but that chance is gone. It's up to us now."

They had just watched Odi's Berettas slip from his limp hands to the floor as Cassi produced a Colt .45 from her bathrobe pocket. Now the twins were just standing there, her tears flowing, his mouth agape, neither knowing what to do next.

Stuart said, "You better get over there now before they figure things out," but Wiley was already gone.

~ ~ ~

Wiley wondered how it had come to this as he slipped out of the security closet and slunk down the hall. He knew the answer of course. He had made a Faustian exchange, his soul for the Oval Office, when he committed to The Three Marks to do whatever it takes. He realized now that he had been a fool to think that he could pull it off without genuine sacrifice—as had they.

Peering around the doorway, Wiley could see Odi's back and the top of Cassi's head. She was holding her brother in a supportive embrace, although the Colt remained in her hand.

Cassi spotted Wiley as he entered the room and she backed away from her brother.

"What is it?" Odi asked, obviously studying her face before turning to look around.

"I couldn't leave you alone in your time of need," Wiley said, before Cassi could comment. "I was worried. I'm glad to see that you've got things under control. Shall I leave the two of you alone?"

Before Cassi could reply, Odi interjected, "Shoot him now. Don't let him get to my guns."

Wiley almost smiled when he heard Odi's words. It was as if he was reading from Stuart's script.

Odi's guns lay on the floor in front of the closet. They were a yard to Wiley's left, and a full twenty feet from the Carrs. Wiley held up his hands. "Hey, I'm not the one who came here to shoot anybody. In fact, I'm the only one walking around unarmed—and this is my house."

"Don't listen to him Cassi," Odi interrupted. He has killed lots of people, including Derek, Flint, and Adam."

Keeping his voice soft and in check, Wiley said, "You're sick, Odi. Deranged. Mentally ill. What happened to you over there in Iran? What did they do to you?"

As he spoke, Wiley watched Cassi look back and forth, her face a mask of anguish and apprehension. Sensing her indecision, he held out his hands and said, "Let's diffuse this situation. We don't want anyone doing anything stupid." He slowly bent down and grabbed the barrels of each of Odi's Berettas between thumb and forefinger without taking his eyes off Cassi's face. Moving slowly, he walked over to the aquarium and dropped the automatics in, saying "sorry about this, guys," to the fish. The Berettas sank quickly through four feet of water and clanked against a white coral reef at the bottom.

Wiley said, "Why don't we all sit down and talk."

Cassi looked from Wiley to Odi to Wiley again. She blinked once and then walked toward Wiley with the Colt raised in her hand. Her face was puffy and her eyes were void of expression. In that moment, Wiley realized that he had underestimated the strength of the love that bound the twins. He had bet that Cassi would prefer to believe his trauma-victim explanation over Odi's deeply wounding truth. He had lost.

Wiley's mind raced through alternatives as Cassi drew closer. He could bolt from the room, or he could try to snatch the gun, counting in both cases on her reluctance to shoot him. As she closed the gap he decided on the latter. He wanted this mess to be over. Just before he pounced, Cassi transferred the Colt to her left hand, grabbing the barrel between thumb and forefinger.

Odi yelled, "No!" as Cassi held it up to her left and added it to the fish's collection. "Yes," she said, obviously trying to keep her voice calm. "Let's sit."

As Wiley stared at the three weapons resting impotently on the floor of the tank he felt a surge of relief and a wave elation. He had won.

Chapter 51

Asgard Island, Chesapeake Bay

CASSI LOOKED OVER at Odi through tear-soaked eyes, afraid that her heart would break. Although upset at first, she was now glad that Wiley had broken their agreement and returned early. She did not want to go through this alone. She dropped her weapon in the tank where it settled next to Odi's and then walked over to the couch. Wiley followed.

Odi looked back at her from the other side of the room, his face a mask of desperation. She felt an inexplicable surge of guilt, followed by a sense of foreboding. He walked slowly toward the armchair with his feet shuffling and his head bowed low, the epitome of a beaten man.

In a split second, he changed everything. As Odi drew beside the chair he scooped the marble cigar ashtray off the end table and whirled around like he was holding a discus. He completed one full turn and then launched the rock straight into the center of the aquarium.

The enormous glass panel cracked into a spider's web as the ashtray soared through. There was a catastrophic crash followed by the sound of three hundred gallons of furious water and a hundred doomed fish spewing onto the beige carpeted floor. Cassi and Wiley both shot out of their chairs as the living rainbow began to thrash and flop.

Odi dove into the writhing school toward the nearest Beretta. Cassi heard a gunshot as the Beretta jumped off the floor an inch before Odi's hand. "Don't move, Carr," a new voice shouted from the doorway. "I never miss."

Cassi turned toward the voice as Odi froze.

Stuart was standing there, dressed head to toe in black. Aside from the handgun and accompanying snarl, he looked exactly as he had when Wiley brought him to her loft for brunch. His dark eyes flashed with cold intensity behind silver spectacles as he spoke. "Lie on your stomach with your hands behind your back. If you try another funny move, I'll put the next bullet in your sister."

Cassi looked from Stuart to Odi to Wiley. "Wiley, what's going on? Tell your friend to put his gun away."

Wiley rose and picked the three wet automatics off the floor. "I'm sorry," he said, not meeting her eyes. "You should have listened to your brother."

Cassi felt the blood drain from her face. The room began to spin. It couldn't be. Wiley couldn't ... Wiley wouldn't ... "Wiley ... ?"

"I didn't expect it to come to this. Your brother is a little too resourceful." Wiley slipped the two Berettas beneath his belt and used the Colt to motion Cassi toward the floor.

Cassi had no strength to resist. Stuart pressed her face into the saturated carpet as he bound her hands using thick black zip ties extracted from his pocket. A dying fish gasped for air an inch from her face. She knew exactly how it felt.

She turned to look at Odi. Stuart had him similarly bound and positioned. He was drenched and bleeding from a dozen cuts, some still embedded with aquarium glass. Guilt overwhelmed her as she asked her brother, "What resourcefulness are they talking about?"

Odi said, "I've been a fool. I've been used." He looked up at Wiley. "What are your plans for the explosive?"

"What explosive?" Cassi asked, now totally confused.

"He's referring to the two gallons of custom brew that he gave our mutual friend," Stuart said, unzipping Odi's backpack and pulling out a bottle of what looked like milk. "What he really should be concerned about is this pint." He shook the bottle as Odi groaned. Then Stuart produced a long funnel and Cassi saw tears appear in her brother's eyes. She had not seen Odi cry since the day their parents died. The sight curdled her rage into fear.

"Your brother really is a remarkable cook," Stuart continued. "I think it's time you enjoyed a taste."

Chapter 52

Asgard Island, Chesapeake Bay

ODI GAGGED on the end of the funnel as Stuart forced the tip into his throat. He was pinned on his knees with Wiley behind him and Stuart in front. Wiley had a knee planted between his shoulder blades and was pulling back hard on his elbows to incapacitate him. Meanwhile, Stuart kept one foot on Odi's crotch for insurance as he prepared to pour. Odi sensed that Stuart would joyfully transfer his weight if he resisted, however Odi was not about to do that. He had lost the will to fight the moment they emptied half a pint of Creamer into his sister. He clenched his eyes and listened to the upturned bottle gurgle as his stomach accepted the cold flowing liquid death.

"You're working with Ayden, aren't you?" Odi asked Wiley, once the bottle had been emptied and the funnel withdrawn from his mouth. "Were you working with him from the start?"

"No, we have you to thank for introducing us," Stuart interjected.

Odi kept his eyes on Wiley. "I figured it all out, everything except one key question."

Wiley raised his eyebrows.

"Why do it? You have so much to lose."

"Let's just say that I'm a hero in need of a war."

As Wiley spoke, Odi saw Cassi staring at him, tears still running down her eyes. Odi could not begin to imagine what she must be feeling. Perhaps the Creamer was a blessing. All her sorrows would vanish in about thirty minutes.

Odi had brought the Creamer to Asgard to use on Wiley, so he accepted this turnabout as fair play. Part of him even thought that he deserved it. But he could not accept what Wiley was doing to his sister. She had given Wiley nothing but love and devotion. Now she had eight grenades worth of explosive sloshing around in her belly as thanks.

"The plan to assassinate the Senate Armed Services Committee— was that real, or another red herring?" Odi pressed.

Wiley grew a wry smile. "Oh, the idea Ayden presented was very real. I fear, however, that our mutual friend misled you on the tactics."

"How so?" Odi asked.

Wiley looked over at Stuart, who had been standing there silent and expressionless with an automatic gripped professionally in each hand.

Stuart nodded, his message clear. With the Creamer already congealing in their opponents' bowels, they had nothing to fear from that revelation.

"Do you know what day it is?" Wiley asked, turning back to Odi. "What date?"

"October twelfth," Cassi interjected with venom in her voice.

"Precisely. First there was 9/11. Now there will be 10/12. Just as The Prophet warned."

Odi had not caught on to the calendar aspect, but otherwise he was not surprised. "So it's even bigger than what Ayden proposed? Bigger than the SASC? What are you going to do, take out the Capitol? Two gallons of Creamer is a lot, but it's not nearly enough for that."

Wiley returned an amused smile. "The SASC won't be in the

Capitol this afternoon. They're going home. They're flying home."

Odi felt a frigid iron vise take hold of his heart and begin to squeeze. His parents had died aboard a plane on 9/11. So had many others'. "Twenty-five airplanes," he thought aloud. "That's thousands of innocent souls."

"We're hoping to get six thousand—double the casualties of 9/11 —but we expect it will turn out closer to five. A lot depends on where the planes hit the ground. In any case, it won't make a good advertisement for Baileys Irish Cream." Wiley paused to admire his own wit. "Oh, and just to be accurate, it's only going to be twenty-four planes. SASC Chairman Marshall is not flying home. He's taking a cruise. The Senator is going to England, aboard the Queen Mary 2 no less."

Odi cringed but did not comment.

Wiley continued. "There is one particular operational detail that I'm sure will hold your interest. Believe it or not, Ayden is going to handle Marshall personally. He considers it an honor." Wiley chuckled. "Actually, Ayden's mission will bring terrorism to a whole new level, an elite level. What location could strike closer to home for the world's elite than the fanciest suite on the most luxurious ship? The QM2 may not sink, but a terrorist attack aboard it will strike home with the rich, and evoke a tidal wave of campaign donations."

"How could you, Wiley? How could you become such a monster?" Cassi spit the bitter words through her torrent of tears. "You were a good man, a decent man ... I loved you."

"Love often requires sacrifice, my dear. To answer your question, only a man in full control of his emotions can hope to survive the electoral process. It's part of the hazing ritual. To join the fraternity of presidents, one must prove himself capable of despicable acts—and for good reason. You see, for all their wealth and position, the American people can't afford the luxury of a Commander-in-Chief who will waiver when the time comes to pull the nuclear trigger."

It was obvious to Odi that Cassi wanted to retort, but apparently the words would not come—only more tears.

"We're going to leave you now," Wiley continued, picking up the remote control. "Stuart and I have much to do. You two enjoy the rest of your lives."

Chapter 53

Ronald Reagan Washington National Airport

AYDEN FELT his anxiety peak as he watched Amir reach the front of the security line. He looked perfect. Polished shoes, a crisp navy suit topped with rimless spectacles and platinum tie. A *Wall Street Journal* adorned with a Grand Hyatt sticker completed the disguise. But the scanner would not be looking at the man ...

"Your identification and boarding pass please."

Amir handed the requested documents to the TSA officer. It was ridiculous how many times you had to do this, Ayden thought. Did the bureaucrats really think that terrorists could not afford to go online and buy a ninety-nine dollar ticket?

The Idaho driver's license Amir presented was not real, of course. For that matter, the matching boarding pass was unlikely to be used. The twenty-four martyrs had checked-in online the day before. Each had booked himself on three or four sequential flights under differing aliases. Although Director Proffitt had supplied Ayden with the list of the SASC Senators' flight reservations, plans were known to change as meetings ran long or finished unexpectedly short. With multiple tickets, each martyr would be ready to board with his assigned Senator no matter which flight His Honor actually took.

Ayden watched Amir's progress over the shoulder of the lady in line between them. His colleague was a rock, or perhaps more appropriately, a rolling stone. He acted respectful but bored as the guard finished his perfunctory perusal. Then he put on the requisite thank-you-officer smile as the guard nodded like a dog approving of his biscuit.

Amir put his bag on the scanner belt.

The lady who had been separating them in line stepped aside unexpectedly as her cell phone rang. Suddenly it was Ayden's turn. It took all his willpower to keep his nervous eyes off the guard inspecting Amir's bag as he handed over his boarding pass and driver's license.

Ayden had run each refilled miniature Baileys Irish Cream bottle through the dishwasher six times, so he was confident that the agents, their bags, and the bottles themselves would pass a random swab test.

The luggage scanners might be a different story.

During his discussion with the woman pretending to be Sheila, Odi had asserted that Creamer would pass through security scanners like a bottle of milk. Ayden had repeated Odi's claim with certainty to his twenty-four friends, although as his sweaty palms now testified, he had serious doubts. It was highly unlikely that Odi was up to date on the latest scanning technology. The field was changing too fast. Yesterday Ayden had pushed that worry aside because he had no choice. Now that the ball was in play, he felt weak in the knees.

As Ayden walked through the metal detector, his heart jumped into his mouth. A guard had picked up Amir's plastic quart bag as it emerged from the scanner. Ayden walked to stand behind Amir, straining to hear while trying to make nervous look like impatient. He wished he had taken one of the Diazepam tablets that Arvin had him give the martyrs. His nerves were not well suited for this kind of work.

"Do you have anything unusual in here?" The guard asked, no sign of alarm in his voice.

"No," Amir said, "just toiletries ... and uh, my breakfast."

As the guard held the bag up his face registered comprehension. "Expecting a tough day at the office, eh?"

"You have no idea," Amir replied, his tone remarkably cool.

The fat guy putting on his shoes in front of Amir looked back, saw the bag full of miniature bottles of Baileys, and nodded appreciatively.

Amir was quick on his feet, Ayden noted, not without a touch of pride. He also had a gift for words. Ayden had not told the martyrs what to say in the testimonial videos each had made for release in the coming days. He had just told them to tell the American people why they had chosen to do this. Arvin had pointed out that their testimonials would be much more persuasive if the world could see the un-coached conviction in their eyes and sense the sincerity in their voices. If Ayden had written a text, however, it would have read like Amir's. His arguments were an oversimplification, to be sure, but political sound bites always were. He wiped a tear from his cheek as he remembered the words delivered by the handsome, well-coiffed man before him in flawless American English.

My friends and I do not wish to die. Quite to the contrary, we want the same thing as you. We want to better our children's lives. Unlike you, however, our situation is desperate. Desperate enough to do ... this.

You all harbor a deep desire for world peace. It's in America's blood. It's the default answer in every religious sermon, political race, and beauty pageant. Yet despite all your means and rhetoric, all your promises and potential, and all your fine examples of individual and private efforts, your government is actively working against it.

Your politicians are the problem.

Our action today is a result of their inaction yesterday. We do this destructive act in the hope of building a better tomorrow. My colleagues and I are executing the twenty-five members of the Senate Armed Services Committee in order to shed light on their crimes. The American voters deserve to see the enormous gap that exists between these politicians' promises, and their deeds.

They spout bromides about Christianity, democracy, education, and world peace much as a fountain does water—with great volume and much show but little thought. Then they quietly shovel billions out the back door and into the pockets of their war-mongering corporations in exchange for campaign contributions.

We hope that the sacrifice we make today gives the good people of America the chance to reevaluate the world, to see it not as the 'Us' and 'Them' politicians peddle, but for what it really is: one people under God.

Chapter 54

Asgard Island, Chesapeake Bay

CASSI WATCHED open mouthed as Odi sprang from the floor, instantly recognizing the desperate act of a man with nothing to lose. She remembered his line from the Potchak video: The only antidote to Creamer is death. Since Odi's hands were bound behind his back, he tried to ram Wiley with his head. Cassi wanted to join him but before she could rise she saw Stuart's Beretta flash and heard the sickening crack of metal on bone as he brought the butt down on the back of Odi's charging head.

"You bastard!" She screamed.

Stuart turned to point the Beretta at her face.

She ignored the gun barrel inches from her nose and gave Wiley a contemptuous stare. He and Stuart backed out the door. As Wiley lifted the remote control, Cassi screamed, "Wiley, for God's sake, don't do this!"

"It's already done," Wiley said. Then he dialed the non-emergency code, and pressed the red panic button.

The door slammed closed and Cassi heard bolts sliding into place. Titanium shutters began rolling down to cover the bulletproof windows. In seconds the study would be a fortress. For the second time in as many days, she was locked in a room with a bomb. At least this time she was not alone. And for better or worse, she could not see the clock. On the downside, she was the bomb. Escape was not an option. Strangely enough, Cassi found that fact calming.

She struggled to her feet and used a shoulder to turn on the lights as the shutters dropped into place. She walked over to Odi and knelt down beside him. He had a nasty lump where Stuart's pistol butt had cracked the back of his head, but he was breathing.

"Odi ... Odi wake up ... Wake up. I need your help."

He did not respond.

She repeated herself, louder.

Still nothing.

She gave him a vigorous nudge with her knee and then turned her attention to the floor. She needed to find a piece of glass sharp enough to cut her bonds. Unfortunately the aquarium had shattered like a car windshield. It lay strewn about the floor in a thousand little pieces. She knew that this was a safety feature, but in her case it would do more harm than good. Most of the pieces were far too small to be of use.

After brushing a dead fish aside with her foot, she spotted a triangular piece wedged into the thick carpet pile. It was more round than pointed, and each side was less than two inches long. Still, it was better than any other piece available, so it would have to do. She squatted and found it with her fingers. Picking it up, she rotated it to feel each side. The edges were only mildly sharp. "No problem," she told herself. "You can compensate for sharpness with force." A few seconds later she knew that she had spoken too soon. It was too small and slippery to afford a forceful grip.

She stood and walked over to the desk and leaned against it so that if she dropped the glass, it would not fall far. As she scraped the edge against the tough zip-tie, she continued shouting Odi's name. She knew that he would not be able to change their lot. Death was the only antidote. But that was not the point. Odi would want to face his fate head-on, teeth gritted and eyes opened wide. Since she had put him in this position, she owed him that final wish. For her part, she wanted to go out of this world as she had come into it—holding her twin brother's hand.

Trying to sever her bonds, Cassi lost her grip on the shard more often than not. Each fumble rewarded her with another gash in her palm or wrist. Adding insult to injury, the slippery blood made it even harder to work. She ignored the pain and kept at it. What else could she do? After two more fruitless minutes, however, Cassi realized that her current approach was not going to work. At least not in time. She needed to find another way to free her hands.

She considered slitting her wrists and lying down to die beside her unconscious brother—but only for a second. Wiley had her ire up. She wanted to go out fighting. She wanted to leave a note, an accusatory message from the grave. To do that properly, she had to free her hands.

Cassi turned and began looking about Wiley's desk for something sharp. The desk itself was glass, so there were no drawers. She looked into his pewter FBI pencil holder. It held a miniature broadsword that functioned as a letter opener. Her hopes jumped until she saw that it too was made of pewter, a soft metal. She dumped the pencil holder out onto the desk to test the edges just in case. They were dull as Des Moines. She studied the remainder of the spilled contents. There was the usual assortment of short wooden golf pencils and logo stamped ink pens. Her eye jumped to the single shiny object and she felt a glimmer of hope. Winking at her from the desk was a pair of nail clippers.

She found it slow going, trying to maneuver the tiny object behind her back with slippery fingers and bound hands. Oddly enough, it even left her struggling for breath. She did not care. It was working. The nail clippers were making headway against the tough plastic. She had gotten nearly halfway through when her eyes darted from the zip tie to her hands. The sight she saw brought the terror of the moment crashing home, provoking a guttural scream. Despite the blood she could clearly see that the tips of her fingers were blue.

Chapter 55

Asgard Island, Chesapeake Bay

ODI JOLTED AWAKE to the sound of his sister screaming. He looked in the direction of her voice and asked, "What happened?"

As he spoke, Cassi's hands flew out from behind her back and a shiny object soared across the room. It splashed down near his feet. "Odi, thank God you're awake. Stuart pistol-whipped you."

"Right after Wiley told us of his plans," Odi said nodding, wishing all the while that he could rub the back of his head.

"And made us drink your Creamer," Cassi confirmed.

The urgency of their predicament struck him like a hammer. "How long ago was that? How long was I out?"

"It was about fifteen minutes ago, I think. Look at me." Cassi held up her bloody hands and Odi saw the discolored fingertips. His stomach dropped. They did not have long. The explosive was already sweating, and they had each swallowed the equivalent of eight hand grenades.

"There may still be hope," he said, trying to sound more optimistic than he felt. "Can you free my hands?"

Cassi looked at him with wide eyes and then grabbed the nail clippers off the floor. Ten seconds later Odi's hands were also free.

"We've got to purge our stomachs. Use your finger. Gag yourself." Odi got up on his knees as he spoke and then plunged a finger into his throat after noting that it was not yet blue. The gag reflex came on fast and strong. His throat protested but his stomach began to heave. He ignored the pain. His mind was working overtime now, churning as fast as his stomach. He was desperate to prevent 10/12. He was willing to endure anything for that shot at redemption. He was straining to think of how they could possibly pull off such a miracle when an idea came to him. He pulled his finger from his mouth and shouted, "Wait!"

Cassi looked over at him, obviously scared.

Odi got off his knees and retrieved the plastic wastebasket from the bathroom. After emptying its contents onto the floor, he set it down before her and said, "Vomit into this."

Cassi looked at him funny from the corners of her bloodshot eyes but did not question why.

Over the next couple of minutes they knocked heads a few times over the can, but eventually all their heaves were dry. Cassi had expelled three or four marble sized chunks whereas Odi's effluent looked more like milky peas.

"I've got nothing left," Cassi said, her voice hoarse. "Is it safe to stop?"

Odi was not sure. It did not look like they were accomplishing anything, and there appeared to be roughly a pint of effluent in the bucket, but the penalty for underestimation was severe. "Let's give it a couple more tries."

Thirty seconds later he said, "That's enough."

"Is it really that simple?" Cassi asked.

"I don't know. Probably not. It only takes a few drops to provide a bomb with critical mass. It's time for phase two."

Odi pulled a line of clear plastic tubing from the ruins of the aquarium. "You have to swallow one end. Once you've got it down the right tube, I'll push it all the way down and suck the remaining contents out. It will hurt like hell, but it beats the alternative."

Cassi grew a shade paler, but nodded stoically. His sister was the best.

The next couple minutes went by in a disgusting, painful blur as Odi purged Cassi and she returned the favor. He kept stealing subtle glances at the tips of her fingers, and was encouraged to see that they had gotten no worse.

With phase two complete, Odi ran back to the half bath and flung open the medicine chest. He saw Aspirin, Band-Aids, Triaminic, and Mylanta. "Bingo." He grabbed the green plastic bottle and gave it a good shake. It was nearly full. He tossed it to Cassi. "Drink this. The acid in your stomach catalyzes the reaction. No acid, no explosion. In case we didn't get it all, this should neutralize any Creamer that's left."

Cassi drank half the bottle in the time it took Odi to walk back to her. She gave the Mylanta back to him. Odi guzzled the rest and wiped his lips with the back of his hand.

"What do we do now?" Cassi asked. "We're still stuck here in Wiley's panic room, completely incommunicado. Six thousand people are about to die. Tell me you have a plan."

"Of course I have a plan, Sis. That's why we threw up into the wastebasket. You can help out by getting me some coffee filters. There should be some under the bar."

While she searched, he took the basket off Mr. Coffee. Then he grabbed the wastebasket and set it next to the bar's small sink.

"Here you go. What else can I do?" Cassi asked.

Odi put two clean filters into the basket and positioned it over the sink. "You hold the filter-basket," he said. "I'll pour."

The milky liquid seemed to take forever to drain through the filter. As it dripped out the bottom, Odi studied Cassi's hands. They were regaining their original color. His had never changed. Although he had no empirical evidence, intuition told him that this was a very good sign. "Why don't you wash up and make use of the Band-Aids. To get out of here, you're going to need your hands."

"Okay," Cassi said. " But while I'm doing that will you tell me what's going on?"

"The acid in your stomach causes the explosive to congeal like curdling milk. As the process progresses, the curds combine with one another. Eventually only larger curds are left and they form a crust. The crust sweats a substance toxic to hemoglobin. That is why your extremities turn blue. By drinking the antacid, we raised the pH in our stomachs, halting the reaction. Now all we need to do is keep the pH in our stomach neutral until everything passes into the small intestine, where the pH is too high to catalyze the reaction."

"But the explosive is still there," Cassi said, panic apparent in her voice.

"Yes, but there's nothing to set it off. Think of it as a hand grenade with the pin still in. It's safe to carry around." The thought of adding just don't fart flashed across Odi's mind, but he thought better of it. His sister did not always appreciate his humor.

He used a few more filters to dry out the congealed explosive further. "Is my memory right? Do the bolts on the door enter the frame on both sides?"

"That's right."

Odi began inspecting the frame, looking for the bolts between the cracks. "But not on the top or the floor?"

"I don't think so," Cassi said. "Definitely not on the floor."

"Let's hope you're right. There are only two lamps."

"Huh?"

"There are three ways to detonate most explosives: chemistry, pressure, and electricity."

Odi took a brass lamp off the desk and its twin from the end table as he spoke. He removed the white shades, the shade supports, and the bulbs. He cleared everything else off Wiley's desk and said, "Grab that end. We need to set this down in front of the door."

Cassi assisted without question.

Once the desk was flush against the door, Odi took the lamps and laid them sideways. He lined up the sockets so that they were directly in front of the door bolts. Then he bent the lampshade and used it as a prop to get the level just right.

Once satisfied, he split the explosive in half and then halved it again. Cassi watched him pack one-quarter of the explosive putty between the door and frame at the location of each bolt, leaving a protuberance. With that accomplished he packed each empty light socket, again leaving some run-over. He laid the lamps on the desk once finished, and slid each carefully toward the door until the bits of explosive made solid contact.

"Bring me that extension cord," he asked Cassi, pointing toward the desk. She did so and Odi plugged both lamps into extension-cord sockets. "Now comes the fun part."

Being careful not to disturb the lamps, Odi trailed the extension cord into the bathroom, and then motioned for Cassi to join him. Once she was inside, he closed the solid door. "Crouch down in the corner with your knees covering your chest," he pointed, "and plug your ears."

Cassi did not require any explanation. She rushed to do as she was told.

Odi placed the end of the extension cord over an outlet and then looked over at her. "Here goes ..."

Chapter 56

The SS Norse Wind, Chesapeake Bay

WILEY LOOKED DOWN at his hands as they gripped the yacht's wheel. No white knuckles, no jitters. He had gotten through the Asgard confrontation distancing himself from the spasms of his own heart. He had frozen his emotions, and they had yet to thaw. It had still been the most difficult five minutes of his life. But he had known going in that the third-person approach would be the only way to get through it, and he had prevailed. He had prevailed without a hint of weakness because Stuart had been by his side.

Now that it was over and Cassi's blood stained his hands, Wiley had expected to be feeling sick. He expected to be spending this boat ride back to the mainland retching over the rail while Stuart looked on in disgust. But he was not sick. He had not thrown up over the rail. In fact, he wanted breakfast. Looking from his hands to the mainland he felt only one emotion: relief.

Emboldened by this discovery, he allowed his thoughts to wander to the Tiffany box and the promise it held. It seemed a distant memory now, like a fond but forgotten childhood memory. He pondered this unexpected emotional twist, searching for deeper meaning as the Norse Wind cut through the waves. As they neared the marina, he figured it out. Cassi had been spoiling his dream. This was supposed to be the most magical time of his life, a time of self-realization and tremendous professional growth. Instead, he had been stuck in a quagmire of doubt, bogged down by worthless guilt. With Cassi gone he was unencumbered, free to grow. Her death had lifted a tremendous weight from his back. Destiny was once again marching by his side. He felt powerful, purposeful, and brave.

With Cassi and Odi both out of the way, he expected smooth sailing and clear skies—at least metaphorically speaking. The rising sun had ducked behind a thick bank of clouds shortly after it cleared the horizon. Now the temperature was beginning to drop.

He saw a dock boy standing ready, eager to be of assistance, and for a second his mind flashed to the Marines ever guarding the president. He saluted the boy and eased off on the engines. As the yacht dropped lower in the water, Stuart gave him a funny look. Stuart knew what he had been thinking.

Wiley looked at his thick titanium watch. It was early enough that he could still make it to the office on time.

While tossing a line to the dock boy, a shocking thought blazed through his mind like lightning from above. He let fly a panicked "Shit!"

The dock boy jumped back.

"What is it?" Stuart asked.

Wiley stepped back into the cabin and lowered his voice. "Can you handle the boat?"

"Yes. Why? What happened? What's wrong?"

"We forgot the security video."

Stuart's jaw dropped.

Wiley stamped his foot three times on the deck. "Damn, damn, damn!" He looked at Stuart. "You have to go back!"

"Okay."

"You have to go back to Asgard right now and get the recording!"

"Okay."

"That video will show everything. You have to get it now. The panic room is engineered to withstand assault, but we used a lot of Creamer. If someone heard the explosion or saw the smoke they might have called the Coast Guard to check it out. You have to beat them to it. Hell, you have to be gone before they arrive."

"Okay, Wiley. Get out of here. Go be seen in the office. I'll take care of it."

"The recorder is right above the monitor we watched. It's in the cupboard on the wall. Actually, every monitor has its own recorder. You better take all the DVDs just to be safe. Plus, that way I can say I never got around to reloading the recorders after the last batch ran out."

"Will do."

Wiley picked up his duffel bag and jumped onto the dock. He handed the dock boy a twenty and said, "You can leave us now. He's going back out."

As the boy ran off, Wiley looked back up at his coconspirator. "Don't come back without that video, Stuart. You know what happens to people like us in jail."

Chapter 57

Asgard Island, Chesapeake Bay

CASSI CLOSED HER EYES and held her breath as Odi plugged in the extension cord. She heard a sputtering sound come through the closed bathroom door and wondered if it was the last sound she would ever hear. She had already survived one explosion of late. Was two too much to ask?

Odi tightened his grip on her shoulder. Then she heard a deafening boom. A hard rain of debris followed. It sounded as though a giant were whipping handfuls of pebbles against the walls. Cassi guessed that the stones were really glass shrapnel from Wiley's desk.

Odi held her in place for a few seconds more until everything settled down. A wisp of smoke crept under the bathroom door as they waited. Cassi worried that the house might be on fire. Odi shook his head as though reading her mind. He said, "The smoke is just a byproduct of the blast. It's not a threat." Then he released her arm, stood, and opened the door.

The first thing she saw was a big hole in the wall in the place where the door had been. She shuddered at the sight, joyful though it was. The bomb that wrought that destruction had been inside her body. She would never feel pure again.

Looking around, she felt like an evacuee returning home after a hurricane. There were a thousand little rips in the black leather couch and pockmarks all around the walls. Cassi looked back at the door to the bathroom. Bits of glass were embedded like cupcake sprinkles all up and down the wood. The result was a cross between modern art and a medieval torture device, although structurally it was not damaged. The windows had also held. She realized that without Odi's bomb, they would never have escaped.

"Let's get out of here," Odi said.

"You read my mind," Cassi replied. "Just give me a second to swap Wiley's wet pajamas for my regular clothes."

While zipping up her jeans, Cassi had a thought that would not wait. She picked up her shoes and ran barefoot down the hallway to the security closet. She flung open the door to see six flat-panel monitors, each showing a different room. She found the recorder for Wiley's study and rewound the video for thirty seconds. Before pressing play, she glanced upward in silent prayer. The monitor came back to life with the picture of Odi hurling the marble ashtray into the aquarium. This was better than great. It was fantastic. "I can't believe they forgot this," she called.

"What?" Odi asked, running to stand beside the closet door.

"See for yourself. It's all here. What they did to us is all video recorded."

Cassi sat down on the floor and quickly tied her shoes. Finished, she looked up at her brother and lost her smile. He looked pale. "What's wrong?" She asked, standing up and ejecting the DVD.

"That video may cook Wiley's goose, but it also blows my alibi."

"Your alibi?"

"I was planning to wake up from a coma in Iran once my mission was complete." Odi made quotation marks with his fingers as he spoke.

Cassi understood. She looked down at the DVD in her hand and thought about his situation for a minute. She had temporarily forgotten about Odi's earlier murders. "We'll figure something out later. Tempting though it is, nailing Wiley and Stuart is not our top priority. Stopping 10/12 is. To do that we have to get off this island. How did you get here?"

"Jet Ski."

"Will it fit two people?"

"You bet."

Cassi smiled. "Finally, we catch a break."

Odi led her across the lawn in the opposite direction from the marina. They moved at a slow run, discussing strategy and the events of the last few weeks as they went. Once they cleared the manor house lawn they entered a deciduous forest. A few of the birches still had golden leaves, but most of the limbs were bare. It was beautiful and innocent, the polar opposite of how she should have felt, yet something about being there with Odi gave her hope.

Odi lurched to a halt after about five minutes. Cassi was surprised to find that the forest went right up to the cliff's edge and realized that this was no place to be running blind. She peered over the edge and saw the Jet Ski below.

Odi said, "Oh shit."

"What is it?"

"The keys are gone. I started to take them with me but then figured that they would be confiscated if I was captured so I left them right here on this rock as insurance." He pointed to a flat-topped boulder. "Now they're gone." He bent down and began searching the grass around the rock. Cassi joined him, searching the side of the cliff as well. After a few minutes they decided that it was hopeless. The keys were gone.

"Do you think Wiley took them?"

"If he saw me coming he would have. But I don't think he did. My money is on one of those crows. He pointed at three black figures on a neighboring tree. I thought I was being clever, but it appears that I was outwitted by a bird."

"What do we do now?" Cassi asked

"Go back to the marina and wait for the Coast Guard."

"What makes you think they're coming?"

"I'm going for a swim."

Cassi could not believe what her brother was proposing. "You can't do that. You'll freeze."

"I've got a wetsuit, and the eastern shore is much closer than the western one. It looks like it's only a mile."

"Tell that to the sharks."

~ ~ ~

On any other day, Cassi would have found Odi's plan preposterous. Today it was de rigueur. After watching him disappear into the waves, she walked back through the woods. She heard every cracking twig and each rattling branch but no squirrels or birds. Even the crows were gone. The forest that only moments ago had seemed so refreshing, now felt dead. She found herself acutely aware of being alone. She knew that she had better get used to that feeling. The man with whom she had planned to spend the rest of her life was now destined for disgrace and jail. Or was he? She wondered, feeling a sudden chill.

Cassi drummed her fingers on the DVD in her pocket. She would let Wiley walk if that was the only way to save her brother. There was no question about that. Unless ... Cassi asked herself what she would do if it looked like Wiley would actually become vice president. Would she sacrifice Odi to prevent that? She would have to. No, she corrected herself. What she would have to do was find some other way of stopping Wiley. Some other way ...

She walked past the manor house without stopping and headed straight for the marina. She never wanted to set foot in Wiley's home again. As she stepped onto the cobbled walk, she wondered if she would ever truly understand what had happened. Wiley's actions were so far removed from her current comprehension that she did not know if her mind could twist to an angle that would allow it to make sense.

Of course she would have said the same thing about Odi a few hours earlier and now it was clear that he had charted a rational course. However Wiley's case was different, she decided. He had confessed.

Still drumming her fingers on the DVD, Cassi wondered what it was that had turned Wiley from her? From the life they had, a life that most people would consider ideal? She still believed that he had truly loved her once. Some life-altering event must have occurred. For her sanity's sake, she needed to know what it was. She refused to believe that anything that felt so real could be faked. She suspected that Stuart was the key. She wondered who he really was. Clearly Stuart was not the old college friend that Wiley had portrayed him to be over brunch. Perhaps he was the corrupting influence. Come hell or high water, Cassi promised herself, she would find out.

As Cassi followed the cobbled walk toward the top of the marina's stairs, she looked out across the water. A boat was approaching. Could it be the Coast Guard already? Odi would have to be one hell of a swimmer. But then he was a lot of things. Her heart leapt until she got a better look, then it dropped to her stomach as she dropped to the ground. Wiley was returning.

Chapter 58

Chesapeake Bay

ODI FELT THE COLD WATER of the Chesapeake draining his life —despite his exertion, despite the wetsuit. The bay water could not be more than forty-five degrees. Each time he rolled his face back into the water after sucking in a breath, it felt as though someone were driving a wedge between his eyes. At least the wind was light and the waves were small—for now. The sky was darkening by the minute.

Once his muscles finally warmed and he got up to cruising speed, Odi set his body on autopilot and attempted to focus on the problems before him rather than the deathly cold. He had a cart-full. He had to stop bombings on twenty-four airplanes and one cruise ship. He had to rescue Cassi. He had to catch Ayden, Stuart, and Wiley. He had to do it all in a matter of hours. He had no money, no transportation, no disguise, and no weapon.

Trying to piece together a plan, Odi took a nose full of brine as yet another obstacle marched across the battlefield in his mind. Whatever he did he was going to have to do without being identified or even seen. That was no short order. Cassi had told him that Wiley had issued an APB for a terrorist who matched his description and was using his name. It was a clever move. It blocked Odi from approaching the media, the press, or any government officer—at least today, given his time constraints. With one clever move Wiley had isolated his opponent, and forced him to work alone.

Odi began to prioritize as he stroked and kicked. The first thing he needed was a solid timetable. Wiley had indicated that the bombings would take place "that afternoon." That gave him hope. If it were true, then there should be time for him to call the Coast Guard, for the Coast Guard to rescue Cassi, and for Cassi to call to the FBI in time to stop the suicide bombers.

To confirm the timing, Odi planned to pull the schedule of the Senate Armed Services Committee off the Internet. He would also check the Queen Mary 2's schedule to see when she was scheduled to depart New York. Once Cassi got out word of the attack, the Chairman of the SASC would either be pulled off the QM2 or guarded by the Secret Service. Ayden, however, would not know that. He would still board the ship. Odi would board it too. Ayden was his.

Odi had no doubt that Ayden had purchased his ticket under an assumed name. Odi did not have that option. He did not have time to generate a fake ID with matching credit card. Stealing a set was also out for obvious reasons. He decided that his best chance of getting aboard the QM2 would be to mug and replace a sailor.

The more he thought about it, the more he decided that mugging was the way to go. It should not be too difficult, he tried to convince himself. He would just hang around near the NYC Cruise Terminal looking for a tall white guy with a QM2 duffel bag. Psst. Hey, Bud …

Now that he knew how to leap the highest hurdle, he began thinking about the hurdles that were closest at hand. He still had to get from the middle of the Chesapeake Bay to Manhattan. As Odi considered his options he felt something brush by his foot. It brought him out of his autopilot trance. Sharks were not unknown in Chesapeake waters. He recalled Cassi's warning but brushed it off. What were the odds? He had already been Tasered, left to burn in a gaseous explosion, and filled full of liquid explosive today. The rule of three worked against adding "shark attack" to that list.

He looked up to take note of his position and scan the waves for fins. He had swum further than he thought. That was the day's first pleasant surprise. A few hundred more bits of good news and he would be even.

Odi was able to make out the details of waterfront houses now. They appeared to be very nice, much nicer than Charlotte's modest cottage. As he stroked on, a plan began to take form. He changed his course slightly, heading directly for the nearest bay-front residence rather than the vacant lot he had been targeting. He estimated that he would reach the shore in ten minutes at about eight o'clock. Some of the locals should be leaving their houses at that time, heading for work …

Chapter 59

Near the New York City Cruise Terminal

ONCE THE WAITRESS finally set down their espressos and departed, Ayden asked Arvin, "How did you enter the country?" He heard relief and surprise in his own voice, and tried to mask it with a calmer clarification. "I mean, aren't you on a list or something?"

The Iranian smiled a bemused smile. "Lists only catch people who don't know they're on them. Once you know, they pose no problem."

Ayden wanted to know the specifics of Arvin's assertion, but he was afraid to ask. He did not want to seem naïve. Despite everything that he had already accomplished for Arvin—recruiting Odi, guiding him, deceiving him, supporting him, and finally killing him—Ayden still felt a compulsion to prove himself to Arvin. The man had incredible charisma.

Either Arvin read his face or he just happened to be in a pedagogical mood, for he did go on to explain his assertion. "I flew into Toronto and drove down from there." He grinned and shook his head in amusement. "I barely had to slow the car at the border as I waved a fake passport. If they had turned me around I would have flown into Mexico and crossed via the tomato-picking pipeline. Or," he nodded his head back toward the dark mountain of steel resting in the harbor behind them, "if I felt like crossing the border in style and didn't mind spending some cash, I would have flown to a Caribbean island and convinced a passenger to let me replace him for the homebound stretch of the cruise."

Ayden nodded. You heard so much about border security these days that he had just assumed that entering the US illegally could not be easy. "So all the hype about border security, all the boarding-pass checks and Homeland Security measures …"

"They're just for show. Keeps the voting taxpayers docile while rewarding campaign contributors with fat homeland defense contracts."

"Still," Ayden pressed, "I don't understand why you risked coming personally?"

Arvin reached out across the tiny table and put his hand on Ayden's shoulder. Then he flashed a smile that made Ayden feel warm all over. "This is your big day, Ayden. I'm proud of you. The son of an orphaned Iranian immigrant is about to change the world. This is an historical moment. I want to be able to say that I was there with Ayden Archer on 10/12."

Ayden saw tears forming in the corners of Arvin's mesmerizing eyes. He looked down, embarrassed.

"I've heard from the other twenty-four," Arvin continued after a moment's pause. "Each is in position near his assigned gate. No one had an issue with security. Meanwhile the SASC is still in committee, so you should be able to get to the chairman before his colleagues begin falling from the sky. And," he brought his palms together, "there's more good news. I finally learned the details of Marshall's diet. He goes through a gallon of coffee a day—lots of cream, lots of sugar. So you won't need to mix Creamer into gravy or soup."

"How on earth did you learn that?"

"I had a friend seduce one of his administrative assistants. They're all trained never to mention business, but it's natural enough to joke about bringing the senator his coffee. She said that everyone on the staff brings him a fresh mug whenever he summons them to his office. It's an unspoken rule."

Ayden nodded appreciatively and Arvin switched gears.

"This is for you," Arvin said, handing over an envelope and a small suitcase. "The envelope contains a British passport with your photo and a matching ticket. You're booked into the suite next to Marshall. There's also a credit card for incidental expenses."

"And the suitcase?"

"It contains the uniform of a QM2 steward. I don't have a weapon for you—that would be too risky—but you can use a wine bottle or a Plexiglas towel rod to knock out the steward bringing Senator and Mrs. Marshall their dinner. Then all you will need is Creamer. How much do you have?"

"I've got a whole pint."

"Excellent. That's enough to fill two little pitchers and spike the soup just in case."

The way Arvin said it he made it seem so easy, Ayden thought. Assassinating the Chairman of the Senate Armed Services Committee, getting your car washed, one and the same. He hoped Arvin was right. In any case, Ayden thought, he was about to find out.

Chapter 60

Asgard Island, Chesapeake Bay

CASSI HUGGED the ground behind a sculpted hedge and watched the Norse Wind arrive. It was approaching much too fast. The engines roared into reverse as it neared the dock, making the water boil. The yacht bucked in response but it was too little too late. She watched it career into the iron dock with a deep thud and a grating scrape. Wiley was obviously upset—but he had nothing on her.

The image of Stuart forcing Wiley to do what he had done flashed through her mind, extending a ray of hope. She caught herself grasping for it and shook her head in self-rebuke. She was a professional psychologist, not a teenage girl. She had to face it: the man she loved, the man she had pinned her hopes, her dreams, her very heart on, was a worm.

Stuart jumped onto the dock alone, making Cassi feel all the more foolish. Then insight overwhelmed shame and she understood. They had remembered the surveillance video.

She wondered if Wiley was waiting on the yacht, too racked with guilt to move, or if he was back on the mainland. Sadly enough, she would have to bet on the latter. Wiley was acting purely as a politician now. He would contract out his dirty work.

She continued hugging the hedge until Stuart jogged past, praying to the god of invisibility. Then she low-crawled to the top of the stairs and studied the yacht from above. All appeared quiet, but light was reflecting off the windshield, making it impossible for her to see if anyone was on the bridge.

Grabbing the base of the railing for support, she pulled herself over the cliff's edge until she was dangling beneath the stairs. In that position her feet were still hanging twenty feet above unfriendly rocks, but she was out of the yacht's view. The new vantage gave her a shot of insight. She anchored her feet and pulled the video recording from her jacket pocket. She kissed it and then wedged it into the gap between the top of the cliff and the underside of the highest stair. Now she would have leverage if they caught her. If they didn't, she could always come back for the video. It didn't matter if DVD's got wet, did it?

She brushed that fear aside and began working her way down the underside of the stairs again, aware that Stuart would be returning any second. There was quite a latticework under there. Whoever built the stairs had built them to last. At the bottom she used the dock's bracings to keep above the freezing water. The posts were six feet apart there, so twice she had to stretch her legs in a full split to reach. This left her terribly vulnerable for about five seconds each time, but it was better than getting wet in this weather. Poor Odi. She prayed that he had survived the swim—and summoned the Coast Guard.

She pulled herself up onto the cold iron dock where she was out of view from the bridge and listened. She heard nothing but water lapping the yacht's hull and crashing against the rocks. There was no sign of Wiley but that did not mean that he wasn't there. She wondered how much time she had left. Stuart had undoubtedly reached the security closet by now. He would be less familiar with the system than Wiley, so it would take him a minute to orient himself. He would also note that the explosion had blown out the door to the study and he might take the time to investigate. She wondered if he would note the lack of gore and realize that neither she nor Odi had hosted the blast. If he did, he would bolt for the yacht straight away. She wished she had checked her watch as he walked by. With all the adrenaline now coursing through her system, it was hard to estimate time.

She crawled toward the back of the yacht and pulled herself through the aft gate. After another short pause to listen, she crept to the companionway that led up to the bridge. She crouched there for a moment, trying to picture the contents of the cabin above. She was mentally searching for a weapon. Wiley's binoculars leapt to mind. He had the heavy nautical kind with a thick leather strap. She tried to imagine the scene, mentally practicing her moves. She would barge through the door, grab the strap, and spin into a swing. If Wiley was there, she would knock him out before he had time to react—unless he was ready for her. If she allowed herself to be seen or heard, she would be running into the barrel of a gun.

Cassi took a deep breath and sprang up the stairs as quickly as a frightened cat. Bursting onto the bridge she grabbed the binoculars by the strap and began to pivot. The cabin was in fact empty. Stuart had returned alone.

She scanned the bridge for a handgun just in case. Then she checked the drawers. Nothing. A weapon would have been comforting but it was not crucial. She was about to strand Stuart on the island.

Cassi had little experience behind the wheel of a yacht, just a few playful minutes with Wiley by her side. But she was not concerned about damaging his yacht or any other, so she did not care. She studied the controls for a second to re-familiarize herself, focusing on the throttles and the wheel. Then she pushed the starter. Nothing happened. She pushed again. Zip.

Frustrated now and more than a little bit nervous, she studied the rest of the controls. She saw screens and knobs and switches with labels. She pounded the wheel and cursed the wind. Where was the bloody switch marked go?

She remembered the ship-to-shore radio and enjoyed a flash of hope. She could call for help and get instructions on how to start the bloody boat. She reached up for the mike and caught empty space. Her eyes began to tear as she stared at the socket.

She thought of everything she had been through during this last hour: Wiley's betrayal, Odi's Creamer, the retching, the explosion. Then she thought of Odi plowing through that freezing surf. After all that, she could not allow herself to be foiled by something as simple as the failure to find a switch.

As Cassi considered the option of flipping every switch and hitting each button, she spotted an empty chrome hub to the right of the wheel. The sight of it made her collapse into the captain's chair. Stuart had taken the keys. "The mike and the keys," she muttered. He was one meticulous bastard.

As she flopped backwards into the captain's chair, Cassi heard a sharp crack coming from inches in front of her face. She snapped her head up and saw a spider's web of cracks in the windshield. The web had a hole in the center. The agent in her recognized the hole as a .38 —not that it really mattered. Stuart had returned. The angle of the sun must have changed, allowing him to see her from the top of the marina's stairs. Obviously he had decided to fire straight off, perhaps thinking that she had a spare set of keys.

She rolled out of the chair and onto the floor as she heard another crack and saw a second spider web appear. He was definitely firing from atop the stairs. His intentions and tactics were abundantly clear. Since she did not have keys, the boat was a dead-end trap. Cassi had just one move.

She leapt down the yacht's aft companionway in a single bound and sprinted for the stern. She pumped her arms as she ran, forcing oxygen deep into her lungs. She wanted to glance back to see if she had been spotted, to check if life-threatening bullets were about to fly, but she did not dare. Milliseconds mattered. Without hesitation or a second thought, she sprang with all her might and dove headfirst over the rail.

Chapter 61

Asgard Island, Chesapeake Bay

STUART HEARD the splash and knew instantly what it meant. He bounded down the remaining stairs a half-dozen at a time and ran down the dock toward the back of the yacht, arms pumping, finger wrapped around the trigger guard. Cassi was nowhere to be seen and the turgid waters told no tales. He tried to guess what direction she would swim, hoping to head her off. If he guessed wrong, she would escape onto the island. Then he would have a hunt on his hands. Hunting Cassi represented an unexpected complication, but the thought was not entirely unpleasant.

Stuart scanned the deck. He had not seen Odi on the bridge, but there was even money that he had been on the Norse Wind too. Perhaps he still was. Seeing no signs of life, Stuart returned his gaze to the churning water. He knew what he would have done in their place. He would have created a false trail. He would have thrown something heavy overboard and then hidden below deck, hoping to attack his pursuer unawares.

He spun back toward the main cabin and raised his Beretta. He saw nothing but a pair of seagulls. He waved the gun to shoo them in frustration. They ignored him. He considered shooting one to vent his rage, but only for a second. He had never let emotions get the best of him in the past. This was not the time to start.

As he did a quick sweep of the luxurious craft, checking all possible hiding places, he considered his predicament. Until he destroyed that recording and silenced the Carrs, everything he had spent his life pursuing would be up in the air.

So what was his best move? Stuart wondered. His thoughts returned to Odi. Was Odi with his sister, or elsewhere? Thinking about it, he decided that he had only heard one splash. The odds of their hitting the water at the exact same second were slim. Perhaps Odi had left the island the way he had come—either abandoning Cassi in anger or being unable to take her. The latter and more likely option implied that his boat was too small. In any case, Stuart had to hope that the video recording was still on Asgard. If that murder scene ever made it off the island, Stuart would lose his job, his career, and his very freedom. He had to prioritize his actions in order to prevent that from happening.

He decided to circle the island at full speed on the Norse Wind in hopes of intercepting Odi. If Odi's craft was too small to carry Cassi, it was probably also slow. Perhaps it was even a rowboat. Oh, let it be so. Stuart realized that regardless of the craft, he had a chance of catching the seemingly indestructible agent if he hurried. And if he was wrong and Odi was still on the island, well, they would still be there when he got back.

After fishing the keys from his pants pocket with a satisfied smile, he raced to the bridge and brought the powerful engines to life. Without so much as a backward glance, he thrust the throttle into full reverse and sent the Norse Wind surging backwards into the bay. Though his piloting was careless, his search for Cassi was not. He scoured the surrounding cliffs as he backed the yacht away, hoping to see a flash of flesh or a scurry of movement between the slippery rocks. His adrenaline spiked momentarily when he thought he saw a bobbing head, but it was just a cormorant. No matter, he consoled himself. She was not going anywhere. Soon she would be a dead duck. He turned the wheel and pushed the throttle forward to full, roaring after Odi.

By the time he was halfway around the island, Stuart understood that Asgard was crescent shaped, with the marina in the center of the concave side. It faced west across the bay toward Reedville Virginia, where he had just dropped Wiley. Now that he was on the other side for the first time, Stuart saw that it was much closer to land. His spirits sank. The southern end of the Delmarva Peninsula was just a mile or so to the east. Even in a rowboat, Odi could already have made it.

Something white caught Stuart's eye as he glanced back at Asgard. It was bobbing near the base of the cliff. Was it another bird? He asked himself. No, this was too big. He gave the eastern horizon a quick scan for other craft and then turned the yacht back in that direction. He picked up the binoculars and directed them toward the object. His heart leapt as a Jet Ski came into focus. That discovery solved the mystery of Odi's arrival and ruled out his departure. But why were they still on the island? He wondered. The Jet Ski even had two seats. The answer came to him as he piloted the yacht in that direction. Odi must have stolen the Jet Ski when it was low on gas. Now it was out. The Carrs were stranded on the island. And more importantly, so was the video.

Just to be meticulous, Stuart put a bullet through the Jet Ski's ignition switch and another through the gas tank. No sense in taking chances. Perhaps Cassi had been on the Norse Wind looking for gas.

He gunned the yacht's motor and raced back toward the marina. This time he studied the island rather than the waters around. He felt like a knight preparing to siege a castle. He was just one man, but he had the only weapon, and the king and queen could not cross the moat.

As he rounded the southern tip of the island, Stuart caught sight of another vessel. When he saw that it too was making waves for the Asgard marina, he was glad that he had not wasted ammo on the seagulls. Then he saw the orange stripe and felt a tightening in his chest. The approaching craft belonged to the Coast Guard.

Stuart weighed his options. They boiled down to fight or flight. The Coast Guard vessel was smaller than the Norse Wind, but given that it was the maritime equivalent of a State Trooper, it undoubtedly had powerful engines. Flight would be his last-resort. That suited Stuart just fine. He was a fighter. He wondered how the Carrs had summoned the Coast Guard, and more importantly, what information they had conveyed. Had they been able to send a detailed message, he wondered, or just a simple SOS? Stuart knew that it was a dangerous proposition to intercept the Coast Guard without that knowledge, but he really had no other choice. His goose was cooked if they got that video. He would just have to make good use of his favorite weapon. He would have to rely on guile.

Stuart raced the Norse Wind to the midpoint between the Coast Guard and the marina and brought his motors to idle. He was about a quarter mile off shore. He knew that if the sailors were veterans, they would recognize this as a military move. To counterbalance that, he walked out onto the deck, assumed a casual stance, and waved. Body language would be the key to the next few minutes, both his and theirs.

There were only two sailors aboard the Coast Guard craft. The captain had thick white hair and a leathery face, whereas his younger mate sported red hair and freckles. Both men appeared tense. As soon as they were within earshot, Stuart started to fish. He looked at freckles and asked, "I say, are you headed for Asgard?"

Freckles responded without deferring to rank, much to Stuart's relief. He said, "Yes. We got a call."

Stuart had hoped for more information than that. We got a call was a little too vague. He would have to reply in kind. "I'm glad the call got through. Our radio died."

"Was it you who called?"

That was better, Stuart thought. "I'm Stuart, Director Proffitt's

Personal Aide. We thought we were stranded but as you can see we've got the yacht running."

"I recognize the Norse Wind. It's one of the finest on the Bay," the captain said. "Would you mind if we had a look?"

The captain had a friendly expression on his face, but Stuart read business in his eyes. These guys would want to tread lightly with someone as powerful as Wiley, but their trepidation would only get Stuart so far. He knew it would be a mistake not to indulge them. He could always shoot the sailors in a pinch, he figured, but only as a last resort. They would be missed with the first unanswered call, and then the heat would really be on. "Sure, you're welcome aboard."

No sooner had he spoken the words than Stuart remembered the bullet holes in the windshield on the upper bridge. If the Coast Guard saw them, the gig was up. He would have no choice but to shoot them then. He had to try to keep them away from that part of the yacht.

The two sailors conferred and then the captain climbed aboard. Stuart cursed in silence. Killing them had just become twice as difficult. "It's important that one of us stay with the radio," the captain said, inclining his head toward Freckles.

Stuart extended his arm in a sweeping gesture. "Please, enjoy yourself. She's a beaut."

He sat on the stairs to the upper bridge such that the captain would have to ask him to move if he wanted to ascend. He tried to look relaxed as he waited for the captain to complete the fifty-cent tour and chatted idly with Freckles. It took the captain less than two minutes although it seemed like forever. As he approached, Stuart wondered if it would be better to offer to show the captain the upper bridge if he liked, or if he should wait for the captain to ask. When the captain returned, Stuart tried to read his expression, but got nowhere. The salty old dog kept his features neutral. After a moment of awkward silence, the captain placed his hands on his hips, sighed and said, "This is exactly how I'd like to retire."

Stuart returned a genuine smile. The captain was not eyeing the top of the stairs. "I hear you. Say, I'm sorry if we caused you any trouble. Given Mr. Proffitt's job, we're sometimes quick to panic."

"Say, where is Walter? He on the mainland, or the island?"

"You mean Wiley, I assume. I just dropped him on the mainland."

The Captain relaxed with that response. "So what caused your problem? Did you figure it out?"

"Sure did. A battery cable worked its way loose. We routinely disconnect it whenever we know that we won't be taking her out for more than two weeks. Last time we must not have reattached it tightly enough."

The captain nodded. Apparently he had come across that before. "Please give the Governor Captain Latimor's best."

Stuart inclined his head.

He did not relax until the Coast Guard boat grew small on the horizon. Then he checked the magazine of his gun, found it nearly full, and smiled. He had more than enough ammunition to wreck a couple of Carrs.

Chapter 62

Crisfield, Maryland

CROUCHED BEHIND the rear passenger tire of a shiny blue Buick, Odi had to struggle to keep his teeth from chattering as he watched his mark lock the front door of his house. The rotund middle-aged man carried a travel mug of coffee with a muffin balanced on top in one hand and a generic black briefcase in the other. He shuffled unenthusiastically, and the vacuous look of routine was readily apparent in his eyes. Eight o'clock in the morning and the poor soul was already bored. Odi was about to change that.

The man unlocked his Buick with a remote and hopped into the driver's seat. He placed the travel mug in its holder, lay the briefcase on the passenger seat, and set the muffin on top. Blueberry. Odi slid into the back seat as the man reached out to close his door.

The man jumped at the sound of Odi's door closing as though a rattrap had clamped on his ass. He let out a startled cry.

"Good morning," Odi said, trying to sound friendly. "Where are you going?"

"Who the hell are you?"

Odi changed his tone sharply. "I'm the man with a gun to your back. That was your last question. Understand?"

The man turned to face forward and nodded.

"Now," Odi continued, "what is your name?"

"Les."

"Okay, Les, let's drive to work."

"You want to go to my office?"

"No questions," Odi said, pushing his fingers deeper into the upholstered back of the seat. "No noise. Just drive."

The man reversed down his driveway and turned the Buick north.

"Where is your office?"

"Laurel."

"Is that on the way to the Big Apple?"

Les hesitated, then let out a weak, "Yes."

"The fastest way?"

"Yes."

"How far is Laurel from here?"

"About an hour."

"And New York City?"

"Four to six hours, depending on traffic."

Odi nodded to himself. "Do me a favor, Les, and turn the heater on full. I caught a bit of a chill swimming into town."

Les complied without comment. He was a quick learner.

Odi watched the street signs in silence as Les followed his routine. A few miles down Highway 13 they passed a sign that said Laurel 29 miles.

"I need your cell phone," Odi said.

Les hesitated for a second, and then he reached into his breast pocket and produced an iPhone.

Odi accepted it and said, "I'm going to let you off at your office. Afraid I'll be needing your car from there. Meanwhile, I don't suppose you happen to know the number for the Coast Guard?"

Chapter 63

Asgard Island, Chesapeake Bay

CASSI FELT a sense of dread as she watched the Coast Guard ship head for the western horizon. She cursed herself. She might have been able to signal it if she had been just a few seconds faster.

After pulling herself from the freezing water and watching Stuart race off in the Norse Wind, she had run straight for the house and a hot shower. She had indulged herself for too long, soaking the cold and tension away under the hot shower while the Coast Guard approached and then departed. Now she was trapped in another nightmare—with

Stuart.

The Norse Wind was still out there, idling in the bay. Cassi watched it as she contemplated her predicament. She had expected this to be the worst day of her life, knowing that she would be arresting her brother. As it turned out, that was only the beginning, the opening course, the appetizer. Since then she had also been betrayed by her lover, imprisoned in a panic room, forced to swallow a bomb, left to explode, had her stomach pumped, dangled off a cliff, and dodged bullets. Then she had nearly frozen to death while swimming for her life while under fire amidst jagged rocks. And it wasn't even noon. If only she had shown Odi a little more faith, everything might be different.

As horrible as all of today's experiences had been, and regardless of the fact that each would haunt her for the rest of her life, Cassi knew that they were all about to fade to insignificance. She was currently empowered to prevent the next 9/11. She had information that would save thousands of lives. And she was helpless to deliver it.

Any fantasy of trying to swim to shore without a wetsuit had vanished the moment she plunged into the Chesapeake's frigid waters. She had survived the five minutes it took to evade Stuart, but hypothermia would surely suck the life from her bones long before she made it to the nearest shore.

The Norse Wind taunted her, scoffed at her, winked. It was only a quarter mile away out there in the bay, but it might as well be on Mars. She could never reach it. Could she? Could she survive a quarter mile swim in that water? Could she then climb stealthily aboard the yacht and overpower Stuart, an armed man, despite her hypothermic state? She estimated that the odds were a thousand-to-one against her. In fact, she reasoned, that was probably why Stuart was idling there. Flushing her out was exactly what he wanted to do. But despite all that what choice did she have? She could not sit there safe but mute while twenty-four planes were bombed out of the sky. She would never forgive herself. She would rather die trying.

"She would rather die trying," Cassi repeated out loud. It was so commonplace to utter those words. Did she have the courage to live them?

The Norse Wind roared to life as she pondered that thought, sparing her the opportunity to test her mettle. Her flash of relief vanished as quickly as it appeared, however, when Stuart turned the bow toward the marina. The sight filled her with an odd mixture of hope and dread. She was going to get the chance to save the twenty-four planes. All she had to do was get the keys away from Stuart—before he shot her dead.

Chapter 64

The SS Queen Mary 2

AYDEN LEAPT BACK from the suite's peephole as though it was trying to bite him. He could not believe his eyes. From a distance he had found the tall silhouette and confident walk familiar. Now that the man was closer, Ayden could verify the face. Despite the glasses and slicked-back hair there could be no mistake. Odi Carr was walking down the corridor—directly toward his suite.

How did he get free? How did he find me? What is he planning to do? The questions came to Ayden easily. The answers did not. He had no time for interrogatory now anyway. He had to act.

He backed into the bathroom, a champagne bottle clenched in his white-knuckled hand. He tried to think. He had been planning to whack the steward over the head with the bottle when the steward brought the Marshalls their meal. Could he do the same to Odi? He did not see how. He would have lured the steward into his neighboring suite with a desperate plea—then replaced cream with Creamer and delivered the Marshalls' order himself—but he had no chance of catching Odi with such a simple ruse.

Ayden looked down at his hand, noting that it was beginning to sweat. While the hefty champagne bottle would have been fine for a surprise attack on an unsuspecting steward, it was a pathetic weapon against a primed combat veteran like Odi Carr. But what choice did he have? Odi had come to him. Think, Ayden. Think! What would Arvin do? He asked himself. The answer came as though God were whispering in his ear.

Ayden ripped the do-not-disturb sign from the door handle and slid it between the doorframe and the lock, disabling the latch. Satisfied that the door would now swing open beneath a firm knock, he grabbed the extra polyester blanket from the closet. He folded it in half and placed it on the parquet floor like a rug, a very slippery rug. It would not look right if studied, but Odi was hardly going to be paying much attention to the suite's furnishings as he burst into the room. Ayden would sweep the rug out from under Odi before he realized that he was standing on slippery ground, and then he would give him the good news with the bottle.

Ayden returned to the bathroom and picked up the champagne bottle, certain that he had not a second to spare. "Come on, come on," he mouthed, wiping his sweaty palms on his black steward's pants as he shifted the bottle between hands.

The knock did not come. Nor did Odi attempt to use a key. Ayden waited and listened, assuming that Odi was out there doing the same. After a moment he loosened his tie, hoping to get more blood to his brain. He waited some more. Nothing. Not a sound. Finally, unable to take it anymore, he flung open the door, holding the champagne bottle high.

The corridor was empty.

He backed into his suite, puzzled but relieved that no one had seen him. Then he got it. So much for God's whisper. Odi did not know that he was there. He had come to warn the man in the neighboring suite. He had come to warn Marshall.

Ayden decided to go out onto his terrace. From there he might be able to see if all hell had broken loose in the senator's suite. Ayden knew that would be a bold and risky move—windows worked both ways—but he figured that the pouring rain would help to camouflage him. In any case, everything he did would be risky for as long as Odi was still aboard. And besides, he was in uniform.

He grabbed a black QM2 umbrella from the closet and slipped out the sliding-glass door.

The sky was dark as midnight and the rain was coming down in a torrent. Ayden did not care. He walked all the way to the edge and crouched down with his back to the rail. Despite the downpour, he could see clearly from there into the Marshall's suite due to the lights inside. He saw one end of a dining table through the parted curtains. Mrs. Marshall and a female guest were seated there, drinking red wine and talking with friendly animation. Odi did not appear to be inside. Nor, it seemed, had he raised an alarm.

Ayden was puzzled. Was it possible that he had imagined the sighting? Could his eyes be playing tricks? "No," Ayden muttered to himself. He had no doubt.

Although Odi's plan of action remained a mystery to Ayden, the fact that he now had to switch tactics was clear. Perhaps he could just push Marshall overboard. All he needed to do was get him out on the terrace alone. Of course, given the weather that would require one hell of a trick.

As Ayden sifted through the possibilities, he felt another doubt tugging at the back of his mind. After a few minutes, it came forward. If Odi had come to save Marshall, then he was likely to have warned the authorities about the other bombers.

He sank down beneath the weight of the world until his butt rested on the wet deck. That last thought had taken the wind out of his sails. The flamboyant execution of all twenty-five members of the Senate Armed Services Committee would have captured the world's attention for months if not years to come, just like 9/11. Now that it might not happen, Ayden felt as though he was about to let down a hundred-million kids. That thought was too much to take.

He groped frantically at the corners of his mind, seeking some solution. Nothing came. He watched the rain beat down on the deck around him. Each drop sent a tiny fountain into the air. Would taking out the chairman garner enough attention if the remaining members of the SASC lived? He wondered. The answer came immediately. No. To rivet attention he needed something huge, something personal, something rivaling 9/11. The modern world was numb to anything less.

Sitting there beneath the black sky and pouring rain, he felt as desolate as his surroundings. The emotional rollercoaster ride was not helping. For years he had struggled to make a difference, day by day. Each day had given him little rewards in the form of tiny upturned faces. But the hopelessness of the big picture had always loomed as large as the mob outside his clinic's door. Then Arvin had walked into his life and talked of creating a world where the strong helped the weak and the rich cared for the poor.

Arvin had given Ayden hope that he could actually help cure the world's manmade woes. The tipping-point was near, he preached, his eyes sucking Ayden in. Mankind had the technological means within its grasp. All the shift required was the right catalytic act. Today he, Ayden Archer, was to have tipped the balance. Today he was to have opened the door to a better world. Now everything that moments ago had seemed so certain was suddenly up in the air. Ayden began to shake with a fear that he was about to fail the children.

"No," he said aloud. "Not without a fight." At the very least he would take out the chairman. Perhaps the other twenty-four would also find the means to prevail—at least a few of them. His mind racing, Ayden spied a thread of hope. He was aboard the new Queen Mary. Nearly three thousand of the world's elite were there with him, plus a thousand crew—and he had a lot of Creamer. Given that combination, the power to focus the world's attention had to be in his grasp. Ayden felt it in his bones. He just had to think—think and then act.

He began running through the ship's systems in his head. He knew the vessel's construction inside out. He could not use the airplane approach and make the ship itself the weapon. The heavy oil powering the ship would not explode. But cruise ships were some of the largest, most complicated machines on earth. There had to be another way …

Ayden was soaked to the bone by the time the solution came to him, but it was a grandiose, eloquent, audacious plan. Getting excited, he reminded himself that radical action might not be necessary. He had seen no commotion in the chairman's suite. For whatever reason, Odi might not have sounded the alarm. Perhaps he was afraid of jail. Or perhaps he had tried but been ignored. The why hardly mattered. However, now that he had devised a grand solution, Ayden found that his original plan held far less appeal. Simply assassinating the chairman of the SASC seemed so uninspired.

The question he had to ask himself now was: Did he have the courage? He decided to put off handling that prickly pear for now. Better to see how Plan A turned out.

He was about to get up and head for the bar where he could check CNN and weigh his options, when movement crossed his peripheral vision. He refocused. Someone was rappelling down from two decks above. Someone was attempting to drop onto Marshall's veranda.

Ayden smiled with great satisfaction as he recognized the figure. Once again, Odi Carr had dropped into his lap.

Chapter 65

The SS Queen Mary 2

SEARCHING THE LAVISH CORRIDORS, Odi was trying hard to look like a privileged vacationer rather than a hired gun. As tired as he was, he was finding it increasingly difficult to pretend. Still, he knew that Ayden was somewhere in the honeycomb of those thirteen decks, plotting away, so he would not stop.

His plan for getting to New York and sneaking aboard the ship had worked, but it had been hard on both body and soul. Poor Kostas Tzemos, the Assistant Ship's Engineer whose identification Odi now wore, would soon awake to a pounding headache and a nasty lump. Odi vowed to make it up to him, along with the others. He cursed himself as he thought of that growing list, ashamed of the gullibility at the root of it all. How bloody naïve he had been, naïve and blinded by revenge.

Odi was not sure where this was all going, or how it was going to play out. An hour earlier, he had watched with surprise as Senator Marshall and his wife boarded the ship. He had expected them to cancel after Cassi put out the word. Yet there they were. There were plenty of possible explanations for their presence, he knew, the most likely being that they were just used to living with threats. After two decades in the senate collecting a hundred threats a year, virtually anyone would be numb. As he mulled that over, Odi quickly latched on to the upside of the Marshalls' nonchalance. Without the Marshalls aboard, he was searching for a needle in a haystack. Now he had a magnet for Ayden.

Walking past Marshall's suite again, Odi knew that he was pushing his luck. On his first pass he had been surprised to find that they did not have a Secret Service Agent posted in the hall. He knew that one was undoubtedly on lookout either via a hidden camera or from the peephole of the suite, but he had expected one in a more visible spot as well. This made it less awkward for him to roam the surrounding halls, but it would still be the third time he pinged the Secret Service's radar by passing Marshalls' suite. He knew that was a mistake for any man, much less one with a wanted face, but he had no choice.

Odi was racing against a clock. Although the voyage to Southampton would take six days, he had to find Ayden before Mr. Tzemos awoke and sounded the alarm. Once the alarm went out, his freedom would last about twenty seconds. He imagined that the conversation would go something like this:

"He's about thirty years old, six foot one with broad shoulders, thick dark hair, steely gray eyes, and oh yeah, he stole my glasses."

"Hey Lou, that sounds like the APB we got from the FBI."

"Did he look like this guy Mr. Tzemos?" The police officer would ask, producing a poster.

"That's him! That's the thief who took my ID and stole my clothes ..."

Odi's own wanted status was not the only complication on his mind. The Marshalls' nonchalance continued to nag at him. He had called the Coast Guard as agreed, and sent them to Asgard for Cassi. Was it possible that they had ignored his call? He wondered. Probably not. Could the Secret Service have ignored Cassi's warning? Again Odi's answer was no. The threat was too serious, and she was a FBI Agent. Odi concluded that his concern was the result of exhaustion combined with an over-stimulated imagination. Still, he hated to take the risk of having two corpses prove him wrong.

With the third pass of Marshall's suite yielding no sightings of interest, he went to the Future Cruises boutique and took a virtual tour of the Marshall's split-level suite on an interactive screen. He paid particular attention to the windows, doors, and terrace. Then he turned his attention to the rest of the ship. The Queen Mary 2 was enormous. It covered an area equivalent to four city blocks and carried 3,900 souls. With just one man looking, Ayden could stay hidden there for months.

As he clicked from screen to screen, Odi became increasingly nervous about spending time away from the Marshalls. Ayden had fooled him, he might also be able to fool the Secret Service. Still, Odi knew that knowledge of the ship's floor plan would be invaluable if he had to pursue, escape, or hide. He bit his lip, rolled his shoulders, and decided to invest ten minutes in cramming the floor plans into his head. Fifteen minutes later he shoved a map in the pocket of his slacks and headed for deck eleven.

Odi pressed the button that opened the sliding door to the promenade, and walked into the darkest, wettest day he could remember. Never before had he considered such misery so perfect. He walked all the way to the rear of the eleventh deck and stood alone by the whirlpool. He looked over the edge. The terrace of the Marshall's Balmoral Duplex beckoned to him from two decks below. He pictured the Scottish residence from which the suite drew its name and decided that it was time to storm a castle.

The whirlpool may only have been three feet deep but the railing beside him still proffered a life ring. He took the measure of the rope. The Atlantic raged a hundred feet below and there appeared to be enough rope to reach it. Certain that there were the fifty feet he needed, Odi removed the coil from the hook. He wrapped the ringed end twice around a post and tested the friction. It felt right. He tucked the ring between his legs and hopped over the rail.

The rain beat down upon him and the wind tried to steal his balance, but Odi was not deterred. Stopping Ayden was something he was prepared to die for. He rappelled down just far enough to see through the wet glass of the Balmoral Duplex's picture windows. He saw the companionway connecting the two floors immediately before him. Beyond it he could see through the open door of the master suite. Judging by the visible portion, the top floor was deserted. So far, so good.

He rappelled half way down to the terrace, stopping at the blind spot between the ninth and tenth decks. He adjusted his grip on the rope, and wiped the rain from his face with his free hand. He tried to think of the rain as refreshing, but in truth it just made him cold. He still had that Chesapeake chill. What a day this had been.

He surveyed his surroundings while evaluating his next move. If the Marshall's were home, they would be just below him on the other side of the glass. The dark and rain might hide him from their view, but it probably would not. He was too close to the glass. He decided to jump backwards, out away from the wall. This was the kind of move his CRT colleagues called brave but he knew was decidedly stupid. Today it was par for the course.

He picked his target landing spot and practiced bending his knees twice before finally pushing off. Landing close to the window was dangerous, but there was a bigger penalty for going too deep. The rope made a zipping sound as he flew back in a relatively controlled drop toward the puddled terrace. Two breathless seconds later he landed squarely on his feet between two lounge chairs. He felt an impulse to take a bow but crouched instead. The life ring was still between his legs. He tucked it behind the leg of a lounger where it would be handy for his retreat.

He studied the sliding glass doors three paces before him, the lighting working in his favor. The Marshalls were there. His rainstorm rumba had not been in vain. The distinguished couple was drinking red wine and chatting animatedly with another elegant pair. No one else was visible in the suite. Odi's stomach did a nervous somersault. Where was the Secret Service? Something was either very wrong or very right. Perhaps Ayden had already been apprehended.

Straining to keep his nerves under control, Odi continued to examine the scene. The dining table before the Marshalls held several plates and bowls. The second he saw them, Odi knew he needed to see what was inside. If something was cream based, he was going to have to make a very awkward knock on their rain-streaked sliding door. He decided to sneak closer.

Dropping to his belly, he low-crawled through puddles to the wall. Then he slid sideways until he could peer around the edge of the curtains. The first thing he did was study the occupants, paying special attention to the hue of their fingers. Everyone looked fine and festive. Mrs. Marshall wore a red silk dress with a matching manicure, her companion a jungle-patterned pantsuit with gold jewelry and matching shoes. The men both sported dark suits with bright shirts sans ties. Their gaiety presented a harsh contrast to the torrent outside, and ran contrary to the danger lurking within.

Odi didn't get it. How could they be so nonchalant? He stood up and turned his attention to the table, his stomach seizing that joyous moment to remind him that he had not eaten in twenty-four hours—excluding the Creamer. One of the bowls closest to him held mouthwatering strawberries, the other tempted him with mixed nuts. Further back was a crusty French baguette on a cutting board and a large wedge of ripe Brie. As his stomach grumbled his heart rejoiced. There was no chance of secreting Creamer in any of those. The

Marshalls were safe for now.

While considering the option of knocking on the glass and confirming that Ayden Archer had in fact been captured, a squeak emanated off to his right side. As he pivoted to investigate, someone plowed into his stomach, sweeping him off his feet and into the air. Odi felt himself being carried backwards on his assailant's shoulder but his exhausted mind took a second too long to react. Before he could gather his wits he was falling backwards through space. That sensation and a fleeting glimpse made everything instantly clear. Ayden had just hurled him overboard.

Chapter 66

Asgard Island, Chesapeake Bay

AS THE COAST GUARD VESSEL dropped over the horizon and Stuart piloted into the marina, Cassi sprinted for the house, running as she never had before. Wiley kept a pair of miniature walkie-talkies in the coat closet by the front door. She needed them. As the Norse Wind's motors had roared to life, she had cobbled together the components of a desperate plan.

She grabbed the pair of Motorolas and was out of the house within ninety seconds of Stuart revving the motors. He would be docking by now, she figured. She tested the batteries as she ran to the garden and found them strong.

Flanking the south side of the manor house was a mature and elaborate garden an acre in size. It ran all the way out from the porch to the cliff. According to Wiley, twelve generations of Proffitts had spent their declining years tending to that garden. Wiley was not declining yet, he had told her, so he employed a gardener. It was spectacular during the summer when the flowers were in bloom and the fountains were running, but even this time of year the ancient fruit trees and manicured maze of hedges gave it an elegant grace. This morning, however, Cassi did not notice the aesthetics. This was a battlefield.

She crashed through a hibernating rose thicket, ignoring the protesting thorns. Once she reached the garden's center she plunged one of the walkie-talkies into the dense branches of a spherical sculpted hedge. She secured it at chest level, gauging the distance to be about twenty feet from the front corner of the porch. She turned it on, cranked the volume up to high, scampered back out of the thicket, and said, "Testing." Her voice came back loud and clear. Motorola made great equipment. For a moment she had the feeling that this was actually going to work.

She turned and dashed for the back of the garden, keeping an eye on the marina path as she went. She clutched the second walkie-talkie in her left hand like a lifeline. The garden ended with a thick row of hedges at the edge of the cliff. Wiley's forebears had planted it generations ago for erosion control and to act as a natural fence. Cassi dropped to the ground when she reached them. Then she peeked back over the surrounding bushes and caught sight of Stuart.

He was a couple hundred yards away, moving toward the manor house with a determined stride. To Cassi it appeared as though his forehead was being pulled by a rope, but her eyes were drawn to his hands. He held a Beretta pointed straight down in each. It did not take a psychiatrist to read that body language. He was a man on a mission, and that mission was her death.

She zipped the walkie-talkie inside her jacket's breast pocket and then climbed over the cliff-side and began working her way along the side of the cliff toward Wiley's yacht.

She moved more quickly over the slippery rocks than any sane person would consider safe, knowing that it would not take Stuart more than five or ten minutes to determine that the house was vacant. Even scampering at a dangerous clip it still it took her the better part of five minutes to reach the Norse Wind. Once aboard, she began hastily collecting the few tools her plan required. Her first stop was the closet in the guest stateroom, where she procured the Ping driver that Wiley used to launch old golf balls into Chesapeake Bay. Next she ran to the master bath where she raided the emergency kit for an air horn and a roll of medical tape. She stashed the three items near the aft gate and then ran up two flights of steps to the upper bridge. She grabbed the binoculars off the captain's console, slung them around her neck, and then used a windowsill to climb up onto the cabin roof.

Standing on the slick white roof with the radar station by her knees, her head was about thirty feet above sea level. If she strained her neck, that put her just high enough to get line of sight over the cliff to the front of the house. She had guessed that right. Two seconds into her watch, however, Cassi understood that her perch was both awkward and precarious. The rooftop was swaying beneath her feet, amplifying each little wave. After a couple of minutes of straining her eyes for Stuart, Cassi realized that her previous assessment was wrong.

Precarious was an understatement. A single unexpected gust of wind could steal her balance and send her toppling over the edge and into a fall that would likely break her neck. She had not considered that aspect of the danger when formulating her plan, but she was not going to change horses in the middle of the stream. She did not have another horse. She would have to risk breaking her neck. The passengers on twenty-four planes were depending on her.

She began to wonder what other unanticipated dangers awaited, and stopped herself. She could not afford to ponder them now. She could let neither her mind nor or her gaze wander, even for an instant. If she was not alert during the second it took Stuart to walk through the front door, he was likely to spot her first. Then he would shoot her off the roof of the yacht like a carnival toy. "Come on, Stuart," she muttered through clenched teeth. "Come on."

She heard a motorboat in the distance and her hopes began to rise. Perhaps the Coast Guard was returning. It sounded like a big boat, but she could not risk a look back over her shoulder, at least until it got closer. Stuart would also want to investigate the noise. She continued to study the front of the house, darting her gaze back and forth between the windows, the porch, the front yard, and the big green door. All appeared quiet. She began getting nervous. Had she missed him? Cassi knew that it was all over if she had. She was a standing duck.

The tone of the distant motor changed, bringing the approaching boat back to the top of her thoughts. It was not a change in speed that caused the shift. It was the Doppler effect. The motorboat had continued past the island and was now receding. Cassi was about to turn to see if there was any chance she could signal the captain when she caught sight of Stuart.

He appeared to be more of a shadow than a man at first, all clad in black and darting. She kept the binoculars trained on him with her left hand as she used her right to reach for the walkie-talkie. She brought it to her lips and pressed transmit. "Stuart!"

She saw him drop to one knee as he pivoted to his left. She saw him bring both pistols up smooth as silk and then she heard them bark. As she brought the walkie-talkie back to her lips the Norse Wind was hit by the wake of the passing boat. The rocking motion caught her distracted and unprepared. As her balance faltered she flailed her arms to compensate, but it was no use. With visions of the jagged rocks and cold water below Cassi toppled over the edge.

She saw a flash of white light and felt a searing bolt of pain shoot out of her upper left arm. She heard her humerus snap like a breaking bat. She fell a few more feet and landed with a thud on her back. Shocked though she was, Cassi managed to bring her right hand to her mouth to muffle her scream.

She rocked back and forth for a moment, trying to ease the pain. She was aware that she was lying on the main deck, twenty feet below where she had stood a second before. It took her a second to realize what had happened. She had fallen and landed sideways on the port rail, snapping her humerus. Fortunately she had bounced back onto the main deck rather than into the freezing waters of the bay. Even in her agony Cassi also knew that she was lucky to have landed as she had. If she had hit her neck or back or head on the rail she would already be a corpse.

Still fighting back screams and moans, she brought her eyes to rest on the walkie-talkie. She tried to focus on it and nothing else. It lay six feet away, further aft on the deck. She wriggled in that direction as though it were a desert oasis, her broken arm pulsing fire as she moved. She thought of the fire about to engulf twenty-four airplanes. That image fueled a reserve of strength. After seconds that seemed like hours, her hungry fingers enveloped the Motorola. She sucked in a deep breath and brought it to her lips.

Chapter 67

The SS Queen Mary 2

ODI HEARD the churning of seawater and the pounding of his heart. He smelled lilac perfume, cigar smoke, and brass polish. He felt a thousand drops of rain. Nothing focuses the mind or sharpens the senses like falling helplessly through space.

As the rail disappeared above him he flipped and flared faster than a falling cat, moving with the reflexive conditioning of a hundred parachute jumps. Something red entered his visual field, eliciting a primitive reaction. His arms thrust out of their own accord even before the memory of a lifeboat canister flashed through his mind. His fingertips made contact but the surface was slick and curved so his hands slid impotently down its side. His panic peaked. He was still gaining speed. Knowing that the canister rim was the only thing between him and a watery grave, Odi curled his fingers into butchers' hooks and willed them not to bend. They struck the rim an instant later.

Odi stared up his hands in gratitude and wonder as they clenched the lip where the two canister halves joined. Meanwhile his legs continued to move as momentum swung them under the enormous canister. A split-second later the shock of his legs impacting the side jarred his right hand loose. Dangling on just four slim fingers, Odi felt gravity pulling his body downward as the driving rain pushed him from above. He teetered outward and caught a frightful glimpse of the churning black waters seven stories below. Fear fueled his left hand, turning it to stone. Swiftly but smoothly he brought his right hand up beside its brother.

Thirty seconds after Ayden hurled him over a guardrail, Odi dropped back onto the safe side. His hands continued to tremble as he crouched there on the rain-swept deck, letting it all sink in. Despite being safe for the moment, he felt winded and shaken. He stared through the rails at the bottomless waters below, knowing that for the second time today he was supposed to be dead. He looked up at the huge protruding canister that had saved his life. Its red underbelly was slick with rain, and the droplets scurried across its surface, propelled by the gale.

Odi knew that his survival was a miracle. He felt touched by the finger of God. He did not have to question the intervention of the Almighty. Odi understood. God had a purpose, and Odi knew exactly what that was.

He shook off the water as best he could and brushed back his gel-slicked hair. Kostas's glasses had fallen into the drink, but at this point that hardly mattered. To stop Ayden, Odi had to come into the open. He had to surrender his alibi.

Chapter 68

The SS Queen Mary 2

AYDEN PLAYED with the condensation on the side of his frosty mug, waiting for Breaking News. There had been no word of a threatened terrorist attack, and now that Odi was dead Ayden knew there would not be. He checked his watch and smiled. The planes were in flight. He was moments from making a difference to the world, moments from saving the children—if the bombers had gotten aboard; if they had the courage to swallow; if the Creamer worked; if, if, if …

He took a long swallow of Boddington's and looked around the modern nightclub of the grandest vessel ever to grace the seven seas. Club G32 was dimly lit but brightly furnished. Colorful roving lights moved randomly around, pulsing and flashing with the hypnotic music. Why they called the club G32 Ayden neither knew nor cared. His only interest in G32 was the bank of television monitors it sported on one wall, one of which was tuned to CNN. Even sitting just a few feet away, however, he could not hear the broadcast over the blaring music. He knew that would all change soon. Soon the world would stand on its ear and he would be able to hear a pin drop.

With the announcement of the first exploding airplane, someone would turn the volume up. When the second aircraft blew, even the deaf DJ would take notice and turn the music off. By the third everyone would be standing openmouthed, staring at the reports jamming every screen. That was why Ayden had come to G32 rather than watching in his own suite; he did not want to witness the birth of the new world alone. Oddly enough, he wished Odi could be there, Odi and Arvin.

But he was alone, and that was just as well. He could not permit himself more than a few minutes' celebration. He still had work to do. Once the pattern was established—only SASC-member planes— Marshall's phone would start ringing off the hook. That was when he would order coffee. That was when the chairman would get his Creamer. That was when—

A red banner began flashing on the CNN screen. Ayden stared at the welcome words: Terror Strikes. He stood up and moved to within inches of the hanging screen. There was a volume button on the bottom edge. He turned it up. "… more than a dozen flights. Though details are still sparse, CNN has just received an amateur video. We need to warn our viewers that it contains graphic content." Ayden caught himself grinning ear to ear at the prospect of seeing the first pictures, not for what they would show, but for what they would represent. He wondered what the image would be. A flash in the sky? A plummeting plume? A smoking crater? Or all of the above?

Chapter 69

Asgard Island, Chesapeake Bay

LYING IN A CRUMPLED HEAP on the deck of her ex-lover's yacht, Cassi prayed that his shadowy accomplice was still on the front porch. She screamed into the walkie-talkie. "You're too late, Stuart. Odi's already gone. He swam to the mainland—with a waterproof bag tucked inside his wetsuit. Wanna guess what was inside?"

It was a short message, but it ought to be enough—she hoped. When Stuart's reply came, it was not what she expected. "It was me, you know. Not Sal. Not an accident. I played you like a violin. I—"

She turned off the walkie-talkie. Stuart could troll all he wanted; she would not take the bait. It did not faze her that the daycare center bombing was a setup. That incident was trivial compared to what lay before her now.

She permitted herself a long moan. Her left arm was in agony. She rolled her head and used her right arm to pull her shirt away from her body. She inspected the damage. Her arm looked like a garden snake that had swallowed a mouse. The swelling was intense, but concentrated. Her humerus had obviously broken clean through. The bone was not protruding through her skin, however, and given the level of bruising her veins and arteries appeared to be intact. She would live. She wished she were as optimistic about the twenty-four planeloads of passengers whose lives hinged on her performance over the next few minutes.

She allowed herself one final sobbing wail, then she steeled her will and said, "No more."

Using her right hand to keep her left arm steady, Cassi rolled up onto her feet. White-hot bolts of pain radiated sporadically from her shattered arm. She did her best to ignore them. The painkillers in the first-aid kit she had raided earlier beckoned her with a Siren's song, but she had no time for such a diversion. Stuart's search of the garden would not last forever. Once he satisfied himself that she was no longer there, he would understand that her taunt had been a diversion. He would make a beeline for the boat. She had to be ready.

She staggered to the aft gate where she collected her stash of supplies—the driver, the air horn, and the tape. Once on the hard dock, each footfall sent a shockwave trumpeting up her spine and down her arm where it detonated an explosion. She looked ahead at the marina's staircase, and winced. Each of the thirty-six steps represented a mountain of pain she had to climb. Cassi wedged the driver between her teeth in place of the proverbial bullet, and had at it. At one point she saw a flash of white light and felt herself starting to faint. Still she moved on. She could not help but picture jagged bone grating nerves and slicing flesh. Still she moved on. As excruciating as it was she knew that worse was yet to come. Still she moved on. "Twenty-four planeloads," she repeated to herself. "Twenty-four."

Eighteen stairs into her climb she had to stop. Sweat was gushing from her face. Her heart was pounding two hundred beats a minute, and her arm was so swollen she thought that it might explode. She took a deep breath, and continued, counting each stair off like a battle won. When at last she got high enough she peeked over cliff's edge. Stuart was nowhere in sight. Relief swept over her like a warm wave. Her struggles had not been wasted. The passengers still had a chance—if she hurried. Stuart would be coming any second now. He knew the yacht was what she wanted.

She took the Ping driver from her mouth and laid it down along the base of the fourth stair down from the top, noting with satisfaction that the handrail's supporting brace camouflaged the protruding club-head. She withdrew the air horn from her pocket and unrolled a foot of medical tape. She looked down to take a deep breath and saw that a puddle of sweat was forming between her feet. This was it, she realized, the point of no return.

She risked another peek over the top of the stairs and saw him. Stuart was just leaving the garden, walking briskly in her direction. She shot back down, ignoring the jolt of pain. She did not know if he had seen her too. At this point it did not really matter.

Using her chin and knees and one good hand, she positioned the cardboard roll over the air-horn's button. She pressed down on the roll. The air horn began to blare. She knew the sound was coming but it still frightened her it was so loud. Wrapping as fast as her awkward appendages were able, she tried to lash the roll down so that it pressed the button, but the jet of air caught her jacket and the air horn flew from her grasp. Reflexively, she grasped at it with her left arm. Flames erupted around the break and again a searing flash consumed her eyes, but she caught it. She knew that Stuart was just seconds away. She could not fold. Summoning all her reserves of willpower and strength she continued wrapping until the roll was secure. She scooted four steps lower and stood. She aimed for the roof of the yacht and lobbed the air horn toward the sky with the arcing throw used on hand grenades.

Cassi ignored the missile the instant it left her hand. For better or worse, her only die was already cast. As it arced through the air she slipped under the staircase rail and climbed beneath the stairs. Endorphins were overriding her pain at last. Her body knew that it was do or die. She heard the horn clatter onto the cabin roof as she reached up for the Ping. She followed the sound of the horn as it slid off the roof and plummeted to the main deck where it continued to emit a muffled wail. Stuart would be running full out with the assumption that she was signaling a passing boat.

She strained to hear the sound of pounding of feet. Only then did Cassi realize that her ears were still ringing from the air horn's close-up blast. She felt a surge of panic. She was lost if she could not hear Stuart's approach. She closed her eyes and tried to control her breathing as she focused on nothing but her ears. Better.

Fishing line! The thought leapt unbidden into her head. She should have used fishing line. Now it was too late.

She felt the stairs vibrate before her damaged ears registered the accompanying noise. The muscles in her shoulder went tense. She only had one chance to pull off a split-second move. If she got it wrong, Stuart would shoot her at point-blank range. Twenty-four planeloads of people would die. Battered body or not, she felt primed like never before.

His foot hit the top step hard enough to make it clang. She sprang the millisecond she heard the second footfall—hitting three steps lower than the first. She thrust the shaft of the driver upward along the railing posts until the handrail supports blocked its ascent on both sides. The shaft of the driver now spanned the stairway, creating an unbreakable tripping force. She braced herself.

Chapter 70

The SS Queen Mary 2

SOAKING WET AND WILD EYED, Odi attracted inquisitive glances as he ran through the corridors and down the stairs to the third deck. As he entered the grand atrium, his eyes flashed about in search of a phone. To his left a bartender polished glasses. She was trying to look perky although she was obviously bored. To his right a hostess sat bent over a map, assisting an elderly couple with their shore plans. Aside from them and a half-dozen sad souls mindlessly pouring money into melodious slots, nobody else was around.

The bartender gave him an odd look—half smile, half inquisitive stare—but did not comment. Odi turned his back to her and picked the phone receiver off a table.

"Ship's operator. How may I help you?"

"The Balmoral Duplex, please."

"One moment please."

After three rings a woman voice greeted Odi. "Hello."

"Good evening, Mrs. Marshall, Would you kindly hand the receiver to an agent of the Secret Service?"

Mrs. Marshall did not reply at once. She paused, then said, "Just a minute."

Odi heard the scrunching sound of a hand covering the phone followed by muffled voices.

"Who's calling please?" Said a different voice, a voice Odi recognized.

"Good evening, Senator. My name is Odi Carr. I'm a Special Agent with the FBI. Is there a Secret Service Agent with you?"

"If you are who you say you are, Agent Carr, then you should know the answer to that."

"I know that you're not usually under guard, Senator, but tonight should be different given the threat."

"I'm always under threat, yet here I am. Tonight is no different."

Odi felt the walls closing in around him. This virtually confirmed his worst fear. Cassi had either not been believed, or more likely had not gotten through. At least Ayden had not yet gotten to the Senator.

Or had he? Had the Senator's voice sounded strained? Odi was not sure. "I'll call you back in a minute, Senator." Without waiting for a reply, Odi hung up.

He ran up the six flights of stairs, ignoring another series of murmurs and stares. He hoped that the body heat this generated would help him dry off. He wished he had a gun.

He kept his eyes peeled for Ayden the whole way, but did not know what he would do when he saw him. Attack like a dog, he supposed. Once he reached Marshall's suite, he stood to the side of the door. He reached over to knock, but paused. If Ayden was in there, he realized, he would shoot on sight. "So be it," Odi muttered. He had no choice.

He knocked.

"Who is it?"

Odi recognized the Senator's voice. "Senator, it's Special Agent Carr."

"Hold your ID up to the peephole, Agent Carr."

"I'm under cover, Senator. I don't have my ID. I don't have my firearm either, sir." Odi backed up, raised his arms, and spun slowly around. "Senator, it's crucial that we talk. Thousands of lives depend on it—including your own."

The Senator opened the door. He held a nickel-plated automatic in his hand and wore an expression that made it clear he wasn't afraid to use it. "You've got sixty seconds."

Chapter 71

The SS Queen Mary 2

AYDEN CLUTCHED his sweating beer glass in both hands as he watched the picture shift from the news anchor to the amateur video. His first reaction was surprise. The video was shot from inside a plane. The oxygen masks were down and flailing as wind whipped through the cabin with hurricane force. Although no hole was visible on screen, the Creamer had obviously blown through the fuselage.

The picture was bobbing left and right, the camera obviously held by a trembling hand. No surprise there, Ayden thought. The operator panned left from the oxygen masks to expose a crowd of writhing men.

The elbow of the nearest one, a crew-cut bull with his back to the camera, kept popping up into the air. Though the view was blocked by his rocking back, the crunching sound clarified his unseen movements. He was pummeling someone's face. After a dozen wallops the beating ceased. The bull stood up and hefted a limp form over his shoulder. Despite the bloody nose and swollen bruises, Ayden recognized Khalid's unconscious face. He felt as though he had been kicked in the gut. They had found out one of his bombers.

The camera panned wider to expose an open exit door and the ground a couple thousand feet below. The bull approached it and flopped Khalid forward. Another large passenger took Khalid's hands while the bull retained his feet. Then the cabin grew silent but for the billowing wind and the two burly passengers heaved Khalid out into space. The instant Khalid hit the jet stream his body disappeared from view behind the ship. A flight attendant closed the exit door and the passengers began to cheer.

The screen cut back to the news anchor as Ayden felt the floor dissolving beneath his feet. "That remarkable scene took place just minutes ago after authorities learned that a passenger had swallowed a bomb that was set to go off before the plane could land. Sources in the Department of Homeland Security have confirmed that suicide bombers are believed to have targeted twenty-four planes. In fourteen other cases, the bombs—secreted in miniature Baileys Irish Cream bottles—were confiscated before being armed. As of this moment, we have no reports that any of the remaining nine bombs have exploded. I repeat ..."

Ayden looked away and saw that talking heads now filled every monitor. He took a step back—onto the lizard-skinned boot of a barrel-bellied man. The man did not notice. Like everyone else in the room, his attention was riveted to a monitor. Everyone in G32 had converged on the monitors and the crowd now penned him in. Ayden began to panic. He turned back toward the talking heads and tried to pull himself together. He had to decide exactly what this meant.

The conclusions crashed down on him like falling boulders. The assassination of the SASC was a bust. There would be no grand public investigation. The martyr videos would never be played on the air. The defense budget would not be publicly examined. A billion swords would not be beaten into plowshares. Nothing would change. He had failed the children.

Ayden suddenly felt much older than his thirty-nine years. Arvin's words came back to him as he stared at the depressing report on the screens: "I want to be able to say that I was there with Ayden Archer on 10/12." Ayden felt ashamed. He could sum up his startling new predicament in a series of No's. He had no money, no job, and as of this evening, no friends. He had eliminated Odi, but not soon enough.

His depression mounted until it became too much to bear. A better world had been yanked from his grasp. He could not face the old one. He was ready to take a dive off the bow when he remembered his alternative plan. Hope lifted the rocks from his heart. Desperation lent him courage. He felt born again as he pushed his way through the crowd. 10/12 could still eclipse 9/11.

Chapter 72

Asgard Island, Chesapeake Bay

NO SOONER HAD CASSI LOCKED the Ping into the crook of the rail than she felt its shaft flex and heard Stuart's startled shout. She released the quivering club and popped her head out from beneath the stairs in time to see his airborne body begin to tumble. Stuart must have been sprinting, she decided, because his trajectory was taking him well beyond the steep staircase's base. She watched him windmill his hands in a fruitless attempt to halt his forward somersault as he plummeted through twenty-five feet of empty space. He careened face first into the iron dock, his outstretched arms snapping like twigs beneath the momentum. A fleshy thud and the sickly sound of snapping bones met Cassi's ears as Stuart's terrified scream transformed into an agonized howl. Stuart was tough, Cassi thought, but he was no match for cast iron. "That's for Masha and Zeke," she said with grim satisfaction.

Cassi made a visual inspection of Stuart's hands to confirm that neither held a Beretta before gingerly pulling herself up onto the stairs. Noting that his agony made her own pain easier to ignore, she descended the stairs with slow, measured strides. Stuart looked helpless as a two-pound kitten in a fifty-gallon drum, but she kept the Ping driver cocked back over her head just in case. She was not going to end up like a movie chick.

Her eyes drank in the climactic scene as she descended. Both of Stuart's forearms lay splayed at grotesque angles as though he had been born with a freakish extra joint. That illusion shattered a second later as she watched. While Stuart squirmed a white bone ripped through the black wool of his sweater to glisten like the Grim Reaper's only tooth.

Cassi stood over him, club still poised. She met his eye, and smiled.

With an effort that exhibited tremendous power of will, Stuart brought his wailing under control and began to mutter. "You bitch. You bitch, you bitch, you bitch ..." He continued to wriggle belly down on the dock as he cursed. When Cassi made no reply his words degenerated into moans.

She lowered the club. He was no threat. He seemed unable to move his head but he continued to look up at her with one beady eye. She stifled the impulse to poke it out with the butt of the Ping, choosing to set the club down instead. She used her one good hand to reach into his right pants pocket. Finding the yacht's keys, she pulled the ring out and gave it a jingle. Then she stepped over Stuart's wrecked body and hopped onto the prow of the yacht.

Stuart managed to roll his head so that he could keep her in sight. Apparently he was not paralyzed, Cassi noted. That was just as well. He parted his mouth and looked as though he wanted to say something clever, but neither the wit nor the energy were present. He remained silent.

In stark contrast, Cassi knew exactly what she wanted to say. "You can spend the rest of your life in a six-by-eight cell, or you can roll a few feet to your right and drown. I don't give a damn either way. I'm done with you."

Chapter 73

The SS Queen Mary 2

ODI PULLED A FIRE AXE from the wall as he entered the engine room. One way or the other, he knew it would all end here.

It was a different world from the glorious one he was leaving. Dim lighting bathed the pale green walls. The air was thick with the smells of grease and diesel. The temperature was at least ninety degrees. Odi found it hard to hear himself think over the mechanical noise. The only pleasant surprise that side of the sealed door was the absence of workers. He realized that technicians must be monitoring everything remotely from an engineering room. "So much the better."

Odi had gained admittance to the lower decks by using Kostas's card-key ID, which had yet to be cancelled. He was not sure how Ayden had gotten into the restricted area, but he knew that his traitorous friend was here. He felt it in his bones.

Twice he had tried to lure Ayden to Marshall's suite by ordering pots of coffee. But his nemesis had failed to appear and both times the cream that accompanied the order was normal. That was when Odi concluded that something bigger was up. It did not take him long to figure out what that would be. Or at least where. On a ship, bigger was most likely found in one direction.

Convincing the Senator to put down his big nickel-plated gun and let him go was not so easy.

They had spent a few very tense minutes together while Senator Marshall verified his story. Three questions into the interrogation, Odi understood that the Chairman of the Senate Armed Services Committee had an excellent technical grasp of weapons. Apparently he actually read the briefs and stayed awake during meetings. Realizing that, Odi shifted gears immediately and gave a detailed explanation of how his invention worked. Between the Creamer's chemistry and its creator's conviction, Marshall was convinced.

Once sold, Marshall got the Director of Homeland Security on the phone without further delay and dictated his marching orders. Odi was impressed.

"The SASC Senators are all flying home at this moment," Marshall said. "The planes they're on are all carrying bombs. These are very special bombs, so listen close. They're disguised as mini bottles of Baileys Irish Cream. Looks like each terrorist has four.

"While you bring each plane down immediately for an emergency landing, you've got to have the air marshal aboard make an announcement over the PA. He's got to recruit every passenger to help him find those four bottles. If the Baileys is found before it gets drunk, you're in the clear. If not, the situation becomes more complicated."

Odi nodded as the Senator spoke, reassuring him that his understanding was correct.

"Once the contents of one or more Irish Cream bottles gets ingested, the drinker becomes a very powerful chemical bomb—with a timer of less than thirty minutes. If you can't land within ten minutes of the first sip passing lips, you're going to have to throw the imbiber off the plane—mid-flight."

There was a pause while the Homeland Security Director questioned what he had just heard.

The Senator said, "I've got the man who built the bombs with me here. He says there's no other way. I believe him.

"If you don't find the Baileys bottles right away, or you find any empties in the trash, you need to have everyone look for a passenger developing blue fingertips. That symptom is your warning, but it only appears shortly before detonation, meaning that once you find it you will only have seconds to act. If you see blue you've got to get that person off the plane immediately, or everyone is lost. Have the air marshal open the cockpit door, and throw the bastard into Allah's arms."

Despite what he and the Senator had watched transpire over the next hour on TV, Marshall had held Odi under arrest. The Director of Homeland Security had informed him of the APB. When neither Ayden nor his Creamer materialized during that time, Odi had insisted on hunting him down.

When he finally stood and moved toward the door, the Senator did not shoot.

Five minutes later, Odi was scanning a dim jungle of churning metal in search of Ayden. Due to the time constraint, he did not have the luxury of sneaking around. He had to walk the aisles, exposing himself to fire. He had no doubt that Ayden would shoot him on sight. He just hoped that his old friend did not have a gun.

The glowing flicker of a flare caught Odi's attention, coming from a dozen steps ahead and twenty feet to his left. It came from the far side of an iron tank the size of a submarine. As Odi read the label he cursed under his breath. Ayden had targeted the ship's thermal oil boiler.

Odi knew the mechanics of how ships like this were powered, having studied petroleum chemistry ad infinitum. The heavy oil they used was virtually non-reactive at room temperature. It was the rough equivalent of asphalt. To turn heavy oil into the combustible fuel the ship could use for power, it has to be primed—heated over many hours to liquid form at a temperature of six-hundred degrees. Six-hundred degrees, Odi repeated to himself. This was not going to be pretty.

He peeked around the edge of the thermal oil boiler, and spotted Ayden there. He was sitting in the narrow service passageway between the boiler and the hull. Oddly enough, one of his hands was handcuffed to a feeder pipe. He held a burning flare in the other. Odi saw that he had a dozen more flares gripped between his thighs. He was in the process of lighting them.

Odi stepped halfway out from behind the corner.

"Hello Odi. Did you decide to join me? I'm afraid I drank all the Creamer myself, but if you sit close," he shrugged, "what's the difference?"

"I'm not into suicide."

"This isn't suicide. It's a mission of mercy. The thousands who die today will save millions of lives." He produced the key to the handcuffs as he spoke and then placed it ceremoniously on his tongue as he finished. He swallowed.

Odi could not help but notice the maniacal look in the eyes of his former friend. He did not know what to say.

As it turned out, Ayden was not finished. "In a few minutes the Queen Mary 2 will be rechristened Titanic 2, as she sinks with most of her thirty-nine hundred souls. Oh, some will survive on lifeboats, I'm sure, but given the speed she'll go under it won't be a thousand. 10/12 will still eclipse 9/11. As the media sifts through the wreckage, world attention will finally be brought to focus on the issues that matter most. The money will follow."

"You're only going to kill yourself, Ayden," Odi said, shaking his head. "Heavy oil won't explode."

Ayden scoffed. "Coming from the man who invented Creamer, your thinking is surprisingly conventional. I'm not counting on blowing a hole in the hull, even though there is that possibility—I did down a whole pint. No, my friend, I'm going to burn one." Ayden gestured with the flare.

"A whole pint!" Odi sputtered, unable to contain himself. That much actually might blow a hole through the hulls if the boiler banked the energy of the explosion just right. Ayden's stomach now held the Newtonian equivalent of sixteen hand grenades. Odi dwelled on that image until he remembered the last part of Ayden's sentence. He was counting on burning a hole through the hull.

Odi thought aloud. "When you explode, you'll rip open the side of the thermal oil boiler. Ten thousand gallons of superheated oil will gush out, hit the flares and ignite. In that quantity, the oil will burn at a temperature of around three thousand degrees. Iron melts at twenty-eight hundred ..."

Ayden looked at him and smiled. Then he held his lit flare to the tip of another and it too burst into flame. The extra light revealed the blue tinge of Ayden's fingertips.

As if reading Odi's mind, Ayden shook his left arm, rattling the handcuff against the pipe. "Sorry. I'm not going anywhere."

"I'm sorry too," Odi said, bringing his right hand into view. "But I must insist."

Ayden dropped his jaw as Odi hefted the axe.

WILEY WAS ON TOP OF THE WORLD. Tonight he would solidify his position as America's go-to man on terrorism at the very moment that terrorism returned to the pinnacle of American attention. His move to the White House was but a hop, skip, and jump away.

Fitzpatrick had invited him to record a profile interview for a special extended episode of *PoliTalk*. Fitzpatrick would use it on Sunday, during his comparative analysis of the leading contenders for the presidential election tickets. He was gunning to become the preferred source for election coverage, and that suited Wiley just fine.

They had just finished twenty minutes of raw video when Fitzpatrick held up one hand indicating that the camera should cut as he placed his other hand over his right ear. As Fitzpatrick listened to the news coming over his earpiece, Wiley's cell phone began to vibrate —right on cue. Once his expectation was confirmed by the pallid look on Fitzpatrick's face, Wiley surreptitiously switched off his phone. He did not need to answer it to get the message.

"There's breaking terrorist news," Fitzpatrick said, looking up from the notes he had just scribbled. "Are you okay with going live?" His face was rife with excitement.

This was no coincidence, of course. Wiley had timed things to a tee. His speeches were prepared and his messages ready. The Proffitt-for-Vice-President Campaign was about to launch into the stratosphere. The confluence of events was beautiful. He would not even have to feign surprise at the images of exploding planes and flaming corpses. This was the attack The Prophet had been predicting. He gave Fitzpatrick a take-it-or-leave-it answer: "If you'll cover my back, I'll cover yours."

Wiley knew that Fitzpatrick would hate to surrender his boxing license even for an hour, but he had little choice. To have the Director of the FBI live in his studio at a time like this could make him a network news anchor if not a legend. Nonetheless, Wiley thought that Fitzpatrick said "Deal" a little too quickly. Seconds later, he understood why.

The suicide bombers had failed.

For an hour, Wiley had to sit there looking perky and satisfied as amateur videos showed air marshal after air marshal apprehending Ayden's bombers. It was not hard for Wiley to spin this battle in his favor, but behind his flashing teeth and glowing eyes, he knew that this public-relations victory might cost him the war. For terrorism to top the election agenda, the voters had to be scared. These videos not only calmed them, they gave the whole country the cocky jubilation of the winning Super Bowl team.

"Well, your prediction came true, Director. The Prophet epithet holds. And even more impressive and important than your ability to predict this attack was your overwhelming success in defeating it. We calculate that thirty-eight hundred souls were aboard those twenty-four planes. You saved them all—not to mention their families and the casualties spared on the ground. Why, by this time tomorrow, most Americans will have looked up at the sky and understood that without Wiley Proffitt, a plane might well have crashed on them. Please accept my professional congratulations and my personal thanks."

Wiley was about to comment on the value of a team effort and the dangers of dropping one's guard when Fitzpatrick held up his finger and pressed his earpiece. "We've got more breaking news—also with amateur video." He pointed to the studio plasma screen. "This video was shot just minutes ago aboard Cunard's luxury cruise ship the Queen Mary 2 as it sailed a hundred nautical miles from New York. Like the other videos we have shown you this evening, this was streamed to us from a camera-phone. Our apologies for the low resolution and the jerky quality—the photographer was running while shooting. When you see it, you will understand why."

The monitor cut from Fitzpatrick to the scene of a man running up a set of ornately carpeted stairs. He carried another man over his shoulder, and that man's wrist was spurting blood. His hand had obviously just been severed at the wrist. The camera angle shifted to center on the victim trying to stem the bleeding from his stump. His efforts were not doing much good, and his moans were becoming feeble. Wiley recognized Ayden.

The running man was shouting "Make way!" and "Move!" while the amateur videographer kept repeating "Oh my God."

As the crowd of gowns and tuxedos parted, some cursed while others screamed. The bobbing camera kept tight on the running man's heels as he exited onto the ship's promenade. Without pausing, the running man dumped his handless hostage over the rail, soliciting a gasp from the audiences in the studio and on the video. Ayden's screams crescendoed and faded as the camera followed his plummet.

Then the audience lost sight of him among the churning waves.

The operator panned the camera back to the perpetrator's face and everyone went silent. Wiley felt his blood thin as the camera zoomed in. He was looking into a dead man's eyes.

No sooner had the camera focused on Odi's panting face than the speakers were filled with a water-muffled boom. The camera whirled about to reveal a geyser of seawater. Ayden had exploded a good hundred yards behind the ship, but the blast was still big enough to be both heard and felt.

The studio monitor cut back to Fitzpatrick who was eagerly waiting. "We have learned that the Chairman of the Senate Armed Services Committee, Senator Lawrence Marshall, was aboard that ship and is presumed to have been the bomber's primary target. Would you care to comment, Director Proffitt?"

Wiley's mind was redlining as it raced toward the distant light he sensed at the end of this tunnel. He sat there motionless for several seconds with the camera on him. Finally he nodded as though making a decision and looked into the lens. "Well, now that the cats are all out of the bag, I may supply additional detail without endangering ongoing operations or innocent lives. Your assumption that Senator Marshall was the target is correct. In fact, the twenty-five members of the Senate Armed Services Committee were the primary targets of all of tonight's attacks. Al-Qaeda will stop at nothing to murder defenders of freedom.

"The man you saw throwing the bomber over the rail of the Queen Mary 2 was FBI Special Agent Odysseus Carr. Agent Odi Carr and his sister, Agent Cassandra Carr, have been working undercover in a top-secret operation to combat a specific al-Qaeda cell. Due to potential agency infiltration, their mission was so secret that the brother-and-sister team reported exclusively and directly to me." Wiley paused to let this fact sink in.

"You will recall that three defense corporation CEO's have been executed during this last month." Wiley held up three fingers on his right hand. "That was the work of this same terrorist cell. Those operations showed inside knowledge, as did the attack on our envoy to Iran. So in order to avoid the chance of any leaks in this highest-priority mission, I worked exclusively with a couple of expert field operatives whom I knew I could trust.

"While investigating those killings under deep cover, Odi Carr learned that the next 9/11 was pending. Unfortunately, he was not close enough to the terrorist mastermind to learn the details. In an effort to win him the terrorists' confidence, I added Agent Carr to the FBI's most wanted list. That ruse succeeded, if only just. Technically this operation was a resounding success, but as you saw we were nearly too late. We need to get even better."

"Amazing, truly amazing," Fitzpatrick said. "I certainly thank you for your unprecedented candor, Director. I find it refreshing."

Wiley nodded and relaxed inside as a warm glow suffused him. He had done it! He had covered his ass with the sweetest perfume, and the scent would never wear off. Nobody picked through glowing successes. The fine-tooth comb was reserved for political failures. Of course there would be those in the Bureau who would suspect foul play, but they would not dare to question him now, much less point a finger. This coup gave Wiley the power to castrate his opponents with a flick of his golden wrist.

All he had to do to get the keys to 1600 Pennsylvania Avenue was win over the Carrs. That should not be too hard. He had Odi cold for the CEO murders. Besides, his story made them national heroes. They would be fools to contradict it. Hell, he could even marry Cassi now if he wanted. Even Stuart could not object to having a bona fide hero as First Lady. No one could attack her without reminding everyone of Wiley's finest hour.

The thoughts were coming so fast and furious that Wiley momentarily forgot that he was on TV. As he turned to refocus on Fitzpatrick, Wiley caught sight of Cassi standing at the corner of the soundstage. His bowels turned to water as they locked eyes. As he read the intentions telegraphed by her expression, Cassi held up a DVD.

"... don't you think?" Fitzpatrick asked.

Wiley forced his attention back to his host. "I'm sorry, could you repeat the question?"

"Well, it's good to see that you are human. I was beginning to wonder. I asked if you would be content with the VP slot on the ticket after today. Perhaps you'll consider challenging Carver for president?"

Cassi waved the DVD behind Fitzpatrick's shoulder and gave the thumbs-down sign with her other hand—although that arm was in a sling.

Wiley made a split-second decision—not that he had any choice. He refocused on Fitzpatrick. "No, no. I'm not so ambitious. In fact, I informed the president earlier today that I would not consider running for any office at all."

"Really!" The unflappable Fitzpatrick seemed genuinely shocked.

Cassi nodded but kept waving the damn recording. The message was clear: she wanted more.

Wiley felt an irresistible urge to strangle her but he had to sit there looking affable on the air. He thought of everything he had sacrificed in the course of giving whatever it takes. He thought of Potchak, Drake, Rollins, and Abrams. He thought of a yacht on the Chesapeake, a cabin on Lake Maroo, a clinic in Iran, and a daycare center in Baltimore. He thought of Stuart's smarmy smile, Cassi's agonized eyes, and Odi's brilliant Creamer. He thought of Air Force One, the White House, and the Presidential Seal. He saw his dreams flash brightly before his eyes and he saw his future fade to black. He looked directly at the camera. "Yes. In fact I've decided to let this last operation be my crowning achievement. At that same meeting I informed the president that I was retiring from the FBI. This was my last day in the Director's chair."

Epilogue

Six weeks later. Arlington, Virginia

"ARE YOU SURE this is the right place?" Odi asked the government driver while studying the unfamiliar brownstone.

"Yes sir, this is it. Number twenty-one."

"What's here?"

"I don't know any more than you do, sir," the driver replied.

Odi slid out of the black Lincoln, pulling his duffel bag behind. The brownstone certainly looked more inviting than the suburban Maryland safe house he had been locked away in for forty days and nights while patiently waiting for the powers that be to decide his fate. But looks could be deceiving. Had the offer been a ploy? He wondered. Were they about to take him out?

Standing there on the elm-lined curb watching the Lincoln disappear, he realized that he was alone outdoors for the first time since throwing Ayden from the Queen Mary's deck. It felt good. Whatever his fate, he would embrace it.

He closed his eyes and let the late afternoon sun shine down on his face for a minute. For six weeks he had been chomping at the bit, frustrated by the slow spin of bureaucratic wheels. Once everything fell into place, however, things started moving very fast. One minute he was sitting in his cell, the next he was getting an overview of his new assignment. Five minutes after that he was sitting in the back of the limo.

As he reached for the bell to number twenty-one, his eyes fell on the brass plaque beside the door. He sprouted a satisfied smile. Now he understood.

A grandmotherly lady with lively eyes answered his ring. "Good afternoon, Odysseus. My name is Mary. Please come in."

Mary ushered him into a cozy parlor appointed in yellows and greens. He took a seat in a soft armchair across the coffee table from an attractive woman of his own age. Once Mary disappeared, the woman asked, "Since you're alone I assume that you're here to interview the doctor?"

Odi chuckled to himself at that notion. "In a manner of speaking."

"She's wonderful. My Stephen was having the worst nightmares and," she lowered her voice, "wetting the bed. She cured him in just three sessions. I was going to stop coming after that but Stephen threw a tantrum. He actually looks forward to their talks. Can you imagine? A six-year-old looking forward to talks? The first time I brought him here he was screaming murder. I'm Melanie, by the way." She held out her left hand rather than her right. Odi understood the eccentricity when he saw that her ring finger was bare.

"Odi. I'm glad to hear that you're so pleased. Actually—"

The thick wooden door at the end of the room flew open and a boy with carrot-colored hair came rushing in, cutting Odi short. As Stephen hugged his mother, Cassi stepped into the doorway. She looked radiant.

Odi excused himself and walked into his sister's new office. They embraced the moment she closed the door.

"I can't believe that you left the FBI, Sis, but I'm so glad that you did. You look great."

"I feel great. Better than I have in years. Better than any time since mom and dad died."

Odi raised his eyebrows inquisitively.

"My life is about compassion now—rather than hate. But enough about me. How about you? The isolation must have been terrible. I knew that you'd be okay though, being so tough." She took two steps back and appraised him in full. "You look good, even great."

"I had the use of a small gym to while away the hours."

"I was assured that you were being taken care of, but other than that I was kept in the dark. Then the new Director called me personally yesterday to say that you had reached a mutually beneficial settlement. I appreciated the courtesy, but would have preferred the details."

"Mutually-beneficial, eh?" Odi mused. "I guess that's right. I can't say that I'm entirely comfortable with their decisions, but I agree that the country will be best served in the end."

"You sound dubious."

"Ayden is getting posthumous blame for my killings. They will release the story of his father's unfortunate death as motive and try to keep the profile low. Meanwhile, to complete the whitewash, I'm receiving the Presidential Medal of Freedom for my deep-cover work —and a new job."

"Can you tell me what it is?"

Odi nodded. "I'll command a group of high-tech operatives tasked with identifying and counteracting soft spots in homeland security."

"That's wonderful Odi. I'm happy for you."

Cassi motioned him to take a seat and then asked, "What's happening to your Creamer?"

"That was both my biggest bane and my best bargaining chip. For a while I was worried that they would make me disappear in order to make it disappear. In the end I gather they decided that such an approach would be shortsighted. If I could concoct Creamer, so could someone else. I'm to work with industry experts to design a means to detect and neutralize it. Ayden's contact in Iran knows that Creamer existed, but he doesn't have any technical details, so we should have detection equipment in place long before he or anyone else is able to recreate it.

"But enough about me. I didn't have any access to news while in isolation, and my handlers never answered a single question unless it suited their purposes, so I'm more curious than a boy scout in a brothel. Seeing as how you are doing so well, I guess I'll start with the big one. What happened to Wiley?"

A shadow crossed Cassi's face, but it vanished in an instant. "The official word is that he went overseas for an extended vacation— something about visiting Norway and Scotland to track down his roots. I don't know anything more than that."

"Do you believe it?"

Cassi shrugged. "I try not to think about him."

"And Stuart?"

"There's been little mention of him in the press, and no mention at all of his connection to Wiley. The bottom line is—he drowned. A fisherman found his body. He had two severely broken arms and the autopsy revealed a broken back. The Reedsville Police are assuming that he fell off a cliff onto some rocks and his body washed out into the bay."

"I get the impression that you know better?"

"Some things are better left unsaid."

"I see," Odi said. "So tell me about your new practice. How's it going? From the looks of things I'd say great."

"It is. I'd love to tell you more but I can't."

"What do you mean you can't?"

Cassi blushed. "I have to run, Odi. I have a date."

Author's Note

Dear Reader,

THANK YOU for reading BETRAYAL. I hope you enjoyed it. If you would be so kind as to take a moment to leave a review on Amazon or elsewhere, I would be very grateful.

Reviews and referrals are as vital to an author's success as a good GPA is to a student's.

I know this can be a bit of a pain, so if you do write a review, please email me at tim@timtigner.com and I will forward you the unpublished story behind BETRAYAL, and my thoughts on what happens to the characters next. I thought that would be a fun way to say thank you.

All my best,

Also by Tim Tigner

BETRAYAL, COERCION, and PUSHING BRILLIANCE.

Be among the first to learn of new releases and get a FREE ebook by signing up for Tim's *New Releases Newsletter* at timtigner.com

39821147R00122

Made in the USA
San Bernardino, CA
04 October 2016